The SLIP

Mark Sampson

DUNDURN
TORONTO

Cover image: 123RF.com/file404
Printer: Webcom

Library and Archives Canada Cataloguing in Publication

Sampson, Mark, 1975-, author
      The slip / Mark Sampson.

Issued in print and electronic formats.
ISBN 978-1-4597-3575-0 (paperback).--ISBN 978-1-4597-3576-7 (pdf).--
ISBN 978-1-4597-3577-4 (epub)

      I. Title.

PS8637.A53853S55 2017   C813'.6   C2016-905935-9
                                                C2016-905936-7

1   2   3   4   5   21   20   19   18   17

We acknowledge the support of the Canada Council for the Arts and the Ontario Arts Council for our publishing program. We also acknowledge the financial support of the Government of Ontario, through the Ontario Book Publishing Tax Credit and the Ontario Media Development Corporation, and the Government of Canada.

Care has been taken to trace the ownership of copyright material used in this book. The author and the publisher welcome any information enabling them to rectify any references or credits in subsequent editions.

— *J. Kirk Howard, President*

The publisher is not responsible for websites or their content unless they are owned by the publisher.

Printed and bound in Canada.

VISIT US AT

dundurn.com | @dundurnpress | dundurnpress | dundurnpress

Dundurn
3 Church Street, Suite 500
Toronto, Ontario, Canada
M5E 1M2

For Rebecca

Nothing in the world — indeed nothing even beyond the world — can possibly be conceived which could be called good without qualification except a *good will.*

— IMMANUEL KANT,
Foundations of the Metaphysics of Morals

However unwilling a person who has a strong opinion may admit the possibility that his opinion may be false, he ought to be moved by the consideration that, however true it may be, if it is not fully, frequently, and fearlessly discussed, it will be held as a dead dogma, not a living truth.

— JOHN STUART MILL, *On Liberty*

Monday, November 2

I would have run to little Naomi when she cried out, except I had to get the poppy to stay on. That seemed paramount as I stood in the master bedroom at 4 Metcalfe Street, getting ready for my TV appearance. The producer at CBC's *Power Today* had emailed us all with her fourth reminder since Friday morning. *Okay, folks: We're in Remembrance Day mode as of Monday, so we ask all on-air guests to have the poppy prominently displayed for broadcast. We won't have a box of them in the studio yet, so please bring your own. Should go on the left, over your heart.* Yes, yes. I had a track record for being one of these careless dolts who loses four or five poppies to the wind and just gives up somewhere around November 7. I imagined hundreds of those plastic-and-felt florets I'd bought over the years clogging the gutters of Cabbagetown and the Annex, and the goddamn veterans counting up their gold like Scrooge McDuck. The things were clearly engineered to fall off. It became critical, in that moment, to get it fastened correctly. More critical than whatever else I planned to wear — brown tweed over blue shirt and some pleasantly centrist slacks — or my efforts to sooth the ginger flare of comb-over that sprang across my skull like the facehugger from *Alien*. (Cheryl Sneed, my fellow panellist and long-time nemesis on the Right, would make some green room remark about it, regardless. Either that or the wisp of PEI accent that still warped my rhotics — which I hammered up whenever I was in her presence, because I knew it annoyed her.) And, perhaps, more critical even than what my three-year-old daughter was screaming about down the hall in the bathroom. Grace was on it, anyway. I heard her fly out of Naomi's bedroom with a panicked *Sweetie, are you OKAY?* followed by a quick gush from the faucet. I plucked the poppy off my bureau, fluttered it like a parasol in the mirror. Wait — where *was* my tweed? Oh right, of course. I hurried into the hallway.

"Philip. Philip, are you there?"

I was not. I bounded up the stairs to my third-floor office, zagging around the Dora the Explorer doll lying on the hardwood beneath my feet. Entering my office, I found the tweed where I last left it: thrown over the arm of the futon. I nabbed the jacket and laid it flat across my desk, moving manuscript printouts from my next book (tentatively called "Christianity and Its Dissidents") out of the way. I bent over and manoeuvred the flower over the lapel. I poked the steel pin into the pure virgin wool and pressed the poppy in as deep as it would go. Then I raised the jacket up and looked at it. Already the plastic blossom had slid a few millimetres out of the lapel.

Grace's voice echoed from the hall and through the open office door.

"Philip — seriously, are you there or not?"

Just a minute, dear. I returned the jacket to the futon arm and then moved to the overflowing bookshelf on the opposite wall. I pulled down my author copy of *Corporate Canada Today* (Tuxedo House, 2014) and quickly confirmed a few facts about ODS Financial Group, which would be the subject of this afternoon's *Power Today* interview. Yes, yes. Managing partner since '99: Viktor

Grozni. CFO: the lovely and talented Glenda Harkins-Smith. Market cap before the 2008 crash. Market cap just before Friday's announcement. Number of Canadians with pensions directly managed by. Number of ancillary businesses shareholders had no idea existed. Amount of direct subsidy from the Harper Conservatives since 2011. Yes, yes. It was already there, all of it, in my head. Cheryl Sneed didn't stand a chance.

Time to throw the jacket on and quickly help Grace with whatever she and Naomi were dealing with in the bathroom (the child had stopped screaming, but continued with a kind of hiccupy crying that seemed to reverberate through the whole house) before heading downtown. I turned and reached for my tweed, only to have my gaze hauled to the floor. There on the hardwood lay my poppy, face down like a drunkard.

Oh, that is it, I thought. *Fucking veterans.*

I grabbed the tweed and picked up the poppy before storming back down the stairs. Time for Plan B.

"Philip — Philip can you *please* come here."

I hustled down to the main floor. Stole a glance at the clock on the kitchen wall. Oh *God.* I hurried to the door leading to our basement. *My* basement, since Grace and the kids rarely went down there. More oubliette than man cave, it had a set of stairs that descended almost vertically into that dark, unfinished gizzard. I marched down and popped on the light, which only marginally diminished the darkness, then went to my small workbench with the poppy and jacket in tow. I rested the tweed flat and placed the scarlet bloom onto the lapel. Then I grabbed the industrial stapler I had bought at Canadian Tire to assemble some rather complicated birthday party decorations for my stepdaughter, Simone, when she turned thirteen a few weeks ago. The tool was heavy in my hand, like a weapon. I clamped one end of the nozzle over the flower and tucked the other under the tweed.

BLAM! BLAM!

There. Perfect. Well, not perfect. I held the jacket up once more. Hopefully the CBC's cameras were not so HD that they would pick up the tiny planks of metal that now held the poppy in place.

I hiked back up to the main floor, throwing the jacket on as I did. Moving to holler upstairs to Grace, I turned to see that she and Naomi were already in the kitchen, waiting for me. My wife leaned against the counter, arms folded over her chest, her bottom lip tucked under her top teeth, her head tilted. Oh, she was mad. I briefly scanned the kitchen for the source of her rage. Surely I hadn't forgotten to clean up the wreckage of the Bloody Joseph (my third since breakfast): the inedible stump of celery sequestered in the compost, the tin of tomato juice washed out and blue-binned, the celery salt resuming its place in the spice rack, and various other accoutrements returned to their sentry posts in my bar fridge. But no. The kitchen was spotless, as per our agreement.

"Oh, hey," I ventured. "Look, I'm running late but would you mind —"

"Did you not hear me calling you?"

What was I to say to *that*?

"I'm pretty sure you *did* hear me calling you, Philip," she went on, "because I could hear *you* shuffling in the hallway outside the bathroom as I did."

"I wasn't 'shuffling,'" I said. "I was getting ready for this CBC thing. Look —"

"The tub faucet upstairs still isn't working right."

"Yes, it is," I disagreed, stupidly. I had showered earlier in the day, as had Simone before she'd gone to school. (It wasn't apparent whether Grace had had *her* shower yet.) But she was, technically, right — the tub faucet was still plagued with a peculiar problem: the cold water tap would spew piping-hot water for nearly a minute after you turned it on. It was the latest in a series of bathroom issues we'd been having. You'd think that for the ungodly sum I paid for 4 Metcalfe Street six years ago when we got married, we'd have a fully functional bathroom — not to mention a *finished* basement. But no, no.

"You were supposed to get it fixed," Grace said, "like, three weeks ago. And now —"

"It's on my list. You know it's on my list."

"And now what I feared would happen — what I *knew* would happen if you didn't get it fixed — has happened. Naomi went in there before I realized and turned on the tap and scalded herself."

"I had to take a *pewp*," Naomi informed me with a sniffle, and displayed her reddened right wrist.

I looked at her. "Did, did you poop in the *tub*, sweetie?"

"She didn't poop in the tub," Grace barked. "Philip, you're missing the point. Did you not hear your daughter scream out and start crying?"

I did. Of course I did. But I knew — or at least *assumed* — that Grace had things well in hand. Which she did.

My eyes flicked to the wall clock. *Jesus.*

"Look, what do you want from me?" I tried a half smile. "I fixed the sink up there, didn't I?"

"Yes, you fixed the sink — after I nagged you about it for *five months*. What, do you want a medal for that?"

"Grace —"

"I'm serious, Philip. Would you like a prize for fixing the sink? We could write to the French government and get them to create a new international award for plumbing, and give it to you. They could call it the *Douche d'Or*."

"You're hilarious," I deadpanned, but then chuckled on the inside. She must have been sitting on that joke for weeks.

I shrugged at her. "Look, what can I say? I'm not handy. You know that. This kind of stuff stresses me out, and I have enough stress in my life right now. I'm teaching two courses this term. I've got the new book. I've got the thesis defence I'm chairing in a few weeks, and ..." My eyes floated back to the clock. "I've got this CBC thing this afternoon."

"So you don't have time to pick up the phone and call a plumber, is what you're saying."

"It's not about calling a plumber, Grace. It's about having the headspace to figure out if there are any plumbers left in this city who haven't screwed us over."

"You weren't teaching in the summer," she pointed out. "You could have done it then."

"Yes, but I had a breakthrough with the book, and ..." I pinched my nose, sighed. In that moment, I longed for my old life, before we bought this huge, and hugely expensive, house in Cabbagetown. For sixteen years prior to marrying Grace, I had lived in a loft in the Annex. If the sink broke, the landlord came and fixed it. Which felt like something that only happened in fairy tales, now.

"Look," I went on, "just because I wasn't teaching doesn't mean I had the capacity to deal with ..." And yes, I said it then; the words just flew out of me. "... a bunch of domestic trifles."

"*Wow*," she said, long and slow, and blinked at me. "So I guess what you're saying is it's really my responsibility, because you've got all that," and here she mock-furrowed her brow at me, "*deep thinking* to do."

"Oh, come on, Grace."

But she took a step toward me then, her backside leaving the counter. In one fluid motion, she jutted her hip out, picked up Naomi, and parked the child upon it. Engaging, she was, in that most basic act of motherwork: to hold her child close. Then Grace threw back her thick, curly hair — sporting a henna dye job she'd acquired a few months ago, one I thoroughly approved of when she first modelled it for me, burying my face in its waves later that night, in bed — and looked at me with those wild, emerald eyes of hers.

"I guess what I'm saying, Philip," she said, "is that I don't much care about the tub. Or the sink. What I care about is that you don't really seem all that plugged in to what's happening in your own house."

"Grace, do I need to remind you that I'm appearing on national television this afternoon?" I felt a more *echt* emotion than the one I'd been feigning for the last five minutes swell up inside me. "Do I need to remind you that what happened on Friday is going to make the 2008 crash look like a bad cocktail party? The CBC wants my commentary on it, and they've pitted me against —"

"I don't care," she said. "Philip, your daughter *scalded* herself. And obviously you consider the tub issue to be a 'domestic trifle.'"

"I shouldn't have said that —"

"But you did. You did say it."

"And obviously, you don't care that I'm now very late for this CBC thing."

"You know, you're not the only one with a public persona to worry about," she said. "You're not the only one whose writing is important."

"Is *that* what this is about?" I asked. "That I've somehow disrespected your work by leaving you to deal with Naomi while I got ready? Well, I'm sorry, Grace. I'm sorry I can't just satisfy your ego whenever you want."

"Well, Philip," she said, "I'm getting pretty *used* to your inability to satisfy me whenever I want."

In shock, my jaw sort of unhinged then, like a python's, and my eyes grew wide. "*Oh*," I said, twisting my neck as if testing it for sprain. "Oh!" I looked at her, and she looked at me. "I … I can't believe you said that."

She set Naomi back down and the child scampered off. This was clearly getting out of hand. The flesh around Grace's throat and collarbones had turned an intense red — as if she were aroused rather than infuriated by our exchange. Which was, of course, possible: stranger things had turned my wife on in the past.

"I can't believe you said that to me," I repeated.

"Look, I can only talk about one of your inadequacies at a time," she said. "I need you to focus. What I have a problem with — right now — is that you don't seem all that interested in what goes on around here. You have trouble remembering things I tell you, or ask you to do."

"I remember lots of things," I said.

"Really?" she asked. "What are you doing on Wednesday night?"

Quick — scan your brain! Scan your brain! "I'm … I'm taking Simone to that dance recital at the place up the street. She's really looking forward to it." I grinned, intensely proud of myself.

"And what are we doing next Sunday?"

The smirk slipped from my lips. Oh shit.

"*Philip* — what are we doing on Sunday?"

Something huge. Something important. I scoured hard, dug deep, but it wasn't there. Just a big blank space where what it was should've been.

"Look, I have to go. I'm extremely late."

She refolded her arms over her breasts and sneered at me. "What are we doing on Sunday, Philip?"

"Look, we'll talk about this when I get back," I said.

She gave her head a slight jiggle, her hennaed hair flapping, as if to say, *I guess I made my point.*

"Look, I *have* to go. Wish me luck, okay?"

But she looked away then, staring off into whatever galaxy of indignation floated before her mind's eye.

"Grace, wish me luck."

But she wouldn't.

So I left her there, and made my way to the front entry. Dug a decent pair of Payless shoes from the hall closet and stepped into them. Then I was out the door, finally, and onto Metcalfe Street. Down Carlton and over to the west side of Parliament. Raised my hand to hail a Beck taxi. Miraculously, one pulled up right away.

"The CBC building on Front Street," I said to the driver as I climbed in, then shut the door and sank into the leathery lung of his back seat. I inhaled a long, wheezy breath and tried to relax as we sailed southward. Took a moment to straighten myself and inspect my attire. And it was only then that my eyes fell onto the vast, empty pampa that was my jacket's left lapel.

Oh for *Christsake*!

It's love that sends me to bed every night, but it's hate that gets me up in the morning.

The love is, I hope, obvious to you, dear reader, despite the row I just described. There really aren't adequate words in the English language to relay the kind of passion that consumes Grace and me, the unspoken timbre we share when even the longest, most tiring day is done. I often think it's the passion that *causes* us to have such intense squabbles. Fire can, after all, burn in all sorts of directions. Which made her dig at my inconsistencies in the boudoir so out of left field. I mean — *come on*. Why would she say something so heinous to me?

But let's talk about the hate — the hate that gets me going every day. A term that, I admit, seems overly harsh coming from a self-described deontologist and centrist thinker. But it's true: I often frame myself as the lone *katechon* against what Canada has become in recent years: a hotbed of anti-intellectualism, religious extremism, neo-conservativism and privatization. It's why I dedicated nearly a third of *Corporate Canada Today* to profiling ODS Financial Group, and agreed to share my thoughts on the firm's collapse with the CBC. I was prepared to express my indignation over how its C-suite had made off like bandits — golden handshakes for all! — and I relished the chance to lock horns with my fellow pundit, the grotesquely conservative Cheryl Sneed. Despite holding a mere B.A. in basket weaving earned in 1972, Cheryl has been a top columnist for the *Toronto Times* for nearly thirty-five years now, writing about politics, economics, religion, literature, gender issues, and various other topics she knows nothing about. She ran afoul of me after unfavourably reviewing two of my books — *Capitalism and Other Pathologies* (University of Guelph Press, 2005) and the short, scathing *Stephen Harper: A Biography* (Tuxedo House, 2010) — and we'd been exchanging barbs in the media ever since. Until Friday afternoon, she had been a kind of inverse Chicken Little about the ODS situation, and I looked forward to exposing her various blind spots and hypocrisies. And though there was a wholesale lack of depth to her intellect, she was cagey, often bringing a homespun folksiness to her right-wing arguments. And I had to be mindful of that.

Of course, I wasn't thinking of any of this during the ride downtown. Instead I was thinking: What the fuck *are* we doing on Sunday? Grace had put the bug in my brain and I just couldn't shake it. I knew it was something we had discussed, planned, maybe bickered over a little. But it was now hidden in the fog of my mind. What was it? What. Was. It?

The Beck deposited me at the Canadian Broadcasting Centre — the CBC's imposing Front Street edifice with its blue pillars and red-framed windows and larger-than-life photos of network personalities — and I marched through the doors and made my way to the atrium's front desk. The receptionist paged *Power Today*'s producer, and within moments she came hustling out of the elevators toward me. I expected the first words out of her mouth to be, *You're late!* but instead she said:

"You're not wearing a poppy."

"I know. It must have fallen off on my way over. I —"

"I sent, like, four emails about it."

"I know, I'm sorry. Look, is there anywhere I can —"

"No, there isn't. And there's no time, anyway."

She signed me in and then the elevator whisked us to the upper floors. I'd been on the show before but hadn't met this particular producer. Her name was Lori, a whip-smart twentysomething with a look that balanced sporty with haggard: dark hair pulled into a tight ponytail; bags under her eyes from doing what would have been three people's jobs twenty years ago; nice bum. We came out of the elevators and started Sorkining down a busy hallway as she explained the lineup to me.

"You guys are up first. The ODS story is just too big not to lead with. We're doing two eighters —"

"Meaning?"

"Two eight-minute segments. There'll be a commercial break in between if you need to collect your thoughts."

"I won't. Can't speak for Cheryl, though."

"Sal was going to walk you through his intro and outro but there's no time."

"How is Sal, anyway?"

"There is. No. Time. Once we get you in the chair, I need you to —"

"Philip Sharpe, you whiskey-swilling so-and-so!" I heard someone yell to me. I turned to see my friend Raj approach us through a nest of cubicles and camera stands. "You carpetbagging Maritimer! You salt-stained scallywag! How the hell are ya?" Raj was a freelance videographer, clearly on one of his intermittent contracts with the CBC. I had met him years ago, and would occasionally run into him while doing press chores for my books. Though roughly my age — fifty this year, *gawd* — Raj always struck me as younger, more vital, more unmoored. He was just as likely to be hanging off a cliff-face in Borneo with a camera on his shoulder as he was to be filming downtown Toronto biz-knobs with their *jayus* senses of humour for a corporate video. He and I weren't particularly close. Yet in that moment, I was deeply relieved to spot his familiar face, and I hugged him clumsily when he came over.

"It's so good to see you," I said.

"Likewise — it's been like, two years. I *heard* you were in the hot seat this afternoon."

"I am. They need an expert opinion on this ODS situation, plus Cheryl Sneed's."

He laughed. "I hear that. You know, Rick Mercer was asking about you the other day."

"I know, I owe Rick an email. Do you know if he's —"

"Dr. Sharpe," said Lori, "I *really* need you to come with me."

"You better do what she says," Raj smirked, and whacked me on the shoulder. "We'll talk later. Go eat 'em up. I'll watch you from the booth."

Within minutes I was prepped for the stage: Lori clipped a microphone to my shirt like a prosthesis, then tucked its battery into the ass of my pants with completely non-sexual efficiency. Someone came by to give my brow and cheekbones a light dusting of powder. When finished, Lori shoved me out to the *Power Today* set.

I staggered onto the rise, and there she was: stout, unsmiling Cheryl Sneed, already seated at the large glass table under the klieg lights. She wore a very blousy blouse, but had done something different — and dare I say appealing? — with her hair since I'd last seen her: a certain sensual swirl to her grey-blond locks, a truly noble attempt at attractiveness for a woman of her vintage. Above her left breast sat a pristinely fastened poppy.

"Hello, Cheryl," I said, sitting down in the chair a stagehand steered me into.

"Philip."

"Good to see you."

Her eyes flashed to my tweed. "You not get the emails about the poppy?"

"I lost mine on the way over."

"Understandable," she said. "The things are engineered to fall off. It's how the veterans make their money."

We were soon joined by Sal Porter, the impossibly handsome host of *Power Today*, who also wore a poppy. He shook my hand and took his seat at the end. "Running late today, Philip? We all missed you in the green room."

"Sorry, I was waylaid by ..." What to say? An annoyed wife. Domestic trifles. A yearning vagina. A lapse in memory. What *were* we doing on Sunday, goddamn it? "... stuff at home," I said. Yes, yes. Stuff at home. By now Simone would've gotten in the door from school, and Grace would be asking about her day, verifying homework assignments and partaking in other bits of motherwork before dinner. Wait, what had she wanted me to do with Simone on Wednesday night? Oh *shit*, I'd already forgotten. What was it? What was it?

The final preparatory rituals for live TV unfurled around us — countdowns and cameramen call-outs and such. Lori popped by with a small metallic claw and pried the empty staples out of my lapel without bothering to ask how they'd gotten there. It seemed an overly finicky act, considering she did nothing about the strand of comb-over that was (I would learn later) standing almost completely vertically off my head.

"Are we ready?" Sal asked.

A dance recital! I nearly yelled out. That's what it was! I ran a hand over my bushy red beard. Of course. I was taking my stepdaughter to a dance recital. Grace wanted me to —

The room filled with electric guitar and synthesized trumpets, and a camera came swinging toward us on a crane.

"It's Monday, November 2, 2015, and you're watching *Power Today*," Sal said. "I'm your host, Sal Porter. On this program: evidence is mounting that last month's bus disaster in Italy was in fact an act of terrorism. We'll be on the line with an official in Rome with the latest. Also: Canada's new foreign affairs minister is here to discuss Vladimir Putin and the worsening situation in Ukraine. But first: there's only one story that *every* Canadian is talking about and that is last Friday's collapse of ODS Financial Group. Its sixty-five hundred employees are out of work, but that is just the tip of the iceberg. With so many directly managed pensions and other financial assets vanishing overnight, the impact on Bay Street — as well as Main Street — could be enormous. To discuss the issue, we're joined by two guests:

"Cheryl Sneed is a long-time columnist with the *Toronto Times* who's been covering the ODS situation for months. She won a national newspaper award earlier this year for her profile of ODS's chief financial officer, Glenda Harkins-Smith. Cheryl has just published her first book, entitled *How Feminism Fails Women*. Cheryl, thanks for joining us."

"Thank you for having me."

"And, making his *eleventh* appearance on our show, Dr. Philip Sharpe. Philip is a professor of philosophy and economics at the University of Toronto and the author of ten books. His latest is called *Under the Guidance of Secret Motives: Corporate Canada Today*. Philip, welcome."

"Yes, thanks," I muttered.

"Philip, I want to start with you because you dedicate a large portion of your latest book to profiling ODS, and how a toxic corporate culture there contributed to its problems. In fact, you spent part of your last sabbatical working undercover in its communications department."

"That's not entirely true," I said. "They knew I was there; granted me several interviews with the C-suite, in fact. They just didn't *care*. But I want to correct something from your intro, Sal: you said the impact of Friday's announcement *could* be enormous. I would change 'could' to 'will,' and by 'enormous' we mean 'cataclysmic.'"

"There's no evidence of that," Cheryl excreted.

"Look —"

"No, Philip. You and others have been arguing that this is 2008 all over again, and it's just not true. Most of ODS's assets were either shielded by new federal regulations — regulations brought in by your bogeyman, Stephen Harper, I should point out — or they were *insured*. Only a small sliver was tied up with the securities foreclosed on Friday."

"Cheryl, 37.8 *billion* dollars is about to vanish from the Canadian economy. I wouldn't call that a 'sliver.'"

"Where are you getting that number from, Philip? Because every economist on Bay Street disputes it. And I mean *every* economist."

"Of course they dispute it. They're not exactly inde —"

"Okay, okay," Sal said. "Let's back up here." As he provided a bit more background for his audience and lobbed a couple of questions at Cheryl, I glanced out briefly beyond the cameras and spotted Raj in the control booth. His hands were on his hips but he was still smiling — a good sign that I was doing well. I wondered in that moment if Grace had bothered to turn on the TV at home to watch me. Or was she still seething about the tub faucet or that I couldn't bloody remember what we were doing next Sunday? What was it? Goddamn it, what *was* it?

"Now Philip, you're coming at these issues as a philosopher," Sal went on. "I mean, it's well-documented that your area of specialty is *moral* duty — a kind of categorical sense of right and wrong. So in that context, what was it about ODS that piqued your interest to start with?"

"Well, it comes right back to corporate culture," I said. "The firm began a century ago as one of these genteel and cautious fund managers. But like a lot of corporate entities — law firms and professional services companies and such — it became plagued with an ideology of *internal* competition, starting around the turn of the millennium. Suddenly everyone was slitting everyone else's throat — *within the organization* — to elevate themselves and squeeze a bit more bonus out. From the senior leadership downward, backstabbing practically became a requirement for everyone who worked there. So I grew fascinated by how quickly ODS would betray or even reverse its own business plans, not to mention mission statements or 'core values.' By the end, purge-style *coups d'état* at the senior management level were a weekly occurrence. In the short time I was there, I witnessed whole careers expunged overnight from its corporate history. It was like something out of Stalinist Russia."

"God, I can't *believe* the melodrama you get away with!" Cheryl piped up.

"It's not melodrama," I said. "It's fact. The —"

"If I could just interject here —" Sal attempted.

"It *is*. You know, Philip, your book is so typical of left-wing myopia. You went in to ODS with a thesis statement already calcified in your brain and then you cherry-picked the 'facts' that verified it, ignoring everything else."

"That is *not* true."

"It is."

"Look, Cheryl —"

"No, it is. You went in there convinced that ODS was pure and unmitigated evil. A soulless multinational so driven by short-term profits that it lost any sense of a moral compass. So let me ask you this: in two hundred and seventy-eight pages, why did you make no mention of its Briefcase Moms program?"

I looked at her. "I don't see how *that* is relevant to Friday's —"

"You make no mention of Briefcase Moms — an initiative that Harkins-Smith herself was a direct beneficiary of. Why did you not mention that ODS has been a major sponsor of amateur athletics in Canada? Or that it's been a platinum sponsor of the LGBT community's Out On Bay Street conference? Or that it had work-life balance policies that a daily journalist would *kill* for?"

"Okay," Sal jumped in, "maybe we should switch gears and —"

"Look," I said, unwilling to let him rescue me. "We can talk about all the smokescreens the company threw up to hide its true nature —"

"Oh *please*."

"— but the truth is. No, Cheryl, the truth is: sixty-five hundred people are out of work, billions have been vaporized from the economy, and the C-suite has made off like criminals. We're talking eight-figure payouts, *each*. Money sheltered using complex financial instruments and a level of obscurantism unseen in the history of corporate Canada."

"Well I know from your book, Philip," Cheryl said, "that you interviewed the firm's chief lawyer. What would he say now? Did the senior leadership do anything illegal?"

"That's not the point."

"It *is* the point."

"Okay, we need to —" Sal said.

"Answer the question, Philip: Did they do anything illegal?"

"Cheryl —"

"Because you're the one calling them criminals."

"I said they were *like* criminals."

"So answer the question: Did they do anything illegal?"

"They walked off with *millions* while leaving an economic catastrophe in their wake."

"Did they do anything illegal?"

I turned away from her then. This grilling infused me with a sense of déjà vu from earlier. In fact, it felt as if Grace, not Cheryl, was sitting there at the *Power Today* desk, administering this third degree to me — making that horrific dig about my sexual prowess and then dragging me over the coals about forgetting what we were doing on Sunday. What *was* it? God, I wish I could remember.

"Okay," Sal said, "we're just coming up to our first commercial break, and when we come back we should discuss ..." and he read a few lines from his outro. But as I turned toward them again, I saw the gesture that Cheryl made at me. I'm not even sure the cameras caught it. It was that exact same jiggle of the head, that *I guess I made my point* flap of her hair, that Grace had made at me earlier. The exact same one. I felt the bile rise up in me.

"What they did should be *made* illegal," I said.

Sal stopped suddenly, and he and Cheryl just sort of stared at me.

"I beg your *pardon*?" she said.

"What they did should be made illegal." The words blundered out of me again before I could stop them. And so did these: "The government should pass a law *making* what happened on Friday illegal."

Cheryl let out a smug, choky guffaw. "You can't be serio —"

"I am dead serious," I said. It was like a fever had overtaken my brain, burning behind my eyes and clouding everything around me. "The scope of the catastrophe is such that the government needs to take tough and — dare I say it? — punitive action."

"*Really?*" Cheryl said, twisting her girth around in her chair. "Really, Philip? You honestly think —"

"All right, guys, we do need to go to —" Sal tried to interject.

"You honestly think that would be the *moral* thing to do? Really? Okay, so the government takes months or even years passing new laws to make what they did illegal. And *then* what? What happens to your diabolical C-suite?"

"And then they should be charged *retroactively.*"

"Oh my *God*," she said, swaying in her chair like a buoy.

"I'm serious," I retorted. "The magnitude of this is —"

"Is what?" she barked. "Enough to override centuries of judicial law? I mean, this is really beyond the pale, Philip — even for you."

And just like that, the fever broke and I came out of it. My eyes passed back to the control booth, and I could see Raj through the window. He was no longer smiling. His own eyes were wide, his cheeks sunken. And in that instant, I was convinced that Grace *was* watching me on the television. She and the kids. And also my faculty colleagues at the university. And my students. Everyone.

Oh God — what did I just say? Did I just imply that people should be arrested for breaking a law that does not yet exist? Did I just undermine centuries of enlightened liberal values, values that I had been teaching — and *defending*, against the barbarism of both the Right *and* the Left — for more than twenty years, all for the sake of sending a handful of corporate types to jail? Did I just do that — on national television?

"Look," I sputtered, "what I'm trying to say is —"

"Okay, we *have* to go to commercial," Sal said. "We'll be back, we'll be back."

"*Well*," Cheryl huffed as we faded out, "talk about Stalinist Russia …"

Odious

I hope you'll indulge me, dear reader, if I backtrack now and provide some context around my chthonic journey into the hive of Canada's finance sector. Yes, for three months in the fall of 2012 I joined the workaday masses that streamed through St. Andrew Station in downtown Toronto and up into the charcoal towers at King and York, into commerce's everlasting orgasm at the low end of Bay Street. This was not, as certain faculty colleagues accused me of, some shallow act of anthropology on my part. I took this sabbatical not to specimen-ize a society, but to bear witness to the practical application of ideas I'd been grappling with since my Oxford days, ideas that culminated into my successfully defended D.Phil. dissertation in 1993 and its subsequent publication as my first book (*Decanting Kant: The Categorical Imperative in the Age of Neo-liberalism*, OUP, 1995). What to say: I was and still am an unapologetic deontologist; and I wanted to see how Bay Street's increasingly unfettered cupidity affected real people at the level of their morals, their sense of duty to themselves and each other. ODS's chicanery had been making headlines for half a decade by 2012, and the company seemed a fitting target for my experiment.

But perhaps Cheryl Sneed *was* right: when I showed up for the first day of my entry-level position on their national Comms team, I was fully expecting a cruel, cutthroat environment.

So I was thrown for a loop when they gave us all laptops in the first ten minutes of orientation. The HR manager leading our pan-departmental training session handed the machines out as if they were bento boxes, while we, a cohort of about fifteen, sat in rows of tables in the classroom-style meeting room. I was parked between two young women hired as financial analysts — both of whom, I recall, having vaguely pornographic names: Tiina Cherry (spelt with two phallic *i*'s) and Regina Wetmore. The laptops we were assigned were the slickest I'd ever seen — putting to shame the dud I used for my work at U of T's Philosophy department — but the girls barely blinked at the handout.

Orientation revealed that ODS was in Year Three of its latest corporate piatiletka: The ODS Way (2010–2014), the goal for which was to re-establish billion-dollar revenues by the end of "Fiscal 14." The HR rep, using a Microsoft PowerPoint presentation full of Microsoft Visio diagrams, walked us through how this overarching mission statement was to control our behaviours in every interaction while on company time. This *was more like it*, I thought. A downright fascistic approach to human manipulation: the relentless sloganeering, the buzzword indoctrinations, the pressure not to use any independent judgment that wasn't "laser-focused" on the company's profitability. I raised several reflexively comic protests during this presentation, but my jokes fell flat. Yet despite these subversive queries, I did not achieve the pariah status I assumed I would. In fact, Tiina and Regina — who seemed to have become BFFs during the mid-morning coffee break — invited me to join them for lunch.

In the afternoon, I settled into my assigned cubicle, which was right outside the office of the communications manager who hired me. "Orientation go okay?" he asked, coming out when he spotted my arrival. He was a tall, breezy technocrat named Stuart, with thick curly hair and a meticulously trimmed soul patch, so unlike the red mass of fur that engulfed my face. He took me around to meet the rest of the team, an ensemble of marketing types and quondam journalists and social media specialists. Everyone knew who I was and why I was there — someone even claimed to have read my one confirmed bestseller, *The Movable Apocalypse* (Bibliophilia, 1998) — and everyone was friendly. But it was a friendliness singed by stress, by worries over looming deadlines and relentless project plans, by evening GO Train schedules forever present in the back of their minds.

Stuart and I reviewed the complex nondisclosure documents I had signed — outlining all of the proprietary elements of ODS's business that I'd agreed would not make it into my new book — and then he set me upon the task for which I'd been hired. The company's enormous, labyrinthine website had been written in a kind of business pidgin, and it was my job to rewrite a large section of it into lucid English. The firm was happy for the free labour, and this was exactly the kind of work *I* wanted during this operation, since it would put me in contact with multiple divisions of the company — its fund managers, its corporate advisors, its legal team, its various ancillary offshoots — and give me a view into their world. The job itself was a simple simulacrum of journalism: do a bit of research, go interview the relevant experts, cobble together the web copy, et cetera. Stuart even suggested I could do much of it from home, and I was tempted by the prospect: to be in my own book-lined office, a Bloody Joseph to sip, Grace beyond the closed door doing her thing with the kids. But no. My true subject matter was ODS's corporate culture, and I needed to be in the thick of it.

And what to say of that culture? ODS believed in competition, believed it in its bloodstream. Saw it as the one agora that everyone was obligated to participate in. The next sale, the next business relationship, how one chaired a meeting or approved a business plan — it *all* became about beating somebody else. This created an air of antagonism that hummed like white noise throughout the organization. These men and women, caught up in a kind of radicalized individualism, battled one another not only for the pre-eminence of their effort and ideas, but for the chance to vanquish the effort and ideas of others. Everyone I spoke to seemed cast in a sarcophagus of anxiety. And where did this feeling spring from? One word summed it up: change. Change was the siren call of liberalized markets; it was the only constant these people could count on. A failure to adapt to this kind of mindless dynamism would spell their downfall, and it bred a particular strain of human fear that brought out the worst in these people's natures. Their only relief came, it seemed, from ducking down to the Path beneath Bay Street, that enormous mazelike shopping mall, to partake in some retail therapy as a reminder of why they had signed up for this life in the first place. I myself went down there for lunch sometimes, and would even run into Tiina and Regina in one of the Path's countless food courts. The girls were always kind to me — smiling sprites who welcomed me and my tray of tasteless pad Thai to their table. Yet some simple probing revealed that they were already overwhelmed by their workloads, as if they had been with the firm for years rather than just a few weeks. And as I looked around the food court, *everyone* seemed to be in the same boat, shackled by years of compounded stress that may have come on in just the last four hours. *What kind of life was this?* I thought. How could these people not form a pitchfork-wielding jacquerie to overthrow their taskmasters? But this was Bay Street's monopoly on their reality. It was all they knew.

My "official" interviews with members of the C-suite provided some insight into the *fons et origo* of this so-called culture. I got twenty minutes with each of them, including the reclusive Viktor Grozni himself. I was frustrated (though impressed) by the way they were all able to stay unflaggingly on message, as if the firm's business models and mission statements were as finely engineered as a Lamborghini. They all pleasantly dismissed any notion that their company was in trouble.

Only Grozni, that acne-scarred oligarch, got openly hostile with me. "You're not wearing a tie," he smiled as he extended his hand over his desk when I entered his surprisingly spare office. "Most men wear a tie when they come see me."

"Oh, Viktor, what is a tie anyway?" I smiled back, accepting his hand. "It's just an arrow that points to your penis." The interview went downhill from there. I questioned him — politely at first, then more sternly — about the cutthroat nature of ODS's business culture, and he retorted with buzz phrases like "excellence" and "competition" and "high-performing environment." When I suggested that his brand of competition forced employees to engage in some rather predatory practices, he welcomed me to name the regulations they were violating. When I suggested the federal government had created the very landscape that made such behaviour possible, he said, "Yes, isn't it great that Canada finally has a government interested in growing the economy after so many decades of suffocating socialism?" And when I suggested that he had a *moral* obligation to good corporate governance — considering how many Canadians had their pensions wrapped up in this racket — Grozni looked at me as if I had spoken Martian. As our exchange grew more heated, I began to see him as the embodiment of that great Greek term *pleonexia*, which John Stuart Mill — enlightened man that he was — had written so eloquently about. Grozni's was not your garden-variety greed, but rather "the desire to engross more than one's share of advantages … the pride which derives gratification from the abasement of others; the ego which thinks self and its concerns more important than everything else …" The impression Grozni left me with was that my viewpoints were outdated at best and dangerous at worst. He even said to me, near the end of the interview, "The Canada you knew, Mr. Sharpe, is long gone." "It's Dr. Sharpe," I corrected him, "and I think you're wrong." He just chuckled once, as if to say *I can't fathom a world where someone like you could prove someone like me wrong.*

Back in the CBC studio during the commercial break, I was tremulous. As a stagehand came by to re-powder my brow — I was tacky with sweat by this point — my imagination began to corkscrew out of control over how my gaffe might be reverberating around the country. My heart raced as I looked over at Sal and Cheryl, who sat cool as breezes at the other end of the desk. Their poppies hovered over their breasts like beacons of respectability, while mine was probably fluttering somewhere among the eaves or gutters of Parliament Street.

I gestured to Sal to lean back in his chair with me, and spoke to him *sotto voce* when he did, even though Cheryl was sitting right between us. "Look, when we come back, can I have a chance to clarify what I just said?"

"Sorry, buddy," he replied, "but that segment went way over. We only have about five minutes left, and I have several other points I want to cover."

He sat back up and I reluctantly followed. The three of us waited in silence for the commercial break to run its course. Cheryl's face held a patina of diplomacy, but I knew what she was thinking: that she had bested me, that by hijacking Sal's role as interviewer she was able to cast *me* as the extremist and *herself* as the voice of moderation. With less than five minutes left, I would need all of my intellectual heft to turn things around. In the seconds before we came back, I looked up once more at Raj standing in the booth. His head was now bowed over his phone, his brow furrowed. Oh God — he was probably on Facebook or Twitter right then, watching the obloquy and snark over my blunder flood in. Was Grace there, too, gingerly defending my moment of indiscretion? Or was she still steaming over my fecklessness as a father (*Philip, your daughter* scalded *herself*), my bedroom shortcomings (*I'm getting pretty* used *to your inability to satisfy me*), or, worst of all, my complete ineptitude at keeping track of our social calendar? Oh Jesus, why couldn't I remember what we're doing on Sunday?

A countdown proceeded, and then the electric guitars and synthesized trumpets returned. "And we're back," Sal said when they stopped. "We're talking about Friday's collapse of ODS Financial Group with Cheryl Sneed and Philip Sharpe. Now Cheryl, you've taken some heat over your coverage of ODS. Even in the last few weeks, as the company entered its death spiral, you've remained ultimately optimistic. Can you explain why?"

"Well, of course the foreclosure of the firm is by no means good news. I know this has put undo stress on both individuals and the market. But I just don't buy that this is some kind of apocalypse brought on by corporate malice. The truth is, ODS made some big gambles that didn't pay off. But the Canadian economy is strong; it's *resilient*. And so, too, are the people who worked for the firm. The good ones will find a way; they *always* do. I mean, just anecdotally, I heard from several of my sources who said that people were on their cellphones Friday afternoon, reaching out to contacts and finding other work. Some had secured new jobs before they left the building."

"And you're also convinced," Sal went on, "that the pension funds that the company managed are still secure? That this hasn't left a big gaping hole in —"

"So you feel the company has no obligation whatsoever," I said to Cheryl, cutting Sal off, "that this is a morally neutral situation as far as the business is concerned. You don't see what ODS did as categorically wrong."

"You're not exactly in a position to talk about right and wrong, Philip," she replied without looking at me, "considering you just argued that ODS's executive team should be arrested for crimes that don't yet exist."

"That's not what I said."

"It *is* what you said."

"It's not what I *meant*. Look. I think what you're doing is obfuscating the bigger issue here. The reality is, last Friday represents the culmination of what Canada has become after nearly ten years of Stephen Harper: this kind of neo-Thatcherism; this normalization of greed and dog-eat-dogism; this complete disregard for the community at large. What we've witnessed is our country giving neo-liberal economics a monopoly on all things moral."

"Oh my *God*," Cheryl said, rolling her eyes. "Again with the melodrama."

"It's not melodrama."

"It *is*. Why don't you just admit what this is really about for you, Philip? You didn't like ODS's C-suite as *people*. You found them smug; you found them indifferent to your abstract ideas about duty; and you found them ruthless when it came to the tough decisions needed to keep the business afloat. And now you just wish someone would come along and arrest them."

"That is *not* true." I nodded toward the camera in front of us. "Canadians need to understand what is really going on here. Friday represented a failure of the social contract we're supposed to have with our leaders. And not just with our *corporate* leaders, whom we've given the right — apparently — to make as much money as they want. But our *civic* leaders, our government, whom we've given the right to protect the *general* will, to have a bird's-eye view on how the actions of a few can harm the lives of many."

"Wow," Cheryl said, her voice sodden with sarcasm. "Straight from the pen of Jean-Jacques Rousseau."

"Okay, we only have a couple minutes left," Sal interjected. "Let's talk about severance packages. We know the senior leadership walked off with huge payouts, but as for the average employee —"

"In the end, Cheryl, what I'm talking about here is magnanimity. About graciousness." The two of them just stared at me, as if they weren't sure where I was going with this. Truth be told, I wasn't so sure myself. "We've watched as freedom of the markets has trumped all other freedoms — not the least of which being our *moral* freedoms. We've all but abandoned civic virtue and good governance in favour of a rigid ideology — the ideology of economic liberty, of wealth as an end in itself. And when that ideology crashes and burns so spectacularly, as it did on Friday, the system itself should be magnanimous enough to punish those responsible. To *allow* us to punish them. *That's* what I meant earlier."

"Okay, guys, let's get back on track with —"

"I assure you, Philip," Cheryl sneered, "that I have no idea what you're talking about. And I'm beginning to think that you don't either."

"You don't see how it's all *connected*?" I asked. From the corner of my eye I could see Lori giving Sal a desperate signal to wrap things up. "This monopoly of market thinking?" I pushed on. "This fetishizing of the self? This abandoning of duty to the mentality of acquisition, to this belief that economic value is the only value? This is nothing more than a *bastardization* of the liberal traditions this country was founded on."

"I just don't see it that way," Cheryl said. "I think you're taking a bunch of vague notions and just extending them onto a situation that, while dire, is relatively straightforward. I think you're saying these things to grind a political axe against the business community."

"That's because you're cynical," I said. "I mean, Sal called you 'ultimately optimistic' earlier, but the exact opposite is true. I think you're deeply pessimistic about how human beings can exist with one another. If you thought about these concepts for half a second, you'd know just how harmful Friday's events are to the fabric of what Canada is supposed to stand for."

"Well, Philip," Cheryl said, "I don't believe these ideas are as penetrating as you think they are."

"Well, Cheryl, I would love nothing more than to *penetrate* you with these ideas," I retorted, "but I worry you wouldn't *enjoy* it enough."

There was a collective gasp in the studio, which I confess I didn't hear at the time. Cheryl's face puckered and Sal sort of gaped at me.

"Okay, we gotta go," he said, turning back to his audience. "The foreign affairs minister is up next. When we come back."

"And we're out!" Lori yelled over the cameras.

Within a second, a duo of stagehands climbed onto the riser and began helping Cheryl out of her microphone. As soon as they finished, she was up and out of her chair, fuming off toward the green room without even saying goodbye to us. Neither of these handmaidens turned to assist me then, but just clomped back off the stage without acknowledging my existence. So I unclipped my own microphone, leaned forward to dig its battery out of my pants, then set the whole tangled mess on the desk. Lori came by quickly to collect it. I tried to make eye contact with her before she, too, departed, but her face was just one inscrutable scowl.

I looked at Sal and he looked at me.

"That could have gone better," he said.

I threw my hands up, as if to indicate: *This is the world we live in now.* I got out of the chair and left the stage myself. By the time I reached the corridor beyond the studio wall baffles, Raj was standing there waiting for me.

"What the *hell* was that?" he asked.

"I know, I fucked up big time." We began to make our way down the corridor as I searched for something to wipe the makeup off my face. "Can you believe I said that — on *national* TV?"

"A lot of people are gonna be pissed at you."

"Tell me about it. You don't just undermine centuries of judicial principle like that and expect to get away with it."

"Dude, *what*?" Raj said. "No, no, I meant —"

But then I spotted it — a men's room. I rushed over and pushed through its swinging door, heading for the paper towels and sinks while Raj waited for me in the hall.

"Look, I need to get out of here," I told him when I came back, all fresh-faced and flushed. "What are you doing right now? Are you allowed to leave?"

"I can leave," he said. "I've been here since, like, six this morning. But Sharpe, listen, don't you want to …" He was maybe going to say, *Don't you want to talk about what just happened?* But I could tell that he could tell that, no, I didn't want to talk about it. I didn't want to *listen*. I felt covered in the cold mud of shame over saying something so horrifying about those ODS executives, so philosophically inconsistent, on live TV. To talk about it right now would be to relive the whole thing.

Just then two CBC interns, a couple of skirted go-getters, walked by in the hall. They must have caught my bumbling performance on a monitor somewhere, because they both turned and tossed me a glare of appalled incredulity as they passed. One of the girls even made to stop, perhaps to say something rude to me, but her friend pulled her away. "Okay," Raj said. "Let's … let's just get you out of here."

"Great," I replied. "I say we head to Cabbagetown. I need to be on my own turf. I'll take you to my local for a drink or six."

"Sounds good to me."

Out on Front Street, the afternoon had turned to evening. We had rolled our clocks back over the weekend, and the abrupt onset of twilight was still jarring, seeming to swallow the entire city like an ominous premonition. We hailed a Beck. I told the cabbie, "Parliament and Carlton," and we soon joined the rush-hour traffic battling to get out of downtown. The Beck felt less like an escape pod and more like a tumbrel, and I imagined impoverished serfs pelting me with fruit as I was taken away to a final, grisly end.

Raj and I sat in silence as we made our glacial progression. I leaned back against the seat with closed eyes and pinched my nose, my mind churning with a thousand regrets. To break the quiet, Raj opted for idle chit-chat.

"Say, Sharpe."

I looked at him. "Yeah?"

"Do you still make that killer cocktail of yours?"

"What, the Bloody Joseph?"

"Yeah."

"I do. I had three of them earlier today."

He laughed. "That drink is off the chain, man. You gotta make me one of those again."

"I meant to have a fourth, but ran out of time." I harrumphed. "Maybe that's why I was so off my game today." Of course, I knew that wasn't true. One final Collins' worth of that fierce concoction — infused with brawny Jameson as a substitute for effeminate vodka — would not have put me in a better frame of mind. I knew damn well what had lay at the root of my distraction. A vision of her, holding up our daughter and speaking those words to me — *you don't really seem all that plugged in to what's happening in your own house* — flooded my mind.

"I'll have to have you over," I said to Raj. "Just not for a little while."

* * *

We arrived in Cabbagetown and the cab deposited us at an Irish pub called Stout. This early in the evening we were able to nab a spot near the enormous fireplace, finding leather club chairs to sink into and a low table in front of us. Raj seemed impressed by the aura of the place: the tastefully exposed brick; the warm mahogany woodwork; the beige piano in the corner; the separate menu for craft beer. I borrowed his cellphone — I don't *do* cellphones — and he helped me send a text to Grace: *Hi, it's Philip. At Stout with friend Raj. Back later.* Soon, a young, attractive waitress came by — "Hello, Professor, great to see you again," she said with authentic enthusiasm — and we ordered a couple of pints from the cask. When they came, Raj and I cheered each other and then I downed nearly half of mine in a single gulp, dribbling a bit onto the top of my Payless when I returned the glass to the table. The waitress was right on it, coming by with a napkin so I could wipe up, then took it away with a sunny "No *problem*" when I finished.

"You know," I said after she was out of earshot, "that was the first time today a woman has been kind to me."

Raj laughed. "Oh really?"

"Yeah." I squeezed the bridge of my nose once more. "I had a terrible fight with Grace before I left the house today."

"Dude."

"That's why I was such a mess on camera."

"Dude, look." And he gave my knee a manly shake. "Try not to worry about it, okay? Maybe it's not as bad as you think."

I looked at him. "Are you kidding? Raj, this is a huge blow to me intellectually. I mean, I'm supposed to be a leading expert on Immanuel Kant. I'm supposed to *know* what it means to talk about the categorical imperative, about universal law — law that applies

to everyone in *every* circumstance. What I said was the worst example of the hypothetical imperative I can imagine. This idea that
we would imprison certain people and then think up a reason why,
and do it out of spite. Do you know what I mean?" He didn't
seem to, but he let me continue. So I talked about these ideas as
we ordered food and more pints. Talked about them as we ate and
drank. Was still talking about them long after the waitress had
cleared away our plates and we ordered yet more pints.

"I'm sorry," I finally said to him, "to go on like this."

"It's okay."

"Tell me what's new in your world. Where are you living
these days?"

"I'm back on the Danforth," he grinned. "Rented myself a
sweet little place out near Donlands. Big kitchen; open porch at
ground level out front. You should come out and see it sometime."

"I'd like that. And will you be at the CBC long term, do
you think?"

He chortled. "Fuck no. Is anyone? More budget cuts are coming and I'll be gone. I'll go freelance for a while until I can figure
out what to do next."

Ah, the peripatetic life of a confirmed free spirit. I marvelled again at how Raj's unbridled existence seemed to infuse
him with a youthfulness that had long abandoned me. Over the
next two pints he told me about various "gigs" he'd had prior
to taking this latest contract with our alleged public broadcaster: the trip to Asia to film a documentary about Japanese
whiskey-making; a sojourn to Alabama for some corporate vid-
eos and the after-hours run-in with bona fide members of the
KKK; the Guelph start-up that paid him obscene amounts of
money to film some CollegeHumor knock-offs, only to fold a
month later. Through it all, Raj seemed fearless in the face of not
knowing where his next paycheque would come from. And as I

vicariously lived through his adventures, I felt the slightest pang of remorse that I was now safely institutionalized — institution-alized, perhaps, in more ways than one.

"And have you seen Henry around much?" I asked him during a lull.

Raj gave a derisive snort. "*No.* That guy got married. Now I never see him. Kind of like *you.*"

"Hey now!"

"Just kidding. It pisses me off, is all. Henry used to be such a good journalist, you know. One of the best in the city. I mean, he did that killer interview with you for the *Star* when your book on Islam came out."

"This is true."

"And now what's he doing? Nothing. Fucking corporate communications. What can I say about that guy? Henry got fat and boring and, now, fucking married. I don't even recognize him anymore. He's well on his way to moving to the suburbs and becoming one of these lobotomized Stepford husbands who, like, helps his wife around the house and talks to his kids and shit. I mean, I can't relate to someone like that."

"No, obviously," I said with shifty eyes. I chuckled at his clever term, since I knew the type well. Grace was always inviting her friends over — a cheery cabal of cocksure feminists with their affably dull Stepford husbands in tow — for brunch. I remained engaged in their table banter only because these men found so many interesting ways to be uninteresting. Thankfully, Grace did not insist I comport to their behaviour. She was just grateful if I still blew below the legal limit by the cantaloupe course.

Wait.

That was it.

Brunch. Brunch! Brunch! Brunch! *That's* what we were doing on Sunday. We were hosting yet another brunch, and had invited my literary agent over in the hopes that she might look at Grace's new children's book. Of course. This fact re-emerged in my mind, as solid as a cinder block.

Raj looked at me queerly. "You're having a whole conversation over there, aren't you — all by yourself."

"Sorry, I have to go," I said. "Let's get the bill. I have to go."

Out on Parliament Street, Raj and I hugged and then parted company — he walking northward to Castle Frank Station, and me hoofing my way home. I didn't know then that he had pulled out his phone to check Facebook as he went, and, when he did, saw something there that twisted his face into a rictus of panic. He told me later that he had thought of doubling back to find me, or at least calling out my name down the street. I probably wouldn't have heard him anyway, caught up as I was in the mental airstreams of my triumph, a parallax of pure, sweet recollection.

I got back to 4 Metcalfe Street to find it dark, the little stained-glass window above our door like an extinguished lamp, the eaves above it pregnant with shadows. Grace and the girls had clearly gone to bed. What hour was it, anyway? I wandered into the kitchen, opened the fridge absently. Moved to the dining-room table, took a quick flip through the day's papers. Then I staggered upstairs to our bedroom, ready to face my fate. But stepping in to the faint light of a street lamp coming through our curtained window, I could see Grace was asleep on her side of the bed, her back turned to me. I was suddenly awash in guilt. As penance, I didn't even bother to go brush my teeth in the ensuite. Just stripped my clothes off and onto the floor, then crawled in next to her.

Tuesday, November 3

I must confess I don't really get the Facebook. Sorry —
Facebook. Grace corrects me every time, grinning impishly at
my occasional inclusion of the definite article as evidence of
my fuddyduddiness and outoftouchitude. Yes, I have a Facebook
account and yes, I have "friends." Mind you, I don't as a policy
accept friend requests from strangers, current students, former students who have not yet graduated, any of my colleagues in the
Philosophy department, or fellow authors whose books I've hated.
I don't quite grasp how all the notifications work, and I only visit
the site a couple times a week. This, according to Grace, makes me
anti-social. She has 1,382 "friends." I have 46.

Which made what happened in the morning all the more baf-
fling. I wish I could say I awoke feeling ebullient and ready to put
the previous day's unpleasantness behind me, only to be dragged
into the muck by what I discovered when I checked my email.
But this was not true. I awoke feeling like a shithead, and had my
shitheadedness confirmed when I staggered up to my office desk,
turned on my laptop, and discovered I had received *eighty-seven*
notifications from Facebook in the last fourteen hours. This, I

figured, was roughly the same number I had received in *total* since joining the social network in 2009.

I hunkered down and started scrolling. My inbox was flooded with names I didn't recognize, strangers commenting on a post added by one of my "friends" in which my name had been tagged. I clicked through to the post and saw that it was — of course — a YouTube clip of yesterday's appearance on *Power Today*. There were so many comments that Facebook could not display them all; could not even say how many there were. The "see previous comments" link taunted me but I refused to click on it. The ones I *could* see were bad enough:

Jake, that's NOT what I said. I'm no fan of Sneed but at the end of the day, Sharpe still shouldn't have …

Well put, Paul! This kind of language is such *a big part of our culture now. I hope U of T shows some backbone and takes him to task about …*

Ha! "Sharpesplaining" — love it! It's great to see that pompous ass finally getting what he …

And one that cut me straight to the gills:

Did anyone else notice that HE WAS THE ONLY ONE NOT WEARING A POPPY!

I slapped the laptop shut.

Wandering downstairs, I felt the gravitational pull of my waiting family and girded myself for a flurry of opprobrium from Grace. But to my surprise, she rushed right over when I emerged in our kitchen to give me a hug, her chest pressing into mine, her mouth at my neck. As we held each other for an abnormally long time, I looked over to see the girls at the breakfast table: Simone was watching us over her toast, her head tilted with a kind of placid fascination; Naomi, meanwhile, sat obliviously spooning Frosted Flakes into her mouth and eyeing up a colouring book splayed out before her.

"It's really bad," Grace said as she let me go.

"Yeah, I get that sense. I just checked Facebook."

"Oh, Philip, how could you *say* something like that on TV?"

I threw my hands up. "I don't want to talk about it, okay? Hopefully this will all blow over in a day or so."

"Are you *kidding*?"

"Grace —"

"No, seriously, come with me." She was about to lead me over to the little alcove workspace she kept off our book-lined living room, but then paused in front of the girls. "Simone, you have ten minutes to be out the door. That includes teeth-brushing. And, Naomi, sweetie, don't hold your spoon with a fist, okay. Hold it like a pencil."

With this quick dispatch of motherwork done, we went to her busy little desk and she manoeuvred herself into the wheeled chair. This was where my wife, the indefatigable Grace Daly, wrote her monthly column, called The Motherlode, for a glossy women's magazine. A popular missive about the trials and ecstasies of full-time mommyhood in the twenty-first century, the column created a certain mythos around Grace as a walk-on-water parent and did much to extend what she straight-facedly referred to as her "personal brand." I liked her pieces well enough, but was often (and silently) struck by what she elided rather than included in them. I felt she didn't always, for example, pay proper due to her wealthy North Toronto parents who provided her multiple levels of encouragement and support and helped to get her where she was. As for me? My own contributions to child-rearing, not to mention my tenured U of T gig that financed this whole operation, made virtually no appearances in the column at all. Anyway. We had experimented with having Grace upstairs in her own office when we first moved into 4 Metcalfe Street, but she soon preferred to have her workplace here, close to the epicentre of the domestic action. On one wall of the alcove, she had hung a framed copy of the epithalamium I had written her — my sole foray into poesy, which I was embarrassed by, but which she nonetheless cherished. Atop her desk sat piles of notes, stacks of magazines, a bright mauve teapot, and a small wireless printer. On the desk's corner rested the manuscript for her as-yet-unsold new children's book, which despite taking nearly two years to write was only about 15,000 words long. And, in the middle of it all, was Grace's own laptop, her chief conduit into a world populated by friends and supporters, but also enemies, frenemies, and near strangers. Yes, unlike me, Grace was fully immersed into the world of social media, a tool to connect with her cadre of fellow authors, stay-at-home moms, and other allies. But it could also, I found, bring out the worst in her. She might lose large portions of a day engrossed in a flame war over some esoteric sliver of the women's movement, and she spent a lot of time lurking on the Facebook walls and blogs of women she vehemently disagreed with. This had led her to tape up a second note over her desk, a flash card of Sartrean parody that read HELL IS OTHER FEMINISTS. She says she keeps it there ironically, but I know it's something she sometimes believes.

She opened the laptop and went to Facebook. At the sight of her navigation bar's beckoning red bubbles, I could tell she, too, had several notifications waiting for her. She scrolled through her newsfeed and sure enough, there was picture after picture of me, with Facebook's Greek chorus chiming in under each.

"Look, I told you I've already seen a lot of this," I said.

"Yeah, and what about this?" She opened a new tab and went to Twitter, a site I can't even begin to comprehend. There we found a relentless stream of censure, with the two words of my name smooshed together and placed behind the tic-tac-toe sign.

"Grace, I don't want to look at that."

"Or this?" She went to YouTube and found the *Power Today* clip: 748 comments underneath it. "Or this?" She went to cbc.ca/news and there was my picture above the scroll.

"Oh, for Christsake, boys," I grumbled at the screen, my PEI accent returning in a burst. "Slow news day or wot?"

She wheeled back around to face me. "You have to do something about this."

"Like what?"

"Well, we all know Cheryl Sneed is a troll, but you could start by apologizing to her publicly."

"Apologize to *her*?" I said. "She's the one who drew those comments out of *me*. Anyone who watches that clip can see it."

"Philip, are you serious? Do you honestly think —" But just then her eyes flashed to something behind me and she was up and out of her chair. "Simone Beauvoir Daly, it is *November* — you are *not* wearing that."

I turned to see that my stepdaughter — in the process of going upstairs to brush her teeth — had also changed into a fuchsia tank top, its skimpy straps revealing the tiny nubs of her shoulders. She and Grace began squabbling about this wardrobe choice, which carried them back upstairs.

I returned to the kitchen, tousled Naomi's hair on the way to my cupboard, then got out the tin shaker and Jameson to start my own breakfast. I noticed Naomi had now abandoned her Frosted Flakes and had taken up a crayon. "What are you colouring, sweetie?" I asked as I went to my bar fridge to dig out the necessary accoutrements.

"Dine-soars," she replied without looking up.

Ice cubes: check. I cracked about half out of the tray, and they clanged noisily into the tin. Tomato juice: check. Horseradish: check. Tabasco sauce: check. I looked back at her. "Can I see?" She held up the book to reveal a not-to-proportion T. Rex and triceratops now bludgeoned with crayon. "Another Vermeer in the making," I declared, then pulled open my vegetable crisper. Took out the celery, then scrounged. Scrounged. Scrounged some more, moving aside torn and empty produce bags. Oh crap.

Grace and Simone appeared back in the kitchen then, the latter now wearing a grey wool cardigan over the offending tank top. "Philip," she asked as she opened the family fridge and pulled down her lunch, "are you still taking me to that dance recital tomorrow?"

"Of course I am," I replied, beginning to assemble my concoction despite the fact I was missing one of its chief ingredients. "Why wouldn't I?"

"Well, something bad has happened, right?"

Grace and I looked at each other.

"What's going on?" Simone pressed.

Grace and I looked at the floor.

Simone then pulled her rhinestone-covered iPhone out of her cardigan's pocket. "I got a text from Sarah last night," she said, scrolling. "It reads, 'My mom says your stepdad's a real dickhead.'" She pushed the screen toward my face. "Do you want to read the rest of what it says?"

"No, I do not."

"Okay, you're now late," Grace said. "You have to go. Right now."

"*Fine*," Simone sighed, giving a roll of her eyes. She grabbed her bookbag off the counter and threw on a coat from the front closet. "Okay, bye!" she yelled, and then was out the door.

"You know," Grace said, "she's convinced you're going to renege on taking her tomorrow."

"Well, I'm not," I replied, dropping a celery stalk into the now completed Bloody Joseph and raising it to my lips. "And *another* thing: I finally remembered what we're doing on Sunday."

"Oh, really?" She gave me a smirk that I could only interpret as an olive branch.

"Yes. We're having people in for brunch — Jane Elton included. And you want me to steer her in the direction of 'Sally and the Kitchen Sink.'"

Grace took a brief but longing glance over at the chaos of her writing desk. "Do you think she'd look at it?" she asked.

"I don't know. She's not taking a lot of kids' lit these days. But we'll see."

"Anyway," she said, turning back to me, "I'm sorry I gave you a hard time about it right before you went on the show. I felt bad about that."

"Yeah, well. It was quite a thing to have on my mind when I was supposed to be routing Cheryl Sneed."

Grace made a face. "So it was *my* fault?"

"I didn't say tha —"

"*I'm* the reason you said that horrible thing to her?"

"Look, Grace, you need to underst —"

"Let me remind you, Philip, that I wasn't upset about the brunch. I was upset because your daughter scalded herself and you didn't seem to care."

"Okay, I don't have time for this. I have class later this morning. I should be up in the office finishing my prep."

"Fine. I have to go to the Loblaws anyway. Naomi has a play-date early this afternoon, and I want to get back with the groceries in time."

Wonderful, I thought. *What a wonderful day you have ahead of you.*

"Naomi, sweetie, let's get your shoes on. We have to go." She took the child's near-empty cereal bowl, scraped its mushy remnants into the compost, and put the bowl in the dishwasher. She then turned to me. "Do you need anything from the store?"

I gazed briefly at my bar fridge. "I need *lemons,*" I told her with not a small hint of desperation.

* * *

Two hours later, I stood on Parliament Street waiting for the 65 bus to whisk me north to the Castle Frank subway station. There, in front of me, sat a *Toronto Sun* news box with my picture in the window.

Oh Jesus, you have to be fucking kidding me.

But no: there I was — my comb-over like a frond splayed across my skull, my red beard thick and untrimmed — taking up the tabloid's entire front page. Alongside this mug shot ran a vertical headline that said:

"Penetrating"
Insights
on
ODS

Oh, please! I thought. Did my heinous remarks against those executives really warrant a front-page blast? And since when do *Toronto Sun* readers care about philosophy anyway? I couldn't bear to take in the subhead, let alone deposit my loonie and read the entire article. Does the *Sun* even run articles? Isn't it all just scantily clad girls and salacious headlines?

I turned away from the box just as the bus pulled up. As I boarded, I worried about the stares and judgments of my fellow commuters. Thankfully, they were few in number that late in the morning, and didn't seem much interested in looking up from their phones.

"Freedom exists," I had said, back in September, in the opening lecture to this, my survey course on the Enlightenment, "because it serves the interests of power. To understand this is to understand everything — from Herodotus to Dick Cheney." A ballsy opening salvo, for sure, but one I felt necessary to establish what I considered to be the *nomos* of the period in which I am an alleged expert. That lecture hall teemed with a large congress of young people — still tanned and tank-topped from their summer vacations — who may have possessed, as a result of cultural theory courses or Mel Gibson movies, an opposite view: that the entire trajectory of Western civilization placed "freedom" in opposition to "power." It was my mission to disabuse them of this fallacy; an eight-month pollarding that would allow sturdier branches of intellectual curiosity to grow. I knew that some of these students would go on to become vocal critics of the Enlightenment; others would end up as Bay Street biz-knobs; still others would resign themselves to a life packing groceries at the Loblaws. But I liked to think that I nonetheless laid down an explanatory foundation — even a subconscious one — of the culture we were all saddled with. The kids knew coming in what to expect from a Philip Sharpe survey course: the readings would be lengthy and intense; writing assignments would come at them fortnightly, along with two major research papers and an exam at the end of each term; extensions would not be given under any circumstances. And yes, I had certain trammels about cellphones and tardiness, but I made it clear that, in exchange for these limitations on their personal freedoms, they would be allowed to engage in a different *kind* of freedom: the freedom to question me, to challenge each other, to debate the ideas captured in their readings. They were here to be *scholars*, to be thoughtful contributors in discussions during their group work and in the broader class. Indeed, the freedom to speak their minds was the *nomos* of this course, because it served the interests of *my* power, as their professor.

I had been making great strides with this batch over the last two months. They had started out as a predictably costive crew during my lectures, and their early assignments were plagued by pleonasms and leaps in logic. Now, they could be counted on to volunteer answers to my Socratic queries; and their essays were sharper and more succinct, in no small part thanks to the efforts of my brainy, uncomplaining TA, Sebastian, an ABD ("All But the Dissertation") fluent in four languages who earned his $8,000 a year poring over and improving these students' sentences. What's more, the kids were just beginning to grasp the chief tenet I wanted them to take away from this course — that the relationship between freedom and power was far more paradoxical than the current culture wars would have us believe. This relationship — while finding its origin in the ancient world (and how could my early lectures *not* pay passing nods to *The Republic*, *The Nicomachean Ethics*, and various Periclean *bon mots*?) — truly came to fruition during the Enlightenment. And far from being one homogenous groupwank about "individual freedom," this epoch possessed codependent contradictions that helped shape the very core of Western identity and what we might still unironically refer to as civil society. Eloquent extrapolations on this earned me what I hoped to see across that sea of student bodies: nodding baseball caps, nodding ponytails, and, yes, nodding hijabs, their corresponding hand-clasped pens scribbling, scribbling.

Which made it all the more difficult to walk into that lecture hall on Tuesday morning and discover an atmosphere of unmitigated tension — airborne and palpable. Sebastian came bounding up to me from the front row when I appeared through the double doors near the stage and took me aside. "Sir," he said, almost *sotto voce*, "are you interested in cancelling class today?"

"What for?" I asked.

He sucked air through his clenched teeth. "People are sort of upset with you." I looked beyond him and, sure enough, I was getting the stink-eye from several of my young charges.

"No," I said. "We'll proceed."

Sebastian nodded in acquiescence. I have to say I liked the boy a lot. He was going to make a great professor one day, in the highly unlikely event he landed a job. But he still spoke to me in the way that all TAs did — as if I possessed a sack of gold coins that I would give him at the end of the year, if only he was worthy enough.

As I moved to the lectern and took out my notes from my satchel, I could tell that two months of hard work had been undone. The class sat before me glaring, as silent as tombstones. It was like the first day all over again.

I took a long, deep breath. "Don't believe everything you read in the papers," I said, unsheepishly as I could, into the abyss. I could have said more to them; probably *should* have said more, facing head on what they had seen and read on Twitter and Facebook and in the *Toronto*-fucking-*Sun*. They could have asked me questions and shared their "feelings." And we could have related what I had said on TV — that abominable blunder — to what we'd been reading and discussing all term. It *was* applicable, after all; and I was even a little impressed that my slip had caused such a shockwave through these tyro philosophers.

But I didn't. Chalk it up to cowardice, I suppose. Instead, I took up my copy of *Foundations of the Metaphysics of Morals* — a book I had first inhaled as a fifteen-year-old in Charlottetown, one that ripped through the fog of adolescence like a sunbeam — and held it aloft in a gesture that said, *You've read this, yes?* No acknowledgement, one way or the other. I pressed on, making a few biographical comments on Immanuel Kant and situating him into our somewhat jumbled chronology of the Enlightenment. Then I asked the most basic question one could to anybody who'd read the book. "Okay, people, in a nutshell, what is Kant's categorical imperative? How does he define and explain it in the context of our reading?"

Nothing. The girls merely scowled at their desks or examined their cuticles. The boys lay slumped in their seats as if poured there by a cement truck. A few of the faces threw tight little smiles my way, but they were full of unmistakable malice.

No matter. I slogged on, working myself into a lather about Kant and his immeasurable contribution to both the Enlightenment and all of Western thought. I threaded a careful needle with our previous readings, explaining how Kant's works had added a crucial shading to those of his contemporaries, how his introduction of deontology to the mix had crystallized so much of what the Age of Reason was trying to articulate about human nature. "It's clear to even a casual reader what the categorical imperative means to the study of ethics," I said, "but what about reason itself? What does the categorical imperative contribute to our notions of the rational?" Dead silence. Not even the gentle susurrus that often preceded class participation. I plugged on, detailing the difference between Kant's categorical imperative and his hypothetical imperative. "What bearing does this distinction have on what we discussed before — about, say, the courts or even industrial relations?" Nothing. "Okay, what does it say about one-on-one interactions between people? How we *treat* each other?" Nothing again. *Okay, kids,* I thought, *how does it relate to what I said about those corporate assholes on television yesterday that's put this bowling pin up your asses?* But I bit my tongue.

As we approached the end of our eighty minutes together, Sebastian and I unveiled their next fortnightly writing assignment. This was another element that set my course apart, and, to be honest, contributed most to the libellous pouting that took place about me on ratemyprofessors.com. I did not believe in handholding or steering students toward certain thesis statements. Doing so ran counter to what I considered to be the true spirit of scholarship. Sebastian worked the laptop to make their essay assignment appear on the screen behind me. It was, in total, a lengthy quote from the second section of *Foundations of the Metaphysics of Morals*, followed by the word "discuss."

I read the quote aloud, explained a few things in it, then asked if anyone had any questions. Their silence lingered for a moment. But then one young man, wearing his baseball cap backward, raised a beefy arm off his desk.

"Yes?" I asked, pointing at him, gratitude flooding me like a fever.

"What does Kant mean by 'rational being'?" he smirked. "What would he consider to be an *ir*rational being? Like — a *woman*?"

"Shut *up*!" the pretty young lady sitting next to him, obviously his girlfriend, screamed. She didn't so much punch his shoulder as shove it angrily with her fist. Two other girls, less pretty, sitting in the row in front of him, twisted around in their seats. "Asshole!" "You're such a *prick*!"

Clearly some residual argument from before I entered the room. Clearly. As the commotion died down, I waggled my furry face at them, a gesticulation that said: *What the* fuck *are you people on about?* But no explanation came.

"That is *all*," I snarled, gathering up my notes, and fled from the lectern.

Sebastian and I spoke little as we made our way through University College and up its ornate staircase that led to my office, where we needed to discuss Thursday's group topics. I unlocked my office door — decorated with black-and-white images of Kant, Hume, Rousseau, Locke, Mill, and Descartes, as well as a five-by-twenty plank of PEI driftwood with the phrase SAPERE AUDE ("*dare to be wise*") embossed on it — and we entered my large, book-choked lair. Too many books, in fact. The *tsundoku* spilled out of over-stuffed shelves and across the floor and onto the chairs. (Grace had said that if we bought a small cottage in the Kawarthas — something she'd been hankering for us to do for a while now — we would have extra wall space for books, since we didn't seem to have a square inch left at 4 Metcalfe Street or here.) Sebastian moved some out of the way so he could sit, and I took my place behind the desk, turning on my green-shaded banker's lamp.

I glanced at my desk phone. The red message light was flashing. I *never* got messages on this phone. I raised a finger at Sebastian in a give-me-a-moment gesture and picked up the receiver, trying to remember how the fuck I accessed voicemail on this thing. I figured it out, and discovered I had seven messages waiting for me. The first was from Roberta Rosenbaum, a reporter with the *Globe and Mail* whom I dated briefly in the late '90s when I first began freelancing for them, and with whom I was still friendly. "Oh, hey, Philip, it's Roberta R.," she sang into the receiver. "I bet you can guess why I'm calling. Just hoping you could give me a statement abou —" DELETE. The others were from media outlets as well: reporters from the *National Post,* the *Toronto Sun,* two AM talk radio stations, the *Toronto Star,* and, bringing up the rear, the CBC. I deleted each without listening all the way to the end.

Hanging up, I looked at Sebastian. "*Reporters,*" I said, rolling my eyes.

"Did you want me to …" and he motioned to the door.

"No, no. Stay. We have work to do."

So we did our work, going over the group topics with stunted, false alacrity. Like me, Sebastian had Kant's text practically memorized, and I marvelled again at how seasoned he seemed for someone not yet thirty. He took the lead in figuring out which passages to focus on and the discussion prompts we'd give the students. I agreed with each of his choices, but with a kind of torpid distraction. When he noticed this he stopped and looked at me.

"Sir …"

"Hmm?"

"Do you, do you *want* to talk about what happened yesterday?"

I said nothing.

"I don't mean to pry," he went on. "But *are* you going to make a statement about ..." and he nodded toward my phone.

"I don't know," I sighed. Then I looked at him. "What do *you* think I should do?"

He made that lips-pulled-from-clenched-teeth face again, his throat a brief spasm of dismay. "I think you need to say something. Even if it's a blanket apology to Sneed so we can all move on. That would be better than nothing."

I gave a weak chortle. "My wife said the same thing this morning. I ... I don't know if I can do that."

"Look," he said, "I know there are lots of people in this department who hate your guts, who'd love to see you eat a big mouthful of crow over this. But there are also plenty of us who respect you deeply, who know that what you do makes an incredible contribution to the political discourse in this country. And *we* want to see you eat crow over this — *because* we respect you."

"You know, Sebastian," I said, finding his *Gefolgschaft* touching, "you really are wise beyond your years."

He tried to smile. "*Sapere aude.*"

"*Sapere aude,*" I replied. "Okay, we can wrap up here. I think we're in good shape for Thursday."

"Sir ..."

"Look, everything will be all right," I told him. "Don't worry, okay. I'll see you Thursday."

"Okay."

When he was gone, I wheeled over to my computer to check email, and discovered I had an additional forty-one notifications from Facebook waiting for me. I gaped at the list of unfamiliar names. *Oh, people — get a life!* I began batch-deleting them when I spotted another message sitting among the rabble. It was from U of T's dean of Arts and Sciences. I opened it and read:

Philip:
I need to talk to you about this escalating situation.
Please come by my office tomorrow morning, 8:30.
You don't have a class. I checked.

My stomach filled with annoyance and dread. In the twenty-two years I've been billeted at U of T's Philosophy department, I have only been summoned to the dean's office in this manner once before. And it did not go well.

I hit REPLY.

Sure, Tom. I'll see you then.

I arrived back at 4 Metcalfe Street about an hour later in an anxiety so thick I was practically vibrating from it. As I came inside, I was greeted by the screams of Naomi and her playdate friend racing through the house in what looked like a game of tag. They came zooming past the front entry just as I was slipping out of my Payless.

"Hi, Daddy!"

"Sweetie — sweetie! No running in the house, okay!"

She cackled at the absurdity of such a request, and the two went tearing through the kitchen together.

"Naomi, what did I just say!"

I followed them in but then stopped when I spotted Grace sitting in the living room with her friend Stacey, the other girl's mom. Grace's mauve teapot sat on a trivet on our coffee table, surrounded by mugs and a plate of cranberry scones. Stacey — a mere whiff of a woman despite having three kids of her own — was the author of a couple of collections of short stories, and had known Grace for years. I often marvelled, though, at how their friendship seemed to be based almost entirely on the mutual need to gossip about other people they knew in the "writing community." It was all, it appeared to me, that they ever did when the two of them got together.

They stopped talking when I appeared in the arch of the living room. Grace brought her bright green eyes up to where I stood, but Stacey just turned away, as if she couldn't bear to look at me. Her corncob-coloured hair fell in her face as she did.

"Did class go okay?" Grace asked.

"No. It did not." I raked my fingers through my bushy beard. "And the dean wants to meet with me first thing tomorrow."

"*Shit.*" Maybe Grace was going to say something more — something comforting to me. But if so, she was cut off then by the sound of one or both of the girls' bodies slamming into the cupboards in the kitchen, followed by a raucous round of giggling.

Grace was on her feet. "Naomi Woolf Sharpe-Daly — please come here." The child obeyed, immediately. "Did you not hear your father say no running through the house?" Naomi nodded, a little embarrassed. Then, her tone softening, Grace said: "Why don't you and Kim go colour some dinosaurs? Do something *quiet.*" The child agreed, and scurried off.

Grace returned to the couch, assuming a position that I always read as *I am the queen of all I survey.* Which, of course she was. I felt wholly redundant in the wake of it, as if I were little more than a functional piece of the furniture, or perhaps a helium balloon, attracting the eye with its novelty, but ultimately pointless. I looked at my wife, hoping she would finish what she'd been about to say. I thought: *C'mon, Grace. Assure me that everything is going to be all right. You owe me that. I wouldn't be in this mess if it weren't for YOU.*

But she said nothing. She and Stacey acted as if they were waiting for me to leave. Which they were. I clued in, then: they were, before I came in the door, gossiping about *me.*

"Anyway," I said. "I guess I'll head up to the office and work on the book for a while."

Grace nodded, as if to say, *Yeah, you do that.*

I stopped by the kitchen on my way. Saw atop the counter the big bag of lemons she had brought me back from Loblaws, those bright yellow shapes shimmering through the plastic. I thought then to backtrack and thank her for picking them up. (We'd been working harder to say thank you in this house.) Instead, I just tore open the bag, pulled a lemon out, then took the remainder over to my bar fridge and dropped them into the vegetable crisper. Then I began to quickly assemble a Bloody Joseph. Not that one assembles a Bloody Joseph quickly, and I could feel Grace's and Stacey's eyes burning me in the back of my head as I poured and squeezed and shook over my martini tin. Waiting, they were, for me to just hurry up and disappear into this huge, overpriced house.

Upstairs, in the book-lined silence of my office, I checked email once again. *Eleven* more notifications from the Facebook. Fuckers. I was just reaching for the mouse to delete them when another email appeared in my inbox. I startled a little when I saw that boldfaced name and subject line:

Rani Sumita
What the hell, Sharpe???

Such a vertiginous feeling, to see her name there. It had been a while. I felt my stomach sink, but also my lips twist into a smile. This was the effect Rani always had on me: a cocktail of apprehension and intrigue. I swallowed hard. Had my slip made it all the way across the pond? Opening a new tab, I went to the BBC News website. I needed to scroll a bit, but sure enough there was a thumbnail photo of me with hyperlinked text next to it that read "Philip Sharpe's on-air gaffe." The article behind it was probably written by one of Rani's colleagues, and she would have no doubt seen it.

I went back to my email, opened it. It read:

> What the hell, Sharpe!!! Are you serious?? What the
> FUCK are you saying over there?

Not exactly helpful.

Should I respond? I thought. *No, just leave it for now. There is work to do, and with all this tension between you and Grace, the last thing you need is get into a flirtatious exchange with Rani. Just leave it. For now. There is work to do.*

So I shut down my email, and launched Microsoft Word. Got busy on the next chapter of my counterintuitive book about Christianity and its dissidents. *In paradoxo veritas.*

The Jugglers Arms

Don't reach for your pen, dear reader. I am well aware of the missing apostrophe that haunted the name of my father's pub like a phantom limb. That truant squiggle was the bane of my childhood, the pea under my intellectual mattress, at least since age eleven when I read Strunk & White for the first time and learned that something was amiss. Despite its punctuational malfeasance, Little Frankie's business on Dorchester Street in the heart of old Charlottetown had been what the locals called "an Island institution," and he and I lived in the large apartment above the pub. It's all gone now, torn down and replaced by a dog park. But whenever I get into one of these scraps with Grace, whenever I feel the constricting squeeze of my domestic situation, I'm often taken back to my PEI youth, to my days inside the dour, smoky caverns of my childhood home.

Indeed, the wordplay in the pub's name may have conjured images of an old-timey British tavern, but the Jugglers Arms was not, as they say, an upscale establishment. It was dark and dingy, with cadaver-grey floors and a low ceiling and a cigarette machine in the lobby. The pub's one redeeming quality remained the small music stage where the occasional prospects (including, my father was proud to point out, a young Stompin' Tom and a shy schoolteacher named Anne Murray) appeared before the larger, more profitable Friday- and Saturday-night crowds. Yet it was Little Frankie's weekday clientele, the farouche farmers and blue-collar whatsits and tourism operators drinking their way through another PEI winter, that gave the dive its inimitable spirit. I often think that it was these men, more than Frankie, who raised me; and in my early teens it became my job to deliver their food and bus their tables as they glowered and argued over their pints of Schooner lager and Labatt 50.

I should also describe Little Frankie himself. My dad was prone to both bursts of pride and fits of rage when it came to me, and his mood swings were about as predictable as a punch in the face. Part of the problem was that the Jugglers Arms had not been Frankie's first, or even third, ambition. He had left Prince Edward Island at age twenty to pursue a series of unlikely opportunities: first a brief stint at academics (he fancied himself a scholar, despite having failed two grades); then a briefer stint in the Canadian military (he missed the Korean conflict by mere months); and finally a six-year career as a busy but unsuccessful featherweight in Halifax's pro boxing scene (retiring, reluctantly, in 1960 after suffering his eighth concussion). He returned to the Island shortly thereafter and took a job slinging drinks at an eatery on the outskirts of Charlottetown. Despite his short stature and now cauliflowered ears, he managed to attract the affections of the woman who would become my mother — a tall, red-headed, bedizened beauty who worked alongside him as a waitress, and who was not above exploiting her Rubenesque cleavage for tips. They soon married and decided to launch their own bar together, downtown.

Problem was, they squabbled about what kind of establishment it should be. Little Frankie insisted on the name the Jugglers Arms, but because he didn't know where the apostrophe was supposed to go, he left it off his signage completely (much to the consternation, years later, of his know-it-all son). I suppose he envisioned the place an upmarket pub where Kingsley Amis types would sit around drinking port and discussing important issues of the day. My mother disagreed. She said what tiny Charlottetown really needed was a strip club, and she was more than happy to be the Island's first (and, if necessary, only) exotic dancer. This threw Little Frankie into a paroxysm of prudishness, and the two of them rowed and thwarted each other at every turn. Thus, with two equally far-fetched ideas about what the pub could be, the Jugglers Arms opened in the early sixties with a muddled identity, one it kept to closing day — that of a slightly seedy but loveable dump.

My mother grew deeply unhappy there, and made sure my father knew it. She began to doubt whether she'd even *want* to take her clothes off in front of the down-market bums the bar was attracting. She was constantly threatening to leave, and Frankie soon encouraged her to do so. Then, the unspeakable happened. Despite her best attempts at birth control, my mother fell pregnant with me in 1965. My existence proved to be the straw that crushed the camel, as the various bodily indignities of motherhood soon filled her with torrents of disgust. Shortly after my second birthday, she abandoned me and Little Frankie and fled to Montreal, where, rumour had it, she took work in a burlesque house. My father felt betrayed, naturally, and spoke ill of her at every opportunity. (Indeed, throughout my childhood she was known simply as "your nymphomaniac mother"; though, to be fair, "nymphomaniac" was how Frankie described *any* woman whose sexual appetites outpaced his own.) Still, this turn of fate presented my father with yet another ambition, one he declared with great drama to the pub's slouching, indifferent regulars: I Shall Raise the Boy Myself. He grew giddy at the prospect of bringing me up the way he wanted, without feminine interference.

And I'll give the guy credit. Despite our poverty — and we *were* poor, more or less, the pub falling victim to long winters of slow business and my father's various get-rich-quick schemes — Frankie made sure to provide me with everything that a young, insatiable mind might need. When I showed an early voracity for reading, he bought me a leather-bound set of the Harvard Classics, which we displayed on a bookshelf near our large bay window overlooking old Charlottetown. I devoured these tomes, which included everything from Homer and Aesop's Fables, to Cervantes, to various founding documents of the United States. When I went through a science phase, he got me a subscription to *Scientific American*; when I got hooked on journalism, he landed me a tour of the local CBC outlet. Frankie also educated me about music. While downstairs the pub played a nonsensical cocktail of honky-tonk songs and Top 40 hits, upstairs in our apartment he insisted we listen to real music, which for him meant classical. Being a barman, he was also particular about booze. While his regulars were happy to drink the swill on tap or the cheap spirits he kept behind the bar, upstairs Frankie insisted I learn the difference between a single malt and a blend, between a transcendental Gewürztraminer and a passable Chardonnay. Why did he go to such lengths? Well. It was clear he regretted not being better educated himself, and he loved living vicariously through this little *sprezzatura*-showing redhead he was raising. Every report card got displayed on the fridge; each academic commendation got bragged about to the pub's staff.

Of course all this would come back to bite him in the arse; and it started when, at age eleven, I first began pointing out the missing apostrophe on his signage. "Did you know," I said, which was how I often began sentences at that age, "that there is a typo in the pub's name?"

"You don't *say*," he replied in his collared bar shirt, walking a keg of beer across the floor of the backroom. "Too bad you weren't here when me and your nymphomaniac mother launched this joint. Here, grab the other end of this, would ya?" As I took one handle of the keg in both hands and we lifted together, I asked him, "Are you going to fix it?" but he answered me with a single dismissive snort. I asked again at age twelve, and age fourteen, and several times at age seventeen. By then I was reading Freud for fun and writing a monthly column on teen issues for the local rag, the *Evening Patriot*.

"Look," I said to him during one particularly dead afternoon, "you can either put an apostrophe before the *s* or after, it doesn't matter. Though if you choose the latter, you really need to add a second juggler to the logo."

"Are you out of your fucking mind?" he said. "Philly, if I did that it's not just the sign out front that would need to change. It's every matchbook, every coaster, every bloody ashtray. I can't afford to do that."

"But it's *wrong*," I replied. "We look like illiterates."

Frankie put both hands on the bar and leaned toward me. "Philly, Islanders don't care about shit like that. The twenty-eight people in this town who know where apostrophes go would never drink in this dive anyway." He went on to remind me that upstairs in the apartment he and I could gab at length about the intricacies of the English language, but down here in the pub it was strictly business. He said that when I was on his clock, I should spend less time jaw jacking about typos and more time keeping up with food and drink orders. And then he said something hurtful about the piss-poor job I did cleaning the bathrooms the previous night.

That was the other thing about Frankie. For all his love for me, for all his pride in my "big brain," he had a preternatural talent for pointing out my incompetency when it came to manual labour. I chalked it up to him being a boxer: he always knew how to hit you where it hurt. The irony was, when Frankie felt I was getting a bit too "uppity" with my booksmarts, he would take me down a peg by intimating that it was *my* fault the pub was struggling as much as it was. (And true, I did lack a certain acumen: by age sixteen I had read and grasped the entirety of Shakespeare, but still couldn't settle the till properly, or help the dray men park their trucks, or remember how to reassemble a bar tap after cleaning it, no matter how many times Frankie roared instructions and belittled my efforts.) He loved the sight of me reading and doing homework, but more generalized idleness incensed him. He said that a real man didn't just loaf around. If a man wasn't working, or thinking about work, there was something profoundly flawed about his behaviour. Indeed, Frankie was forever on the lookout for people who were getting through life more easily than we were; and for all his parental illusions, he was, in the end, just another stressed-out entrepreneur, and my self-esteem was the furthest thing from his mind.

And so who filled in the gaps? As I mentioned, much of my upbringing fell to the *patria potestas* of my father's regulars. Oh God, they were awful men — beaten down by their hardscrabble lives on Prince Edward Island; by their grinding blue-collar jobs; by the dull, interminable winters; and, most specifically, by the fishwives they regretted marrying. Oh, that was the truth of it. And that's why a quarrel with Grace now will stir a memory of these grizzled old-timers, will cause the black bile they instilled within me to rise. I'm ashamed to say that I made a childhood pledge never to get married because I didn't want to end up like my father's regulars. They told me that getting married was not something any man would *choose* to do; it just sort of happened to you, like going bald or developing a paunch. These men questioned what function their wives actually served. Sure, they'd say, she cooked your meals, and cleaned your house, and raised your children, and occasionally had sex with you, but otherwise what was she *good* for? Housewives certainly didn't contribute much to civilization, to say nothing of the household income. These Andy Capp types often complained about arriving home from the most soul-destroying workday and having to endure a barrage of nagging the minute they walked in the door — and from someone whose most stressful part of the day appeared to involve catching little Sally as she came down the kiddie slide at Rainbow Valley. These men knew that there must have been some advantage to having a crabby, indolent, entitled, irrational, unemployed person in their house, day after day, but they had long since forgotten what that was.

Even as a boy, I was *appalled* by this barroom misogyny, but I also feared it. It's not that I was afraid I would ever see eye to eye with these men — many of whom, despite being born in the 1920s or even '30s, opposed female suffrage on principle — but that I would come to resent someone as much as they seemed to resent their wives. It didn't help matters that Little Frankie often egged them on from behind the bar, declaring what a blessing it was that my nymphomaniac mother had decided to scram. I even had an image in my mind, a frightfully detailed paracosm, of the shrew *I'd* marry if I wasn't careful: a squat, pear-shaped woman with a mass of curly hair like a cobra's hood around her head, a permanent sneer contorting her pug face. I had a vision of this person standing at a kitchen sink somewhere in a perpetual state of fury, an utter Andes of backfat greeting me as I came in the door from a job I hated. In this vision, we would row every night, and I would say the most scalding things to her — the kind of things Frankie often said to me.

Well, no. No, goddamn it. I would not become *that* kind of man — the type who just let hurtful things slip out of him about the female sex because he felt trapped in a life he didn't want. I would rather be alone than carry such antipathies toward an entire gender. And so, in my efforts not to become a misogynist, I grew deeply suspicious of women. I avoided them when I could; dated sporadically; turned away the affections of any young thing who challenged the trajectory I had laid out for myself. I thought: *No, no. Study hard. Keep your eye on the goal. Don't get distracted. Your destiny is not a domestic one. You are meant to live a life of the mind.*

It worked. I graduated high school in 1983 with a full scholarship to the University of Toronto. I would do my bachelor's and master's degrees there, and then move on to Oxford for a doctorate. Little Frankie was, of course, button-popping proud of me. I still remember how we hopped around the apartment like madmen when that first acceptance packet arrived in the spring of grade twelve. But then an abrupt realization hit my father — that me leaving PEI meant that I would leave PEI, and he was shocked at how hard the empty-nest syndrome hit him. During my U of T years, he would call me every Sunday, long-distance charges be damned, and listen in rapture as I described whatever academic discoveries I was making. But he grew morose if I dragged my feet about visiting home. Truth was, the Jugglers Arms was struggling and Little Frankie couldn't afford to help much with my education, and thus I had neither the resources nor the inclination to make frequent trips back to PEI. One Christmas I stayed in Toronto to take a bookstore job, and the following spring I abruptly cancelled a trek home after landing a posh research post with the Philosophy department. Both decisions plunged Frankie into despair. "I need the money, Pop," is what I told him. "My scholarship doesn't cover everything, you know." But the truth was, I was avoiding home. For all of Frankie's fluster about missing my presence, I knew what *really* awaited me on even the shorter trips to PEI — a bar apron, Frankie's griping, and the dreadful, dreadful men he served.

I should point out that Frankie's calls to me became daily for a while in 1988, when the PEI premier held an island-wide plebiscite on whether to build a bridge — a "fixed link" — to the mainland. The issue had divided Islanders for decades: you were either in favour of a bridge in the abstract or vehemently opposed on principle. My father fell into the latter camp, as his debacles in the wider world had turned him staunchly provincialistic upon settling home for good. "If they build a bridge, would we even be an island anymore?" he'd ask. "Maybe they'd have to change our name to Prince Edward on a Stick." The fear was, naturally, that a closer connection to the mainland would ruin "the Island Way of Life" — whatever the fuck *that* meant. (I confess I'm not the best person to describe it, since I spent most of my childhood either working like a dog to help Frankie keep the Jugglers Arms afloat, or studying.) Anyway. At the time of the '88 plebiscite, I was halfway through my M.A. coursework, and I remember reading about the vote results in the paper while lounging on a couch in my beloved Hart House at U of T. "You'll have to get the pub sign fixed now," I joked to Frankie that night on the phone. "You'll be competing with a bunch of come-from-away bar owners who *know* how to use punctuation."

He didn't find that funny.

Indeed, throughout the four years of the fixed link's construction (1993–1997), Little Frankie declared, repeatedly, "I will be in the cold fucking ground before I drive on that bridge." This, sadly, proved to be true. My father died of lung cancer on March 2, 1997 — almost two months to the day before the bridge opened. He left the Jugglers Arms to his employees, and the pub limped along for another six or seven years, but then closed and was torn down. By then, PEI *had* changed — just as Little Frankie had warned. Lots of mom-and-pop places pulled up stakes, and Islanders shopped at the Walmart and the Home Depot and the Indigo that arrived in the post-bridge age, and didn't think much of it. Perhaps people longed for a more sophisticated night on the town, and my father's dive just couldn't make a go of it anymore.

During his final days, Frankie expressed a number of regrets to me over the phone — chief among them that he had obviously polluted my mind against marriage, since I was now in my early thirties and still not hitched. He blamed himself for surrounding me with men who clearly hated and resented women, and for saying so many horrible things about my nymphomaniac mother. "You know I was just messing around, right?" he told me. "Anyway, forget all that shit, Philly. Just meet somebody, eh. Build your life with them. Believe me, dying alone is no fun. It certainly ain't for wimps like me." But I didn't listen. By then, I was back at U of T, now an assistant professor, and battling my guts out for publications and teaching experience in order to secure tenure. Sure, I was dating — I *always* dated, intermittently — but I had my head so far up my own arse that I couldn't really heed Frankie's advice. I certainly couldn't fathom the likes of Grace Daly, whom I wouldn't meet for another ten years yet. And yes, she and I butt heads about a lot of stuff, and doing so often conjures these awful reminiscences of mine. But still. I do wish that she and Frankie could have met. He'd have been insecure around Grace at first — her spooky good looks, her confidence that bordered on the sensual, her intelligence, her ability to be the most dominant voice in any room — but I like to imagine that he'd eventually grow to like her. And like who I was with her.

Anyway. When Frankie was just about to cash his cheque, I flew home to be by his side. I made sure to throw him lots of reassuring blandishments about what a great dad he'd been. I mean, I'm not an ogre. But these words proved a poor balm to all the guilt and disappointment that came spewing out of him right at the end. After he took his last breath and everything was calm, I kissed him on the forehead and thought: *Oh, Pop. Why were you so tough on yourself, there? You shouldn't have been. Look, you worked hard your whole life. And you did the impossible: you raised me on your own, and you raised me right. You did. You helped me become the intellectual* you *always wanted to be but couldn't, and you taught me the value of hard work. And sure my childhood was mostly miserable, but so what? I am by any measure a success now, and it's mostly because you pushed me. So I hope you didn't kick yourself too hard in the arse on your way out.*

Did he raise me right?

Wednesday, November 4

In the spew of rush-hour bodies, I came out of the St. George subway station to find a veteran selling poppies on the sidewalk near the bank machines. He stood dressed in the typical garb of our honoured war heroes: black beret sporting the Canadian Legion emblem atop his liverspotted skull, a navy blazer over grey slacks, a row of ancient medals across his left breast, and his own poppy perfectly pinned above them. At his sternum hung a tray on a chain around his neck, as if he were selling cigars at a prizefight.

I got into the lineup in front of him even though I was nearly late. Somehow I had lost track of the morning despite my refusal to read the day's papers, the *Star* and the *Times* and the *Globe* and the *Post*, after I brought them in from the porch. No doubt my slip had found its way to their various op-ed pages, and I couldn't bear to see my unconscionable gaffe ridiculed in black and white. No doubt all the columnists were howling for my blood. Grace and I spoke scant words at the breakfast table as we got the kids ready for the day. I think she knew I needed to be at the top of my game for my meeting with the dean, and thus opted to say little to me lest we have a repeat of what happened on Monday. All she did say was, "So you *are* taking Simone to that dance recital tonight?" and I replied with a tetchy, "Yes, Grace. I said I would, and I will."

"Because she'd be really sad if you didn't."

"No, I know. Look, I am *absolutely* taking her."

Now, in the precious minutes I had left, I stood in line waiting to replace the poppy I had lost. This veteran was chatty, asking people if they would like him to fasten it onto their lapels for them, and some said yes, and some said no thanks, and the line moved slowly. C'mon, c'mon. When it was my turn, I dug a pinch's worth of loonies out of my pocket and manoeuvred them into the vet's little tin jar.

"This is actually the second poppy I've bought this year," I told him, trying to smile as he selected one from his tray. "The first fell off."

"Would you like me to pin it for you," he asked, his voice frail. "It may stay on better."

"Well," I said, and glanced at my watch.

"Come on, it will only take a se —" But then he got a good look at me. At first his face registered embarrassment, as if I might be the son of one of his expired comrades and he should've recognized me off the bat. But then his eyes narrowed. "Wait a minute," he said. "Aren't you that bloke the papers are all talking about? The one who —"

"I'm sorry, I have to go," I replied, plucking the poppy from his hand. "I'm nearly late."

I looked behind me as I hustled off, and sure enough, a few people in the line had suddenly ID'd me as well. I felt exposed, vulnerable, as if a greasy film coated my entire body. I worked like hell to get the poppy attached to my lapel as I shambled up the street, desperate to gain this one small shred of respectability. I finally got the thing poked through the fabric by the time I reached the corner of Bloor and St. George Streets, where the drowsy Philosophy department offices lay hidden in their big blanched tower.

As I mentioned, this was the second time in my career that I had been beckoned to the dean's office for a dressing down. As I sat in the reception area, waiting to be summoned by Tom Howardson (his churchy, chinless secretary giving me stink-eye glances over her computer screen), I thumbed the plastic fern sitting in its plastic pot near my chair and pondered how this drubbing would go compared to last time. Truth was, I didn't hate Tom. He was from my own department, an epistemologist with a handful of decent publications under his belt and a similar teaching philosophy to mine. I could respect an epistemologist. But he'd only been in the role of dean a couple of years, and his predecessor was someone who despised me with every atom of her body. Dr. Sandra Birrell was a postcolonialfeministwhachamacallit from the English department and the ring leader of a clique of arts faculty colleagues I unaffectionately referred to as the Foucult: a band of French theory–inspired anarchists whose sole ambition was to take down Western civilization via tendentious scholarship. I drew their distain, naturally, and not just because I was an "Enlightenment groupie" who still taught Dead White Males at their face value. No, if there's one thing sclerotic academics really hate, it's when one of their own refuses to stay in his lane, an orgulous polymath publishing all kinds of crazy crap in the mainstream media. That described me to a *T*, especially after my second book, *The Movable Apocalypse*, became an unexpected bestseller. All of a sudden I was a regular on the talk-show circuit, discussing everything from American foreign policy to the latest Frida and Diego exhibit at the art gallery. My essays got published in real magazines, not unreadable academic journals. *Globe* Books might ask me to review the latest CanLit doorstopper (*The Brewmaster's Catamite*, or whatever it was called) or hack out a thousand words on what best to read while lolling in a hammock. I even wrote, for a short time, a philosophy-based dating column called The Charming Ethicist for a free weekly in Hamilton, and was only canned after several readers complained about my advice's overreliance on eighteenth-century courting rituals. All of this left a mildew of professional jealousy on Sandra and her cadre, and as dean she waited patiently for some pretense to arise where I could be frogmarched into an early retirement.

Her best chance came seven years ago when I published *Understanding Islam: An Atheist's Perspective* (Tuxedo House, 2008), a deeply controversial book and my first with our nation's largest publisher. The press chores had been lengthy, and yes, I said some divisive things about the Quran, about suicide bombers, Sufism, and a woman's "right" to wear the burqa in a voting booth. When I returned to campus, Sandra demanded a meeting. "There have been some complaints, I won't lie to you, Philip," she began before I'd even managed to sit down in her office. "About your book. And what you've been saying. In the media." This is how she talked (and wrote): in choppy fragments, as if she opposed proper sentences on theoretical grounds.

"From Muslim students?" I asked.

She didn't answer right away, and went on: "I'm all for academic freedom. Don't get me wrong. I'm wholly committed. To academic freedom. But you *can't*, Philip, just bring outside perspectives — especially one as Eurocentric as yours, okay? okay? — to such a sensitive topic beyond your specialty area."

"Actually, Sandra, I consider that to be the very *definition* of academic freedom." I pressed her again about whether it had been Muslim students who had complained. Again, she didn't answer.

"Enrolment," she said instead. "Enrolment is so crucial. To your department. I don't have to tell you. We are, totally. Under the microscope. We are. And I can't have some of the student body feeling alienated. Okay? By a high-profile professor. Especially one who carries as heavy a course load as you do. We need to keep our numbers up."

"Because the Philosophy department is a 'business,' right?" I asked, quoting a line she had let slip during a faculty meeting a month earlier. "You know, Sandra, I could've sworn you were a Marxist." *That* got her blood up, and our argument went to a whole other place. She said Muslim students might well feel "threatened" taking a course from me now, thanks to what I had published. That incensed me. "I'm going to ask you one last time. Was it a Muslim student who complained?" I already knew the answer. It hadn't been a Muslim. It had been a couple of grad students from the Cultural Studies department. I knew this because they had confronted me about it on Philosopher's Walk, and turned me down when I invited them up to my office for a frank discussion about my book. "It wasn't, was it?" I said to Sandra. "And how do I know this? Because Muslim students are lined up outside the registrar's door to get in to my courses. They are lined up outside *the fucking door.* And believe me, it's not because they're dabbling with apostasy. They *want* to learn about Western thought — as *Muslims.* They're curious and open-minded, and know that different perspectives will strengthen, not weaken their faith. And far from being the delicate flowers you think they are, they are tough, they are participatory, and they are very generous in sharing their culture and beliefs." This last part was especially true. I had spent more than two years meeting with a rotating group of Muslim students as research for my book, and they graciously talked about their faith and family life, helped me through turgid translations of the Koran during my five complete readings of it, and even taught me the rudiments of Arabic grammar.

At this point, Sandra misquoted Edward Said's *Orientalism* at me, which evidently was the only book on the East she had read, and I discredited Said in about five seconds flat, and then cited four other prominent books on Islam that she hadn't read. By now we were screaming at each other, and she got down to her real point: that if I wanted to be out gallivanting around talk shows and op-ed pages and getting paid to say provocative things about cultures that weren't my own, maybe I should consider quitting the department and becoming a full-time journalist. And I said, Oh yes, because in 2008 *that's* where the real money is — in publishing and in —

The door to Tom Howardson's office opened. "I'll see you now, Philip," he said, and disappeared back inside his cave.

I stood quickly, nearly giving myself a head rush. His secretary frowned at me over her computer screen. "Your poppy's about to fall off," she said. I looked down and, sure enough, the thing was hanging onto my lapel by the last millimetre of its pin. I patted at my chest as I staggered into Tom's office, hoping to press the blossom back into place before he reached out his hand to shake mine. But then he didn't.

"Close the door and have a seat, Philip," he said instead, and I obeyed. "I don't know where to begin," he began. "You've created an awful lot of work for this office in the last thirty-six hours."

"No doubt I have." I must reiterate, I didn't hate Tom, and certainly wasn't intimidated by him. He wasn't the sort who instilled fear in others. A goofy, gangly man at six-foot-six, he had a face that was pretty much all neck, with two googlie eyes and a tuft of hair geysering out of the top of his head. From a certain angle — i.e., this one — he looked like a tweedier version of Beaker from *The Muppet Show*. Being an epistemologist, he was one of the few profs in the department who didn't hate me on principle, and I tried to stay on his good side during his reign as dean. Yet, in that moment, I was still seething in the memory of my confrontation with Sandra seven years ago, and maybe I projected some of that rage onto Tom before he even started.

"I can't tell you how many phone calls I've fielded about your comment on the CBC," he went on. "Journalists. Students. Parents. Faculty members. Sandra Birrell, for one, is calling for your immediate termination."

"She would," I said.

"Look, Philip, I'm trying to strike a diplomatic stance here. I don't know if you saw the quote from me in this morning's *Toronto Star*." He conveyed this query with a serif of satisfaction, since it was clearly the first time Tom Howardson had any reason to be quoted by the *Star*. "I tried to be as fair to you as I could."

"No, I didn't see it," I replied, brushing invisible lint off the thigh of my slacks. "I've been avoiding this ridiculous fervour as much as I can."

"Well, I'm baffled by that, Philip. I really am. Why you wouldn't just come out and apologize for what you said — nip this whole thing in the bud — is beyond me."

"Because I think this 'whole thing' is blown out of proportion," I found myself saying. Hearing this made Tom's googlie eyes doubled in size, but I plugged forward. "No, I'm serious, Tom. Yes, I got mixed up on the air and said some things I shouldn't have. But that *wasn't* who I really am. And anyone who has read my work, or taken a course from me, or *knows* me personally, knows that."

"Well, first of all, that's not true. Since you published that book of yours, *The Marxist's Palinode* — what was it, three years ago now? — people around here think you've taken a steep turn to the Right —"

I rolled my eyes at him. "Oh my God, Tom —"

"And second of all, what you said on the CBC was beyond the pale. It was, Philip, *beyond the pale*."

Wow. He did look like Beaker. Especially with his eyes bulging like that. I couldn't stand that I was being chastised by a puppet. "I'm not apologizing," I told him. "The Internet trolls and the *Toronto Star* can have their fun, but it's been two days. People just need to fuck off."

He sat all the way back in his chair then. "I'm sorry to hear you say that. I truly am." He opened a drawer in his desk and took out a piece of paper. "The VP of strategic communications has penned this press release about your gaffe. She asked for my feedback on it, and I advised that we hold off on putting it out until I talked to you first, to see if I could get you to apologize on your own. But since you're digging in your heels, I have no choice. I'm recommending," and he flapped the paper, "that she release this to the media later this morning. It condemns, in no uncertain terms, what you said on Monday. I think you should read it."

I stretched across his desk so that he could pass the page to me. I settled back in my chair, my eyes about to glide over the words. But then I changed my mind. Slid the printout back at him. "I'm not reading that," I said. "You do what you feel you need to, Tom."

Somehow his eyes bulged even more, and he began to tremble. Now he *really* resembled Beaker. "You need to listen to me, Philip. You need to listen well."

And I would have, too, except I noticed that, as a result of my reaching across his desk, my poppy had once again fallen off. It lay on the floor, at the tip of my right Payless. I stooped to pick it up, but my foot shot out as I did, kicking the poppy under his desk. It came to rest next to the far right leg. Beaker was talking, but I wasn't listening — captivated, I was, by that scarlet bloom mocking me from a distance that was so near and yet so very far away.

"MEEP MEEP MEEP," Tom was saying. "MEEPMEEP disrespectful. MEEP MEEP MEEPMEEPMEEP wildly inappropriate. MEEP MEEP."

I nodded without looking at him, hypnotized now by the poppy. I slid down in my chair as discreetly as I could, and stretched a clandestine leg under Tom's desk. Frantic now to snag the poppy under my Payless and drag it home — and do so without accidentally playing footsie with my boss.

"MEEPMEEPMEEP," he went on. "MEEP MEEP Ms. Sneed MEEP MEEPMEEP MEEP. MEEPMEEPMEEP tenure, Philip, but that doesn't mean you can just MEEP MEEP MEEP MEEPMEEPMEEP."

I was so close. Another inch and a half would do it. I wanted that poppy. I wasn't giving any more of my pocket change to those goddamn veterans. I'd now gotten as far down in my chair as I could without being completely horizontal in it, my outstretched toe tapping at the floor like a ballerina's. The poppy was right there — it was right there! — but just out of my reach. I couldn't get it. I just couldn't.

"MEEPMEEP MEEP your reputation?" Tom asked. "MEEP MEEP MEEEPMEEPMEEP MEEP press release?"

"Well, let me ask *you* a question," I said, sitting up and zoning back in. "Where were your press releases when I published *The Marxist's Palinode*? Where were this university's press releases when *Why the West Still Matters* won a Stowaway Award in 2000?"

"Philip —"

"No, Tom. The truth is, you people are incredibly ungrateful. No, you are. I make one slip-up on TV and you're all over me. But you've never once acknowledged that my work brings more attention to the Philosophy department than all the other professors' combined."

"Okay, you better just watch yourself," he said. "Tenure isn't what it used to be, you know."

"Well, perhaps we could have a discussion about that with my Faculty Association. They may be very curious to hear your take on my freedom of expression." I sneered at him. "You know, Tom, there was a time when the academy was about more than just over-paid administrators putting out sub-literate press releases. There was a time when an outspoken professor was treated like more than just a PR problem."

"Okay, we're done. I'm sorry. We're done. This press release is going out, Philip. You will have to deal with the fallout as you will."

I stood up to leave. "Unbelievable," I muttered, and thought about climbing under his desk to nab the poppy. "Fucking un-believable."

"Philip, look," he said, his tone softening somewhat. "I'll be honest with you. I often think that you don't really need this university. You're such a big deal now — and I don't say that fa-cetiously. You could've become a full-time writer years ago, if you wanted. I think this job may be more hassle to you than it's worth."

I looked at him in bafflement. *What are you talking about, Tom?* I thought. *I overpaid for a huge house in Cabbagetown six years ago. I'm supporting two kids, one of which isn't even mine. And I have a wife who doesn't work. Of course I need this job.*

Back in my book-cluttered office at University College, I checked email. Seven new notifications from Facebook. Good. Things were starting to die down. Above them I could see that a second email had just come in from Rani in London. The subject line, far more sedate than her first, read simply:

Okay …

I opened it.

Hiya,

All right, I just re-watched the full clip of you on CBC.
I mean, what you said was still AWFUL, but you did
look a bit painted into a corner. Were you distracted
by something? You didn't seem like your usual sharp
self, Sharpe. Trouble in paradise, perhaps?

Look, a lot of people are ragging on you right
now, but I know you didn't mean to say what you said
to that woman. Anyway, if you want to talk about all
this, give a ring on my mobile: 07870 663 926. I'm
here if you need me. For anything. ;)

Love and rockets,
Rani

Oh God, why didn't she just tear me to shreds like everybody
else? It would've been easier to read than — than *that*. I hovered
over the REPLY button for a second, but then backed off. *No*, I
thought. *Don't do it. Don't.*

I returned to my inbox, to the list of Facebook notifications.
It was then that I realized that all seven were identical: they were
for an event invitation, each one forwarded to me by one of my
forty-six friends. The subject line read: EVENING OF PROTEST:
SOLIDARITY IN DEMANDING PHILIP SHARPE'S RESIGNATION:
Hosted by U of T Women's Studies Dept.

The Women's Studies department? Why were *those* people
getting mixed up in all this? They didn't strike me as a group particularly interested in judicial process — especially when it came
to marauding capitalists. Why would they care about what I said
on the CBC? I returned to my inbox and found a message from
Sebastian. He had forwarded the exact same Facebook invitation
to me, and included a note:

Sir,

I really think you should come to this. Everybody is going, and it would be a good chance for you to clear the air. Yes, it'll be a hostile environment, but I and your other supporters will be right there. You won't be alone. Think about it.

Sebastian

The boy was right. I should go. I should go to my protest. It would be a ballsy move. An opportunity to speak my mind, hear what others had to say, and find a resolution to this absurd "scandal." Yes, I should just gird myself and show up to my own effigy burning. Face the outrage head on and clear the air with everyone.

I clicked through to the invitation. Wow. There were 517 people listed as "Interested" in going. One of them, I could see, was Roberta Rosenbaum, the reporter from the *Globe* whom I used to date. That cinched it. She'd give me a fair hearing, for sure. I looked over at the event's date and time.

Shit. *Shit!* It was for *tonight*. What the hell? I stared at the date to make sure I wasn't hallucinating, and then my stomach sank to the floor.

I went to Google then to look up a number, and picked up my phone when I found it. (The red message light was blinking again — more journalists, no doubt, looking for a statement from me.) I dialled.

"Toronto Dance Studio."

"Hi, yes. I'm calling to confirm that you still have a recital happening there tonight."

"Yep. It's still on."

"It hasn't been cancelled by any chance?"

"Why would it be cancelled?"

"Ah, no reason. Thank you for that."

"Thank *you*."

I hung up. Sat in silence for a long time. Grace's words rang in my mind like a bell: ... *she's convinced you're going to renege on taking her ... you don't really seem all that plugged in to what's happening in your own house ...* But then I was lured away from these thoughts by the Facebook invitation, still on my screen. Its gravitational force.

Okay, Sharpe, I thought. *This is one of those life decisions. This is where the good men are separated from the louts.* Sapere aude.

Actually, it wasn't a hard decision. I knew what I had to do.

Higher Learning

ut first, a few words about Rani Sumita.

B I'm not one to gambol through the false paradise of nostalgia but when you've been to Oxford you can't help but self-mythologize, at least a little. I arrived at Balliol College to begin my doctorate in the fall of 1989, during what I can only describe as the backwash of Thatcherism. I had high hopes that there was no better place than here — here being England, with all its class obsessions and new-found bootstrapism — to be a young philosopher looking to excoriate the rising tide of neo-liberal thought. And I *was* young: twenty-four years old, imagine, and still sporting a full head of my tomato-coloured hair and a well-trimmed goatee as precursor to the greying red mass that inhabits my face now. I felt buoyant as I came to Balliol on my Commonwealth scholarship, certain I would break new ground by braiding Kantian thought to trendy economic theories. I was not interested in the ternary structure of a North American Ph.D. (coursework-comps-dissertation, *blah*) and wanted something more for myself. Yet Oxford took mere weeks to prove less an institution of higher learning and more a Gothic theme park, one that both *was* itself and *performed* itself relentlessly. I lasted four months in Holywell Manor, the grad student residence for Balliol, and by January of 1990 I had taken a room on Walton Street in nearby Jericho.

How to describe the ensuing year, before Rani sashayed into my life? I don't think I was prepared to have my bubble burst so spectacularly about what jolly old England had become under Thatcher. How could a country that had provided us Shakespeare and Purcell now provide so little to so many of its own? I remember hordes of homeless people gathered in front of the co-op on Iffley Road, vaguely threatening to me and my presumed "Yankee" accent. Class resentment seemed to be in the drinking water. The town of Oxford itself displayed lots of public wealth and hid lots of private poverty. If you were a gownie, you remained insulated from the latter as long as you stayed inside the castellated walls of your college. But if you were a townie, then despair was like a spastic tic you couldn't shake; despair had become your way of life. This, mind you, in no way diminished the jingoistic roaring that shook the pubs of Oxford in the summer of 1990 during the World Cup. England did very well and then it didn't, getting eliminated by the host country, Italy, in the third-place match. I feared for my life while riding the bus or walking home from the Bodleian Library during those summer weeks as townies worked themselves into a lather of nationalism. I thought: *Are you all insane? Have you forgotten just how much the country you're rooting for has screwed you over?*

Well. Thatcher got hers that November, I need not remind you — the knives of her own party turning on her after so many years of mindless loyalty. But the damage had been done, and I knew even then that the legacy of Thatcherism had put something permanent and heinous into the world economy, a near-religious fanaticism of market thinking that would supply my academic work with decades of fodder.

For my first fifteen months at Oxford, I carried on pretty much as I had at U of T for my first two degrees. Everyone attending

Oxford was, by default, brilliant — as if intellectualism was a hobby you'd had since you were five — and I accepted my *moira* of solitary bookishness and deep immersion into the Enlightenment's lasting influence on current affairs. But I did socialize. Here, look at me go — taking the bus across town to go on dates with chatty café waitresses or fellow students at Balliol. I was a regular at all the well-known pubs of Oxford — Turf Tavern, the Bear, the Mitre, and of course the Lindsay Bar at Balliol. Yes, I avoided the Canadian Club, but who didn't! I even joined the Oxford Union, that famed and notoriously Tory debating society. Why? Mostly for the cheap photocopying in its library — and the polemics! Yes, yes. Despite the union's Anglo-Saxon stuffiness, its overt conservatism, its stature as mere training ground for Britain's future political elite, I really loved attending the society's parliamentary-style debates on Thursday nights. From the packed gallery above the debating floor, I would watch each combatant take his or her place at the despatch box and, surrounded by frosty portraits of notable past union members, deliver a fierce, argumentative speech. It was here that I learned how arguing could be an art form, and I found myself glowing at every incisive joust, even if it scored a point I fervidly disagreed with.

Then, one chilly evening in January of 1991, I attended a debate entitled "The Rushdie Fatwa and the Limitations of Free Speech." The discussion started out surprisingly limp: there were predictable plaudits about the importance of novelists in society; there were politically correct assertions about respecting the sensitivity of other cultures; one bloke, clearly a Thatcherite, argued that Rushdie's free speech wasn't "free" at all, considering how much his now round-the-clock security was costing the state. It was all a bit ho-hum. It was all a bit too obvious.

But then, from the front row of the gallery, I watched as a young woman wrapped in a red-and-orange sari appeared from behind her team's bench and took her place at the despatch box directly below me. Her sari was trimmed in gold that matched the large, feathery earrings that dangled from her ears. Her forearms were adorned with intricately wrought bracelets, her fingers covered in rings. Her hair was pulled back into a long, thick braid that reached beyond her shoulder blades, and her two eyebrows were really just one, meeting above a stare of deep, penetrating brown. When this young woman spoke, her accent was an alluring mix of East Indian and East London, a cockney twang curling around an enunciation that conjured distant oceans. I don't want to say it, and you, dear reader, don't want to hear it, because it's a terrible cliché, but she was the most beautiful, poised, and powerful woman I'd ever seen.

She stunned us all with what she said. The Rushdie fatwa, she said, was merely the thin edge of the wedge. Anyone who was paying attention could see that larger forces were gathering, that soon extremists from every corner of the Muslim faith would place Rushdie's death sentence on all of Western civilization. She drew a succinct line between the Six-Day War in Israel, the Soviet Union's invasion of Afghanistan (pronounced with a sexy, defiantly non-English *v* in the middle — Af*vhan*istan), and, now, America's intervention in the Persian Gulf, and how these events would conspire to put a bull's eye on the institutions and values that we held dear. If we wanted to confront this inevitable threat, she went on, the first step was to stop seeing it as a clash between two cultures, because it wasn't. It was a clash between one culture and a group of violent nihilists who renounced the very notion of culture. Rushdie was living this reality now, and soon we all would be.

Perhaps I'm overplaying the impact of her speech in my memory, its prescience. But I do recall rushing down the winding stairwell from the gallery after the vote and having to wait a long fucking time in a lineup to meet her during the milling that followed. An entire conclave of grey-haired Oxfordian men had descended upon this young sari'd woman to congratulate her on her speech, and I hovered impatiently to have a turn. The last of the fogies took forever to wrap up, asking if she had read his own scholarship on Iranian foreign policy, and then described it to her in bone-numbing detail before she could answer. She actually spotted *my* face, youthful and anxious, and flashed me a gently mocking two-step of her unibrow. Finally, the old fart moved on and I sidled up to her.

"Great speech," I said. "I don't want to take up too much of your time, but I thought your points were bang on."

"Wow," she smiled, "where is *your* accent from?"

I laughed a little and looked at the floor. "Canada." Gawd. Even the name sounded bland. Then I added: "Prince Edward Island."

"*Anne of Green Gables!*" she beamed. "Ah, I loved that book as a kid."

"Uh, yeah," I sighed.

"Well look at that," she said, and gave me a cheeky up-and-down. "Another redhead from Prince Edward Island."

We talked, all friendly like, for a few minutes, and I learned some things: how to properly pronounce her name, that she was twenty-four, originally from Goa, moved at puberty to England with her family, and was now in the middle of a master's degree in international studies at Merton College. When I asked how she had come to join the Oxford Union (hers the only brown visage in this evening's taiga of puckered pink faces), Rani told me it was because her hero, the already-iconic Benazir Bhutto, had been a member as a student fifteen years earlier. Actually, our chat was more than a bit friendly — full of flirts and *bon mots* — and maybe the expectation was that I would ask her out at the end of it. Maybe. I'm not sure if you've noticed, dear reader, but I can be pretty oblivious from time to time. Truth be told, all those rings on her fingers ran interference on my intentions. I thought: *Don't people, even if they're from India, leave a particular digit empty to indicate singledom?*

At any rate, our more-than-friendly chat wrapped up and I walked away, realizing only later that I hadn't even told her *my* name.

That would have been the end of it, except I ran into her a week later in the catacombs of Turf Tavern. I was on my way to the bar and she was just coming in with some girlfriends, and we practically walked into each other.

"Well hello there, Prince Edward Island!" she said. This time, she was wearing blue jeans and a buckskin jacket, her black hair loose and spilling over her shoulders.

"Oh, hey," I smiled, and we passed each other like ships, and she leaned in to whisper to her friends as they moved into the pub, and some of them giggled.

I got a fresh pint and returned to my table, stacked with undergrad papers I should have been marking. Rani's table was on the other side of the room, and I grew envious of the animated conversation she and her friends were having. I thought about inviting myself to join them, but before I could, she got up and crossed the floor to join *me*, sitting herself in the chair across from mine without asking.

"You know, I realized," she began, her eyes sparkling in the pub's dimness, "that I didn't even catch your name at the Oxford Union the other night."

"Um, Sharpe," I fambled. "Philip."

"Sharpe Philip?" She smirked. "Are you sharp, Philip?"

"About certain things," I replied.

"Anyway, sorry I prattled on so much." She shrugged modestly. "It was kind of a big night for me."

"No need to apologize. You did very well. I'm sure you'll make a great British prime minister someday."

She roared with laughter. "Um, no." She leaned in then as if to convey a secret. "I'm not interested in running for office. I want to go into journalism, ultimately. But I figured some public speaking experience would help me as a broadcaster."

"Fair enough."

"And you're obviously a student," she said, nodding at the stack of essays on my table. "Not a tourist visiting from PEI?"

"Yeah, no. I'm reading philosophy at Balliol for my D.Phil.," I said. "Specializing in Kant."

"Oh God, *really*?" She grinned. "And here I thought you were cool. How can you love Kant? He's such a bore!"

"He's *not* a bore."

"Oh, but he is. Can you point to a single translation of Kant that isn't unbearably dense?"

So we had at it for a while (a sure sign of our mutual attraction — we were making fun of each other right away), and I was impressed by the breadth of her knowledge, the way she could quote snippets of *Foundations of the Metaphysics of Morals* at me. I also noticed how the Indian portion of her accent would crowd out the English portion when she got her back up about something. All the while, her hands were flashing in front of my face as she talked, and I once again noticed the glittery assemblage of rings on her fingers. Single? Not single? Help me out here.

"Look, I'm delivering a paper on Kant at the end of the month," I said. "It'll be in the Middle Common Room at Holywell Manor. You should come. Let me prove to you that he's as relevant today as he's ever been."

"Oh, I don't know."

"Come on. It's a symposium — totally open to the public. There'll be lots of people; there'll be food."

She did this dainty little cringe of uncertainty.

"Oh, come on," I pressed. "It'll be fun. You could bring your … husband?"

"I don't have a husband," she said.

"You could bring your boyfriend."

"I don't have a boyfriend."

"You could bring whatever guy friend from undergrad you still string along with an occasional night of snogging."

She was about to make an angry face but then said, "Oh, *Steven* — yeah, he'd probably come."

My heart sank. "Great. Bring Steven. We'll have a grand old time." And I gave her all the details.

"Well, Sharpe Philip, I should get back to my friends."

"Okay," I replied.

She got up, reluctantly crossed the pub floor, and eased her heart-shaped derrière back into her chair. One of her girlfriends, who'd been observing us the whole time, leaned in and said, loud enough for me to hear, "I think that guy *fancies* you." And I disappeared back into my marking.

Okay. Let's cut to the symposium. There I was, well-dressed and ready to roll, exchanging pleasantries with the crowd, my brain jiffy-popping with all the points my talk would cover and the performative qualities with which I would deliver them. Still, I found myself staring at the doors, wondering if Rani would actually show up. Holywell Manor's Middle Common Room, all rugs on hardwood and plush leather couches, was teeming with fellow grad students and their professorial advisors, as well as alumni and other fans of Balliol. The event organizers had pulled off an opulent spread of food on a drape-covered table near the back — a gigot of lamb, an assortment of cheeses and caviars, crackers to serve them on, oysters on the half shell, and little displays of small, decorative mangoes. I was just navigating a wedge of Wensleydale into my mouth when Rani and her date arrived, having wound their way through Holywell Manor to find this room. She spotted me and they came right over.

"This is quite an event, Sharpe," she said. "Are you nervous?"

"I don't *get* nervous," I replied. She smiled, and then introduced me to her friend.

As I suspected, this Steven character was a bit of a sad sack. Balding guy with glasses and a beard, ratty tweed coat over collared plaid shirt, a pen displayed prominently in his breast pocket. He seemed somewhat out of place in this room, but Rani informed me that he was in fact an aspiring novelist. Steven confirmed this, saying, Yep, he had been rising at 4:30 daily since the age of sixteen to write a thousand words, rain or shine. He had yet to publish anything, of course. One thing was quickly evident: he was madly in love with Rani, but like any lapdog, grateful for whatever scraps of affection she threw his way.

We moved closer to the food and they began to help themselves. "This spread is a bit ostentatious," I said. "I'm still getting used to all the wealth in here and all the poverty ..." and I motioned to the windows, "out there."

"Oh, I know," Rani said, taking up an oyster shell. "It's one of the first things you notice when you come to Oxford." She gracefully poured the slimy meat down her throat, and her eyes flared at the flavour. "Mmm. Salty."

Steven, meanwhile, seemed utterly baffled by the caviar. He held a small cracker in his hand but couldn't figure out how to get some of the fish eggs onto it, despite there being a tiny serving spoon right there. "Yep, my parents are working class," he said. "They've never been to an event like this."

"That's sort of what my talk is about tonight," I said. "Using a Kantian framework, I'm arguing that globalization will only worsen, not improve, the class divisions already prevalent in Western society."

"*Really?*" Rani asked. Her whole face lit up. "Because I've often said that about India's caste system." She gave me one of her up-and-downs. "Wow, Sharpe, if I had known that, I wouldn't have made fun of you the other night at Turf."

Having abandoned his efforts at the caviar, Steven now took up one of the small decorative mangoes. I watched as he looked around the table and then reached for a cheese knife. He used its dull blade, as best he could, to pierce the mango's skin. He returned to us just as he began peeling back the fruit's flesh. "Kantian? Kant, right? Philosopher guy?"

"Um, yeah," I replied, staring at his hands. I turned back to Rani. "Anyway, I don't want to scoop my thunder, but yes, that's what I'll be talking about."

"Interesting," Steven said. He proceeded then to not so much eat the mango as make love to it with his face. He went on like that until Rani touched his arm, and then he stopped.

The event organizer came by. "Okay, Philip, we're ready to start. Are you still okay with going second?"

"Absolutely," I said, and she hurried off. I turned to Rani. "Wish me luck."

"Good luck."

I was about to ask the same of Steven, but he had turned back to the table, another cracker in hand, and was now trying to resolve his caviar dilemma. Droplets of mango juice shone in his beard.

"You'll want to use the spoon, champ," I said to him.

"Ah, brilliant," he replied.

Soon the proceedings began. I was sandwiched between a guy talking about Spinoza and a young woman talking about Lacan, and we each had twenty minutes to deliver our papers. I don't want to brag, but I pretty much owned the night. The other presentations were competent but a touch dreary. Mine was a zesty concatenation of contemporary economic trends and Kantian wisdom, which I delivered with humour and charisma when it was my turn at the podium. During the Q&A, I was funny and charming and on point, and left everyone in the room feeling as you should after one of these events — *enriched.*

There was much milling afterward. Steven had buttonholed some minor novelist he'd discovered in the crowd, and was sharing his theory on narrative beginnings with the poor, withered bloke. "By the end of the first page, readers should really *know* your two main characters," he was saying. "They really should *know* what kind of novel it's going to be, right from the start." Rani used this opportunity to slink over to me. As Steven droned on, her unibrow did another of its little two-steps.

"He's quite a guy," I said to her.

"He's just a friend." And then repeated it, as if to herself. "He's just a friend."

"I see."

"Anyway, Sharpe, you were *amazing*. Now I really feel bad for mocking you the other night. Seriously. You've converted me on Kant. If *that's* going to be the focus of your scholarship, you're going to have a long, successful career ahead of you."

"Thanks."

"You're welcome." She looked at the floor for a bit, then back up. "So." And here did one of her shy, girly cringes. "Are you interested in having an Indian sometime?"

I blinked at her, then smiled. "What, is that some sort of subcontinental come-on?"

"What? No!" She burst out laughing. "Oh God, Sharpe, you really are a babe in the woods. No, I meant going for a *curry*, you moron."

"Oh, right," I said, excited. "Yes. Curry. Absolutely. Let's do it. Curry. Right. Yes."

So I had my first Indian with Rani. And then I had my first Indian, with Rani.

The next year and a half passed in a series of moments between us that remain scorched in my memory. What do I remember? In the parlance of 2015: a *bunch* of random shit. I remember her excitement when she learned I lived on Walton Street in Jericho, and she took me to the local club there where the U.K.'s "shoegaze" music scene — bands like Slowdive and Ride and a nascent version of Radiohead — was already in full flower. Rani *loved* shoegaze music, those trancelike guitar riffs and ethereal lyrics, and one of my sharpest memories involved her dancing around my room in Jericho to Lush's "Sweetness and Light" in nothing but her panties. I recall being deathly afraid for her whenever I knew she was out on her bicycle navigating Oxford's narrow, medieval streets. (And she did do a faceplant on the cobblestones, once, after some asshole townie cut her off.) I remember taking her punting at Christ Church Meadow — that most leisurely of Oxford activities, the ruralness just sort of creeping up on you — and nearly capsizing us into the River Cherwell. I remember us gathering with friends for pub-crawls that lasted ten hours. (Steven would sometimes come, sitting with his pint and looking like the sensitive novelist he was, perhaps thinking about all the sex with Rani he wasn't having.) And I remember she and I would stagger back to my place afterwards to fuck and then watch episodes of *A Bit of Fry & Laurie*, thinking, *So this is what the Cambridge set gets up to.* I remember describing Rani to my father on one of my rare calls home to PEI, and how excited Little Frankie got for me. "And here I thought you were *scared* of girls," he quipped. I recall she took me for my first brunch, said I should order a Bloody Mary. When I asked the waiter what the base spirit was and he told me vodka, I made a face. "Well, I could swap in Irish whiskey, but then it would be a Bloody Joseph." So he did, and BY GOD I was in love! And I remember meeting up with Rani in the Bodleian's lunchroom — which was basically just a steam tunnel that reeked of mildew — and we'd share stories about whatever intellectual discovery we had made since we last saw each other, which was sometimes the previous day, and sometimes whole weeks.

Yes, that was the other thing. Rani and I never talked about job descriptions, whether I was her "boyfriend" and she was my "girlfriend." Between our academic obligations and the transience of Oxford life itself, such labels seemed twee. We were both addicted to working — especially her. She took a job with an Oxfordshire radio station before she even completed her thesis, gaining experience she hoped would help land her dream job as a producer at BBC Radio in London. She would pull these afternoon shifts at the station and then return to Merton to work on her thesis until the dawn hours. I always marvelled at what a night owl Rani was, the way she could just stay up until morning — even after we'd been out drinking — and work and work and work. I myself was an early riser, and so it often felt that our schedules never synchronized, that our tryst would fizzle out because we were both so immersed in our respective ambitions.

There may have also been, I should say, other men in her life. Steven certainly loomed on the periphery, and there were vague intimations of a male "friend" in London, and of familial commitments back in India. Rani also had certain hang-ups about sex. There were times when she and I were vigorously intimate with one another, but other times when she might stop us at the beginning of something — or even in the *middle* of something — and just leave, just flee my Jericho flat without explanation. I was hurt, but tried to be understanding about it — as much as any twenty-six-year-old male can be — and simply waited for her to return to me. Which she would. We'd reunite, and be ravenous for one another. Once, while deeply inebriated, she let slip that she "loved" me, but then promptly took it back, apologizing as if it were a gaffe. I thought: *Don't apologize. I kind of love you, too, Ms. Sumita. I mean, what are we even doing here? Are we going to be together long term, do you think?* But I never raised these questions, and she never volunteered to answer them. At best, she would just leap into my arms after not seeing me for a while, kiss me like I was the only man on the planet worth kissing. Cling to me like I was some raft keeping her afloat on a dark, dark sea.

By the end of 1992, OUP was showing interest in publishing my dissertation, and I was showing interest in finishing the fucking thing and moving on to something else. I admitted to Rani that, while I did love my time at Balliol, I would always be disappointed that I hadn't been (due to not having earned my undergraduate degree at Oxford) eligible to attend All Souls College instead. All Souls, which didn't even admit undergraduate students, was known back then for its infamous "one-word exam." During this exam, fellowship applicants would be given a single word — usually something basic, like *tree* or *water* or *fundamental* — and had to write about it for three hours, creating a cogent thesis and including whole quotes and citations — *from memory* — taken out of their specialty area. The exams were marked pass/fail, and very few applicants succeeded in getting a fellowship. I was convinced I could pull it off, and would frequently gripe to Rani about my lack of opportunity to do so. This complaining came to a head one dreary afternoon when we were hanging out in my place near the end of Michaelmas term that year. She and I had just wrapped up a feisty, post-coital debate about whether Gutenberg had really invented movable type in the 1400s, or whether it had been invented in China several centuries earlier. Somehow we got back onto the topic of All Souls. "I could write that exam," I grumbled. "I could totally fucking write that exam."

"Oh *God*, Sharpe, I'm tired of your whingeing. Here." She climbed out of bed to fetch a pad of canary paper and a pen off my desk, and tossed them to me. "Put your brain where your mouth is. I'll give you one word and for the next three hours you will write me an essay about it."

"Fine," I said, resting the pad on my knees. "Fuck you. I'll do it. Citations and all. What's my word?"

Her eyes rolled up to her unibrow as she thought about it, and then she looked at me. "*Movable*," she said.

"Movable. Great. Let's do this thing."

She picked her watch up off my nightstand. "You've got three hours," she said, glancing at it. "*Go*."

And so I wrote. I wrote and wrote and wrote and wrote. Rani occupied herself with reading and listening to her Discman, but I barely noticed her once I got into the zone. And what a zone it was — anyone who writes essays will know what I mean, the way you can just vanish into your argument, and how all the points and sentences just fit and work together and *sing*. It was sort of magical, what happened then, the trancelike state I achieved.

After three hours, Rani came over and kissed me behind the ear. "Time's up," she said. I finished off one last sentence, then tossed the pen out of my cramped and aching hand. I gathered up the stack of pages that had accumulated beside me on the bed and passed them to her. She curled up and began reading, and I went to the bathroom and to stretch my legs. When I came back, I could see she was engrossed. After a bit, she looked up at me.

"Sharpe, this is really good."

"Told you," I said.

"No, seriously. This is really fucking good." She sifted back to the first page. "I mean, your thesis statement — about unreason's reliance on apocalyptic language, and how it moves across philosophies and religions and economies to create a durable cynicism — is really well-argued. And then ..." And she flipped forward several pages, "and then here, in — one, two, three — in three paragraphs, you manage to tie together the Iranian revolution, Heraclitus's theory on the unity of opposites, Brian Mulroney arguing for NAFTA, and the poetry of John Dryden. And it all *fits*. It fucking fits." She looked up at me again. "So you just pulled this out of your arse?"

"Yeah, pretty much." I shrugged.

She grinned at me. "You have to do something with this," she said. "Promise me you'll do something with this."

"Sure," I replied. "Sure I will."

And it was a promise I kept. Over the coming weeks, I would work on what Rani and I now referred to as the "'Movable' manuscript," and would slip her fresh pages as if they were *samizdat* whenever I saw her. Sometimes she was critical of what I wrote, and other times she was fawning, but her enthusiasm for it — and for me — never wavered.

But then 1993 arrived, and everything changed. In January, Rani landed her dream job at the BBC and moved to London. During that same period, I flew to Toronto to interview for a tenure-track position back at U of T, and of course I got it. I returned to Oxford to prepare for my dissertation defence and hammer out details with OUP about its publication, but mostly I wanted to see what the future might hold for me and Rani. After a couple of phone calls and letters, she came up on the train from London to see me. We had a very unsentimental talk about where we stood, which, it became apparent, was nowhere. I did float the idea of us just throwing caution to the wind, of perhaps her giving up her new-found role and joining me in Canada, maybe get on at the CBC there, and we could build a life together. But I recognized the ridiculousness of those words the moment they left my lips — what with her dream job and large, noisy, Indian family here in England. In the end, we agreed on the inevitability of parting ways. She actually said, "It's been great knowing you, Sharpe," as she put on her clothes and left my flat in Jericho for the last time.

And so, with defence done, job secured, and first book forthcoming in eighteen months, I moved back to Toronto in August of '93 to take up my assistant professorship at U of T. A year later I got onto email for the first time, and acquired Rani's address through a mutual friend. On a lark, I wrote her a tentative note, thinking it might somehow fail to reach her through the convoluted avenues of the information superhighway, or, if it did, come back with news of a fresh boy toy, or even marriage. Instead, her response was an enthusiastic, *Oh my God, Sharpe, how the hell are ya?? And where the FUCK is the "Movable" manuscript? Send me some more of it, you ponce!* And so I did, and she sent me back some critiques. We found email an agreeable platform for our flirting, and it got pretty heavy at times. We would, of course, knock it off if one of us started dating somebody new, but then it would resume once we were both single again.

Then, in 1996, she confessed to wanting to see me, and asked how that might be possible. I told her that I was delivering a paper that summer at Dalhousie University in Halifax, and she agreed to fly there to meet me. The plan had been to just hang out together, all platonic-like, for a week as tourists, taking in the sites and maybe chatting about the "Movable" manuscript. Instead, we spent nearly our entire time fucking in my Halifax hotel room. We would take occasional breaks to go for a pint at a charming pub on the waterfront called the Nautical, where we sat at a table overlooking the ocean. She'd run her fingers through my inchoate comb-over and say, "You're starting to lose your hair, Sharpe," and I'd reply with, "Am not!" and then, to verify my enduring virility, we'd go back to my room and fuck some more.

That parting of ways, in Halifax, was far more emotional than anything we'd gone through three years earlier in Oxford.

We had a long clingy goodbye in the airport departure lounge, then returned to our respective home bases. A brief period of radio silence ensued. But then, inevitably, the emails and flirting picked up again. Occasionally, there would even be a transatlantic drunk dial. And during times when I wasn't seeing anyone and she wasn't seeing anyone, we'd make plans to visit each other again. If I was giving a talk anywhere in the U.K. or Ireland, she'd figure out a way to come "hang out" with me; and if she flew to New York on a shopping trip with her girlfriends, I'd come down on the bus and we'd slip away together for a few hours. This went on and on — for nearly ten years. No matter how long it had been since I'd last seen Rani, I felt powerless to resist her. What can I say? She lit my candle, every fucking time. And some goodbyes were easy and some goodbyes were very hard. And most of all, I longed for someone else to come into my life who could render moot this nettlesome attachment to her that I just couldn't shake.

But of course, I'm getting ahead of myself. In the fall of 1998, *The Movable Apocalypse* was published, and, as I've mentioned, became an unexpected hit. Philip Sharpe the Public Figure was born. And, of course, I dedicated that book to Rani Sumita. I mean, how could I not?

Thursday, November 5

This is how it went down last night.

We strolled Metcalfe Street together, through autumn's great chiaroscuro, that orange canopy of leaves releasing their strange light despite the fallen dusk, and talked about the movement of bodies. This had all started two months ago with Grace reluctantly allowing Simone to take *Black Swan* out of the library (we're old school that way, here at 4 Metcalfe Street), which, upon viewing, led to an obsession. This then precipitated a request to order old episodes of *Fame* on DVD from Amazon. The show's theme music became the soundtrack of our house for weeks, and provided Simone with a kind of focus that warmed us as parents. *I'm gonna live forehh-ver*, she sang at us. *I'm gonna learn how to fly.* But then came the doubt. Where does a thirteen-year-old learn doubt? Turned out her best friend, Sarah, in that *psh-shaw* tone of hers, had said that Simone was too *old* to get interested in dance, that most girls started ballet at a quarter of her age. (Grace had not put Simone in ballet as a toddler, perhaps including it in her "princess ban.") But we said: Look, if you want to be in dance we can put you in dance. Just for fun. I dunno, she said. Simone, there's a huge studio right at the end of our street, I reminded her. Why don't we go to a recital and see if you're really into it? She grew animated by this idea. You'd take me? she asked. Grace answered for me. She said: Yes, Philip will take you. She said: Philip, you'd take Simone to a dance recital, right? Absolutely, I replied. I will absolutely take my stepdaughter to a dance recital.

So there we were, walking down Metcalfe and talking about arabesques and *pas de chevals* and all the rest, with Simone doing little demonstrations for me in the street. I was touched that she wanted to share this neophyte fixation with me, and have us spend some quality together. But I also felt a bit scandalous, knowing that the protest against me was happening at that very moment back at U of T and I wasn't there. I was here — here — supporting this bright, enthusiastic young human, like a good stepdad should.

We arrived for the show to find only a short lineup. The Toronto Dance Studio was in a huge old church, its bell tower seeming to look out over the entire neighbourhood. I was getting a few stares from other people in the line but they held their tongues at the sight of my now-notorious visage, perhaps because I had a young child in tow. Simone and I worked our way to the box office in the cramped lobby, purchased our tickets and took our programs, and then were led into the main studio space. A large riser took up half the room, and beyond it were the church's stained-glass windows that faced the street, now black-boxed by long dark curtains. As we climbed the riser and found some seats, I spotted the small bar set up on the far side of the room. I said to Simone, "Do you want a drink?" and she said, "Sure. A Coke?" and I said, "Great. I'll be right back." I climbed down the riser and got in line at the bar. Stepping up, I saw that the best liquor they could manage was the Johnnie Walker Red, so I ordered a double. After paying for it, I started to go but then spun on my heels and cut back to the front of the line. "Oh, and a *Coke*, sorry," I said. I paid for it and then double-fisted my way back to our seats.

I handed Simone her drink and she sipped at it slowly, looking around that massive room with her big green eyes.

Soon the lights fell and the show started. I must confess that, while I am progressive and open-minded, I don't have a taste for what one might politely call the "alternative arts." I cringe away from the spoken-rant artists who now infect our literary festivals. I tend not to give change to the unemployed millennial singing opera in a cape on College Street. *This* show proved more alternative than anticipated. The troupe stormed the stage with great violence, swinging their limbs in the air and then falling to the floor dramatically, forming their bodies into pods while some sort of atonal "music" — mostly squeals and long bleeps — blared above them. And then back up the dancers went, swerving and melting into each other's bodies, then pulling away and ducking behind clenched forearms, as if blocking a punch, then back up and throwing their bosoms open to the world. Around and around they went as they spun and clenched and *ached*. This went on for forty-five minutes, and then the lights went up for the intermission.

"What do you think?" I whispered to Simone as the small audience began to mill.

She took a final, thoughtful sip of her Coke. "I'll reserve judgment to the end," she said in an obvious, adorable parroting of Grace. I beamed at her. What a kid.

"Did you want a fresh Coke?"

"No, I'm okay, thanks."

I went to the bar anyway, for another double Johnnie, and made it back to my seat just as the lights dimmed.

The second half was more of the same, but only lasted thirty minutes. When it was over, we stood to go but kept our opinions to ourselves until we were out of earshot of the other audience members. Most seemed to be — based on the congratulatory hugs and reunions that happened in front of the stage — friends and/or family of the dancers themselves.

"So," I said as we strolled back down Metcalfe Street, "what did you think?"

Simone pondered for a bit. "Well, I guess I kept looking for the story," she said. "I mean — was there supposed to be a *story*?"

"I don't think so," I replied. "With stuff like that, we're not really supposed to look for a narrative."

"What do you mean?"

"Well, it's like when we go to the art gallery and look at the abstract stuff. It isn't a linear thing, right? It doesn't have, you know, a rising action, climax, and all that. You just take it in all at once. This is sort of the same thing. When you watch dance like that, you have to imagine the performers are clutching paintbrushes in their hands and their feet. As they move their bodies around, you should try to see the abstract picture they're painting for you." And I mimicked some interpretive dance to demonstrate, which made Simone laugh.

"That makes a lot of sense," she said. "Still ..." And here she thought and thought. "Maybe dance isn't for me."

"You know, it's okay if it isn't."

She paused again. "Maybe I should be a zoologist. You know, when I grow up."

"You could be a dancing zoologist."

"Hmm. No. Maybe just a zoologist."

"Well, you do love animals," I said, thinking of how well Simone took care of our family cat, Constance, which was her chief household chore.

"I do love animals," she agreed. And then, apropos of this, said, "Philip — do you think I'm too young to read *Life of Pi*?"

"What? No. Fuck no. You're super smart. You could read *Life of Pi*."

She nodded once more. "I think I'll read *Life of Pi.*"

And then we were home. When we came in, Grace looked up from the novel she was reading in the living room and asked, "How was it?" and Simone answered, "It was *weird*," and we hung up our coats and I kicked off my Payless. Simone descended into the living room just as Grace was unpretzelling herself from her reading chair, and the two shared a mother-daughter hug. "It's past your bedtime," Grace said, and Simone nodded in acquiescence. But before she headed upstairs, she paid a visit to the enormous, overflowing bookshelves along our living-room wall, found the *M*'s in fiction, and pulled down the tome she wanted. "Are you going to read that?" Grace smiled. "I'm going to *try*," Simone replied. As she headed up to her bedroom, she said, "Thanks for taking me, Philip." And I said, "Anytime, kiddo." And then Grace and I were alone.

"Is Naomi down?" I asked.

"Down and out. Just one story and she was done." Grace hooked her hip into mine and took my fingers into hers. "You did the right thing," she said, looking at me with those eyes. I nodded. Yes. I had done the right thing.

"Can you help me with the recycling?" she asked, and I followed her to the kitchen. There was a tiny swagger to Grace's walk as she looked over her shoulder at me, at my furry, shambling state. She giggled. I giggled back. What were we laughing at? The quiet of the house? This instance alone? This moment of forgiveness washing over us like a wave? She squatted at the cupboard under the sink while I fetched a couple of blue bags from their place in the pantry. As Grace tossed the collapsed cereal boxes and empty Jameson bottles and yesterday's newspapers between my open arms, I thought: *Yes.* There *was* a wave of forgiveness washing over us, and something else washing in. Grace's chest brushed against mine as she reached deep into the cupboard for a rogue cat food can that had fallen behind the blue bin. She came back up and tossed the can into the bag, then paused. Looked at my mouth. I looked at hers. Then she took up the second recycling bag, and I grabbed the other bin, also overflowing, in both hands. Grace opened the bag to me, and I raised up and then just spilled the whole bin in, giving it a good, manly shake. She set the bag, now heavy, on the floor. "You'll take them out?" she asked, and I nodded. She stepped in to me. Grazed her hand around the doughy mound of my stomach. "Okay, I'll see you up there then," she said. Neither of us moved, and we laughed again, in unison. What *were* we laughing at?

She slinked back to the living room and up the stairs, and I hastily tied up the recycling bags to run them outside. When I joined Grace upstairs a few minutes later, we still had the ensuite rituals to go through, the taking of vitamins, the brushing of teeth, the cursed flossing. But then we hurried into bed together. It had been several days for us, we realized, and certainly not since my TV appearance on Monday.

And yet.

Does it count as forgiveness sex if the forgiveness doesn't hold? Think about that. You slip into slumber with your wife in your arms after an energetic bout of fucking, but then stir in the night to find her awake and staring at you. There has been a shift in her disposition. She wants to talk. She wants to talk, and you, by God, want to listen, but the evening's depletions haul you back down into the selfishness of sleep. Stir again, hours later, and she's *still* awake, and now angry at you — or at least annoyed. This is what being in a marriage has taught you, that you have the capacity to annoy the person you love even while unconscious. *Okay, Grace,* you think, *let's do it. Let's have it out, clear the air between us. Who cares if it's 4:00 a.m.?* But no. Sleep owns you, and before you know it, it's morning. You wake to the sound of her up and in the ensuite: the swirl of sink water, the swish of her bathrobe, the toilet's jet-powered flush. She comes out and stands at the foot of your bed to take one last shot at engaging you, and you make every attempt to rouse yourself. But you can't, and it's too late anyway. She has motherwork to do, and like any woman whose chief function is motherwork, she needs to confront the day with a certain amount of urgency.

Okay. I am making it sound worse than it was. Truth is, I made it downstairs less than an hour after Grace. I was in fine fettle and still glowing in the pride of my good decision from last night. As if to reward me for it, Simone called me over from her place at the breakfast table: "Hey, Philip, you thought last night was weird? Check *this* out." And together we huddled over her pink iPad to watch a video of some bizarre interpretive dance she had found on YouTube, and we had a good laugh about it. Grace, meanwhile, was showing Naomi what we do after we've smeared applesauce on the kitchen wall. The child seemed to be taking the lesson in, but then quite spontaneously bolted across the kitchen floor and leaped into my lap for a hug. The morning sacraments went on. Breakfast, breakfast — eat your breakfast, please. Hey, do you wanna show Philip that issue with your math homework? Maybe he can figure it out. Naomi, Naomi, sit on your bum, please. We've got to go soon. What? Oh, I'm helping out at that bake sale thing at the community centre this morning. Didn't I tell you? Okay, okay. Dishes in the dishwasher, everybody. Don't forget to text me at lunch, Simone. Shoes on. Shoes *on*. No, you can do it yourself, Naomi.

And then we had a scant moment alone in the front entry while Simone took Naomi to the bathroom. Grace stepped up to me, looked in my face, twined her fingers into mine. She seemed tired.

"Today's another day," she said.

"Absolutely," I replied, and we kissed. A nice slow forgiveness kiss.

She was about to go but then said, "Oh, I meant to ask: Do you have any cash on you? I don't think this bake sale will have Interac, and I wanted to bring something home."

"Sure thing," I said cheerily, and ran upstairs to fetch my wallet. I knew that Grace was a bit lean this month: she still hadn't been paid for October's Motherlode column. I came back downstairs and, like the good, primary breadwinner I was, slipped her two twenties without a second thought. She didn't even look at the bills as she tucked them into her hip pocket, because by then the girls had emerged from the bathroom.

"Okay, jackets on. Jackets on. We gotta *go*."

And then they were gone. I returned to the kitchen feeling leavened and relieved, and went to my bar fridge. Tomato juice, Jameson, celery salt, lemon, horseradish. Squeeze, dash, shake-shake-shake, pour. I dipped a stalk of celery into the Bloody Joseph and headed upstairs to my office. Settling at my desk, I checked email. There were just nine Facebook notifications waiting for me. This thing really *was* starting to die down. It pleased me to see that one of them was actually from Simone: she had tagged me in a status update on her recently created Facebook account. (Permission granted as part of our birthday gift to her a few weeks ago.) I clicked through and saw she had done the update earlier this morning: *Okay, so maybe dance isn't for me. I didn't really 'get' last night's show. But big thanks to* **Philip Sharpe** *for taking me. Best stepdad ever.*

My heart welled. Wow. What a kid. I went back to email and began deleting the other notifications — all from strangers — without reading them. But just as I returned to Simone's Facebook wall to exit out of it, something happened. A comment appeared, abruptly and ghostlike, under her status update. At the sight of the person's name and thumbnail image — woman with neon-red dye job and severe bangs — I knew instantly that it was not somebody

Simone, or I, or Grace, knew. The comment read: *Best stepdad ever? Hardly. Your stepdad is A PIECE OF SHIT. Too bad he didn't have the courage to face his critics last night. While he was out with you, we were all attending this:*

And then there was a link, pointing to the event page for the protest against me at U of T: it populated the space below the comment. I stared at it, then scrolled back up. Clicked on this trespasser's name and arrived on her Facebook page. Her profile picture showed a tank-topped woman in her late twenties with hair dyed a shade of red found nowhere in nature, and arms and shoulders sporting a colourful mélange of Look-how-transgressive-I-am! tattoos. Her Facebook wall was covered with feminist sloganeering and pictures of cats.

I looked into her dopey, smug eyes. Rage swelled and swooned and spiralled up inside me. How dare you. How DARE you! Where do you get off invading my daughter's Facebook wall? She's just a kid! She has *nothing* to do with this. She doesn't even know what "judicial process" IS!

Truth be told, some papers and some books and, yes, the half-finished Bloody Joseph went flying off my desk and crashed with a percussive bang against my office wall. Broken glass and tomato juice radiated across the floor. I stood there, panting. Then I rushed out of my office and downstairs to the land line. Called Grace's cellphone. No answer, just voicemail. Called Simone's cellphone. No answer, just voicemail. I tried to calm down. I tried to calm down. Going to our mop closet, I dug out the broom and dustpan, the mop and bucket. Headed back upstairs to clean up the mess I had made, thinking this act would somehow settle me. It took forever, but when I finished and put everything away, I felt no calmer. I came back to my office and glowered into the computer screen, into that *face*. I wanted to retaliate. I wanted to say something. But then I realized it was time to leave for campus.

I was quavering the entire trip over, my thoughts swimming in a stream of fury and hopelessness and an acute sense of persecution. When I came out of St. George Station, I barely acknowledged the veteran selling poppies there. I headed over to my office in University College, partly because I needed to retrieve some notes for class, but mostly because I wanted another chance to pacify myself before facing my students. I went inside and closed the door. I found the notes I needed and put them in my satchel. My slow deep breaths weren't helping; I was nearly intoxicated with rage. I looked over at my office phone: the message light was blinking again. *Oh goddamn it, can't you all just leave me alone?* I thought then of poor Simone, discovering that hateful comment on her Facebook wall when she checked between classes or at lunch. *She's just a kid,* I thought. *She's just a little girl.*

Okay, Sharpe. Calm yourself. Just. Calm. Yourself. But I couldn't. And then the phone rang.

I looked at it. Thought: don't answer. Don't do it. Just let it go.

But it kept ringing. So I went over and picked up the receiver. "Dr. Philip Sharpe," I said gruffly.

"Philip? Oh, hey. It's Roberta R. from the *Globe.* Wow, I'm surprised I caught you. I've been trying to reach you for the last couple of days. Listen, I was hoping you would —"

"You want a statement from me?"

"What? *Yes.* Yes, I do." I heard her scramble around for a notebook. "I mean, everybody does. We've been waiting all week to hear your side of the stor —"

"Here's my statement," I said. "Everybody out there just needs to *fuck off.*"

"Um, what?" She laughed uneasily. "Okay, Philip, we're on the record now, so you need to —"

"You listen to me, Roberta. What I said on that TV show Monday afternoon wasn't that bad. It *wasn't.* People need to realize that and move on with their lives."

"Look, Philip, I really don't think —"

"Cheryl Sneed and I are long-time rivals and, yes, we get into it sometimes. And sometimes debates get so heated that we say things we shouldn't. It happens to *everyone*, sometimes. But at the end of the day, what I said on that show wasn't as heinous as everyone is making it out to be. I think people should grow up and realize that there are far worse things in this world they could be getting their panties into a knot over. Okay? So fuck off. Fuck off, and leave me and my family *alone*."

With that, I slammed the receiver down.

And then I felt much better. Like I had defenestrated some great toxin within me and I was now light and airy, like a meringue. Adrenalin coursed through me but I nonetheless felt in full command of myself. In fact, I thought about picking up the phone and calling Roberta back, now that I had relaxed, and clarifying what I'd just said. But no. I looked at my watch. It was time for class.

I arrived in the lecture hall five minutes later. A few of the students were giving me the same hateful stare they had on Tuesday, but most just sat sprawled in their chairs waiting for class to begin. Sebastian came over when he saw me. He was dressed youthfully in skinny jeans, Keds, and a retro Green Lantern T-shirt, but there was a slouch of disappointment in his shoulders.

"Hello, sir," he said.

"Hey, Sebastian."

"You didn't come out last night."

"No," I replied. "I mean, I wanted to. And your advice to me was sound — I *should* have come out. But I couldn't. I had to take my daughter to this dance thing. I promised her. And you don't break promises to a thirteen-year-old."

"Understood," he nodded, though it didn't look like he did.

"Anyway, c'mon," I said, and whacked him on the shoulder. "Let's go. Let's go."

I sidled up to the lectern with notes in hand. "Hello, everybody, welcome back. So I'm going to talk about Immanuel Kant for a little bit longer and then you're going to break into your groups. Sebastian has your questions that he'll hand out."

And that's what we did. My points were short and succinct, and when I finished the kids manoeuvred through the room and Sebastian went cluster to cluster with the discussion topics. I watched as the usual patterns emerged, how one or maybe two students in each group took the initiative, the very types who always did well on their writing assignments and exams; and how others sat back and did virtually nothing — the same types who were always coming to me with desperate entreaties for an extension or a pathetic *ad misericordiam* about their grades. These types were also the ones who took issue with the various trammels I maintained in my classroom. One of these students, in fact, was violating a rule right now. Bored and disengaged, she had taken out her phone and was scrolling through it as the rest of her group chatted half-heartedly about Kant. I gave her a moment to realize the error of her ways, and then moved to the edge of the lecture stage.

"Excuse me — cellphone."

She looked up and nodded her agreement. But her eyes stayed on the screen as she reached for her bag to put the phone away. And then she saw something on that screen, and her face coarsened. She looked up at me, then back at the phone. Mouth melting open and eyes narrowed, she glared back at me with a sudden look of hate.

I watched as she leaned over to a friend and whispered at length in her ear. The two of them looked at the phone together. This friend then got up and edged over to a friend in one of the other groups, and they whispered together. They got their phones out and began scrolling.

"Excuse me, people — cellphones," I said again.

But there was more whispering, more phones coming out. One girl, sitting near the centre of the room, boomed out, "Oh my *God*," as her eyes pored over her screen. She looked up at me with utter contempt, then noisily gathered up her stuff and stood to go. Poor confused Sebastian moved through the aisle as quickly as he could to intercept her. When he did, she yelled at him, "No, I'm not staying here with this asshole. Did you *see* what he said?" Then she stormed out. Sebastian unholstered his own phone and began scrolling. Oh, this was bad. More students, mostly girls, got up to leave, doing so with as much melodrama as they could.

You, dear reader, have no doubt discerned what was going on, even though I didn't at the time. Good old Roberta Rosenbaum, that lovely ex of mine, was an avid user of Twitter, and she had gotten clearance from her editor to run a quote from me on her feed ahead of the exclusive she would publish in tomorrow's *Globe and Mail.*

More people began filing out of the room in great anger. I came down off the stage and approached Sebastian. I'll never forget how he appeared as his face floated up at me from his phone. He looked sickly. Defeated. Like someone had just pulled out the carpet he'd been standing on for the last ten years. *Who ARE you?* his expression said as he shook his head at me in disbelief. And then he, too, turned to go.

"Sebastian, wait —"

But he tossed one arm into the air with his back to me as if to say, *No, I'm done with you, Sharpe.* And then he was gone.

I looked at the floor. Clutched a hand to my beard. "Class dismissed," I said. But by then the room was devoid of all but a handful of muttering man-boys, wondering what the *hell* had just happened.

I returned to 4 Metcalfe Street a while later to find it dim and blessedly deserted. I was grateful, since I couldn't bear to face another human being right now. I even flinched at the sight of the man staring back at me from the front entry mirror as I kicked off my Payless. God, I looked like hell. My cheeks and eyes were sallow. My comb-over looked like an exotic bird that had crash-landed on my head and then died. I needed a perk-me-up, and headed to the kitchen.

Squeeze, dash, shake-shake-shake, pour. I downed the Bloody Joseph in three large gulps and then promptly mixed another. I sucked back half of that one before moving to the kitchen table, where I saw Grace's note to me.

Took Naomi to library. Back later.

Huh. I don't know what it was, there in that insouciant motherly scrawl, but I grew suddenly angry at Grace. Resentful. It seemed to come over me all at once. *What a life of leisure you lead, Ms. Daly*, I thought. *You know, this* is *all your fault. You caused this to happen. You and your* ... demands *on me.* And I felt hollowed out by these thoughts.

I retreated to my office. Only work could provide me with the solace I needed now. I did an hour's worth of prep for tomorrow's graduate seminar, then headed back down to mix another Bloody Joseph. Returning to my office, I began reorganizing the notes on my desk, cleaning up the disorder that my tantrum earlier in the morning had caused. I checked email. There were *117* new notifications from Facebook. Jesus. I batch-deleted the slew without reading them. Then settled in to work on my book about Christianity, and soon disappeared into it. The hours passed. I grew distantly aware of movement through the house: Simone home from school, Grace home with Naomi. Eventually, Simone knocked on my door to call me down to dinner.

We sat in silence, the four of us. Grace had now seen the *Globe* quote, and was beyond words to me. Even little Naomi sensed the tension. I barely touched the salmon steak and baked potato Grace had prepared. I glared at my daughter, my *step*daughter, and finally said: "Privacy settings, Simone."

She just stared, ashamed, into her plate.

"Philip, I've already talked to her about it," Grace said. "She's already deleted it."

"Fucking privacy settings. We *told* you."

"Philip."

I got up then. Threw my napkin down, just like they do in the movies. Headed back upstairs to my office. I couldn't stand to be around these people right now.

I returned to my work. Buried myself in it, achieving a kind of intellectual hypnosis where nothing in this house or beyond could touch me. I worked and I worked. I was only torn out of it when the phone downstairs rang, and a moment later Simone knocked on my door, came in when summoned, and handed me the cordless before slinking away.

"Hello."

"Jesus, Sharpe, have I reached you on a *land line*?" Raj. He chuckled to himself. "I mean I knew this number for you was old, but not *that* old."

"Oh, hey, brother," I said. "Yeah, yeah. You know me and cellphones."

"So, how are you?"

"I've been better," I told him. "You've probably seen the *Globe*'s quote from me today?"

"Yeah, I did. Holy shit. This kerfuffle's gettin' out of hand."

"It really is. You know, I realized the other night, at Stout, that you were trying to talk to me about this stuff, and I didn't let you. Sorry about that. In hindsight, I should have."

"Hey, no worries," he replied. "Yeah, um, anyway. That's not exactly why I'm calling."

"Oh?"

"Yeah, no." And he chuckled again, awkwardly. "So. Anyway. I got laid off from my job at the CBC today."

"Oh, Raj, I'm sorry to hear that."

"Hey, it's okay. I mean, I knew it was coming. I've been in and out of that fucking place so many times. But still." And he paused. "I got to thinking. About your interview on Monday. I mean Cheryl Sneed is a cunt, no doubt. But she did make a good point, about people who lose their jobs and then immediately get on their phones, reaching out to contacts and finding new gigs. And I'm totally that guy. I've *always* been that guy." And he paused again. "But I've been on my phone all fucking day, and there's nothing out there. And I mean *nothing*. Sharpe, you know the economy and shit, right? Are things really as bad as you said on Monday? Be honest with me."

"Hard to say," I replied. "It's been less than a week since ODS collapsed. But yeah, I think things are going to be bad before they get better. *If* they get better."

"See, now I'm scared," he said. "And I don't get scared. I'm not a *scared* person. But I am fucking fifty years old. I've been a free-lance videographer for almost thirty years. And I've got nuthin'. I have no pension, I've hardly any savings, I got rent, I got car payments, I got a deadbeat brother up in Barrie I'm helping out, and I got child-support payments coming out the wazoo. So I'm fucking scared."

It was curious, I thought, how Raj would very often mention the child-support payments leaving his rear orifice, but rarely the children themselves. I knew almost nothing about them.

"I'm sorry to hear all that," I said.

"Anyway, this is why I'm calling. Two other guys who got laid off with me are coming over tomorrow afternoon. They're just a couple of twenty-three-year-olds, but they're good kids. We're gonna smoke some weed and complain about the general state of the universe. But I'm worried about them — even more than I'm worried about me. They are *freaking out* about this layoff. They have no other job experience and no contacts — not to mention student loans in the mid five figures. So I thought *you* might want to come over and talk to them. I think it would be good for these guys to meet another creative type who actually has his shit together."

And I laughed at that. Oh God, how I laughed. "Sure, Raj, I can come over," I said. "I have a graduate seminar in the morning, but I can stop by in the afternoon. You said you're at Danforth and Donlands, right?" And he gave me the address.

"Thanks, Sharpe. I owe you. Try to think of something optimistic to tell these kids, would ya."

"I'll try," I said. "But I'm not optimistic that I can."

And he chuckled at that, too. A dry, hopeless guffaw.

I worked a while longer, and then went downstairs. The kids were already in bed and Grace was now at her little alcove, trying to get some of her own writing done. I could tell it was not going well. Her computer screen was open to Facebook; her hennaed hair was tied up in a bun of creative frustration; and the little manuscript for "Sally and the Kitchen Sink" sat unmolested on the corner of her desk. Usually when Grace found it hard for the words to come — which was often — she engaged in what I referred to as her "procrastibaking," the pans of cookies and muffins and other extraneous sweets arriving in droves out of our oven. But tonight she didn't even have that outlet at her disposal: her purchases from the bake sale earlier today sat stacked on the kitchen counter.

"Hey there," I said, coming over.

She swivelled around. "Hi." She gave me a look. "You missed storytime again tonight."

"I'm sorry. But you know …" And I gestured to the ceiling, to my upstairs office. "Work."

"Of course." She turned briefly then to face Facebook, then pivoted back to me. "You know this whole thing was just starting to die down, and then you had to give that awful quote to Rosenbaum."

"I know."

"You'd think she'd go easy on you, Philip, considering you used to fuck her."

"Grace."

She threw her hands up. "Just sayin'." We stared at each other for a bit, and then she said, "You really have to do something about this now."

I nodded. "Any ideas?"

"Nope. But it's going to have to be huge, whatever it is. I don't think a simple apology is going to cut it anymore." She bore those spooky green eyes of hers into me. "It's going to have to be *huge*, Philip." And with that, she turned back and began shutting her computer down.

"Grace, look," I said, "we haven't really talked about what I said on Monday. Can we talk? I feel like I have a lot to get off my chest."

"No," she said, getting up. "I'm going to bed."

"Really, why? It's only, like, ten after nine."

"Because I'm *tired*, Philip."

"From *what*?" I asked.

Her face pancaked in surprise, then crumbled into rage. "Seriously? Wow. Just. Wow. You really have no fucking *clue* what it takes to keep this household running."

My own anger sparked up behind my eyes. "Oh, what, this again? It was this exact conversation that got me into trouble in the first place, Grace."

"You know what, Philip, fuck you." She slammed her chair into her desk and turned to go. "You created this mess, okay? You alone. So you figure out a way to clean it up. I'm *not* going to help you."

And with tears in her eyes, she crossed the living room and tore up the stairs. I watched her go. Thought about chasing after her. But then I didn't. What can I say? I just didn't.

Benazir

I fear I've given the impression that Grace and I don't like each other very much. You may be wondering: Why are you two even married, if you carry on like this?

What can I tell you? *L'avenir dure longtemps*, my friends. I like to think that Grace and I could see the future in one another from the first night we met. We could see the salad days, the smug confidences, the restful assurances that come with two instantly compatible personalities. It happened at the Arts and Letters Club in Toronto in the summer of 2007. Tuxedo House was hosting its annual party, and twenty-eight-year-old Grace Daly was there because she had just published her first children's book under its Tuxedo Kids imprint. *Rapunzel Saves the Day!* was an inverse of the traditional fairy tale whereby our heroine goes around the kingdom using her long hair to rescue boys who've gotten themselves into sticky situations. The book's release was the culmination of years of struggle for Grace: the disentangling of her life from the man who was Simone's father; the establishment of a successful freelance writing career; and the quitting of her loathsome communications job at a law firm. By the time she strutted in to the Arts and Letters Club that late summer night, she felt like she had *arrived*. With her name tag featuring the cover of her book proudly pinned to her chest, Grace actually *swaggered* into the club, full of all the wide-eyed narcissism of someone who'd gotten three articles published in *Toronto Life* and now had an ISBN number associated with her name. She was determined to meet everyone important in that faux-medieval room, and to make sure they knew who *she* was.

As I say, I was there as well, though somewhat under duress. I always found these events a bit too air-kissy for my liking, but I had just gotten *Understanding Islam* accepted as part of a three-book deal and felt it necessary to make an appearance. I stayed close to my literary agent, Jane Elton, and my editor at the press, a no-nonsense Judi Dench–lookalike named Rosanna. Jane, wearing her standard ensemble of charcoal power suit and a pair of red-frame glasses too large for her face (so large, in fact, that I often referred to Jane Elton in my mind as Elton Jane) was reluctantly accepting chit-chat from the social climbers who orbited around us. Rosanna, meanwhile, was regaling me with insights on the horrendous glass ceiling that existed in the book publishing business. "Sure, the industry is dominated by women, but only to a certain point in the org chart," she deadpanned. "At the very top, it's *all* men." Massaging her mouth with a glass of Chardonnay, Rosanna went on to say that women themselves — especially of the younger generation — were partly to blame. "Don't treat my industry as a way station after your English degree until you land a husband and start popping out babies," she said. "And don't *presume* we're just going to throw you freelance work so you can stay at home even after your youngest is in school." She harrumphed. "Still. I do feel bad for the spinster-types who never get hitched and *have* to work for a living. Their lives must be so dreadful. I've seen whole cubicle farms of thirtysomething editors whose menstrual cycles have synchronized from all the overtime they put in together, just to keep the jobs they have. They *never* advance past a certain point. It's pathetic."

I was horrified to hear all this, and launched into one of my rare screeds about gender equality — and did so just as Grace Daly came gliding into earshot. Working myself into a lather, I naturally placed the blame for all this on the shoulders of neo-liberal capitalism. In a fairer system, I said, women would *own* the publishing business, soup to nuts, considering that they were the ones who bought the majority of the books. In this utopia men would have a harder time getting published, and certainly have no chance of being reviewed anywhere. This seemed to ring a bell for Grace, and she chimed in with how frustrating she, too, found the gender imbalance in book reviewing. Rosanna, perhaps having encountered Grace's type hundreds of times before, wandered off to acquire a well-earned canapé. Jane Elton, too, was indisposed — listening with neutral patience as yet another balding, bearded writer pitched her on his novel — and so Grace and I were sort of alone together in that crowded room.

Chat, chat: fairness this and injustice that. Introductions: *Wait, didn't you write — sorry, I've forgotten its name.* I cringe-smiled. The Movable Apocalypse. *Right.* I glanced at her name tag. *And you're a writer, as well? A kid's book — cool. What's it about?* Chat, chat. Truth was, our conversation fit together as easily as a toddler's six-piece puzzle. No sane person would question what I found attractive in Grace Daly: those smoky green eyes, the cocky jut of her hip, her hair that was, at the time, chopped into a militant Cleopatra bob. She was a witty raconteur, and had me charmed in about five seconds flat. But what, I'm sure you're asking, did she see in *me*? I wasn't much to look at: even in 2007, my comb-over was more performance art than hairstyle, and there was a certain beaten-down, too-much-time-at-the-writing-desk slump to my posture. (She told me, months later, the source of her initial attraction: "You were the first guy I'd met in *forever* who just let me blather about myself." Take note, lads.) At any rate, we spent much of the rest of the party talking, and only separated because we thought it impolite not to mingle. But by the time we ran into each other while leaving, on the sidewalk out front near the smokers, we were both grinning awkwardly over the *fait accompli* that I was going to ask for her number.

I hadn't been on a date in a while. My intercontinental encounters with Rani had dried up over the last couple years (though we still exchanged the occasional flirty email) and I had more or less exhausted the Toronto media scene's supply of least-objectionable bachelorettes. I was nervous as I took Grace out for dinner on Queen West, but my worries proved unfounded. Our conversation flowed as smooth as a fountain pen, despite what she assumed was the bombshell she nailed me with shortly after we were seated. "Okay, so full disclosure," she said, bracing herself. "I have a five-year-old daughter." "Cool beans!" was my reflexive response. Of course, this news made sense. Who publishes a children's book without having a child of her own? Grace painted me then a portrait of little Simone's general awesomeness, and I sat there, PEI accent banging inexplicably through my mind, thinking, *Look at you, Sharpe — being all progressive and dating a chick with a kid. How to be!*

Dating? Hmm. More like: falling for. I had never met someone who could make domestic minutiae — the baking of a pie, the planning of a brunch, the selection of a feminist-appropriate Halloween costume — sound absolutely captivating. Sure, Grace Daly did not know which African country Robert Mugabe was the tinpot dictator of, and her eyes glazed over at the mere mention of Canada's new right-wing prime minister, but I was surprised at how much I didn't give a shit. Grace made it sound like her tiny Parkdale apartment was the most magical place in the world, and that she and little Simone (with the help of her upper-crust north Toronto parents and child support payments from her ex) were on the adventure of a lifetime together. There was something about all that quotidian zestfulness that revealed a loneliness in me that I didn't realize I felt.

So. More dates: movie; art gallery; poetry reading. Then I cooked her dinner at my huge, book-choked bachelor loft in the Annex, a night of candlelight and Dave Brubeck and al dente pasta. This was followed by — well, *you know*. She spent much of the afterplay of that first night gently ribbing me about all the single-guy trappings she noticed around my nest: the dust bunnies, the stack of out-of-date takeout menus on the fridge, the dresser drawer that I confessed had been broken for five years. In the morning, she came out of the bathroom holding up the towels I had set out for our showers and laughing uproariously. "Philip, you do realize that these are *beach* towels, right?" she said, jiggling the faded and frayed items I had bought at Dave's Cave in Charlottetown back in the eighties. "What, they're *towels*," I retorted. "They'll dry you off, good as anything." And she laughed all the more. Truth was, I wasn't hurt by her teasing; in fact, I kind of loved it, how she went about wiggling her way into all the crevices of my solitary life. She was the first lover, for example, to suggest that my upbringing on PEI was less than normal. She'd say: "Your mother did *what*?" Or: "You were *how old* when your father made you start working in his pub? Wow, Philip, you really didn't *have* a childhood, did you?" I got choked up by that. I hadn't realized how much I'd wanted a woman who visited my bed to notice these things about my past.

And yet. I kept asking (and you, dear reader, are probably *still* asking): *What was she really doing with me?* I mean, Grace could've had anybody. She was twenty-eight (*fourteen* years my junior); she was smart; she was funny; she was very attractive; and she was, it should be noted, insatiably experimental when it came to sex. (And still is. To this day she drags me to an annual sex-toy convention at a downtown hotel, in which I spend the entire time as we wander the metropolis of jellied dildos and various lubes and straps clenched in a panic that I'm going to run into one of my students.) So what did she see in this stuffy, comb-over-sporting bumbler? Well. She made no attempt to hide that she compared me constantly and favourably to her ex, a corporate lawyer at the firm where she had worked, when she used to work. His name isn't important, though he *is* Simone's father. I just call him Richguy. In many ways, Richguy was a good guy: he didn't drink, smoke, or swear; he went jogging every morning, and had the same *90210* haircut since high school. Grace met him while still a summer student at the firm, and was, for a time, desperately in love with him: from the vantage point of her cramped cubicle, he seemed well-positioned to provide her with the life she really wanted, the life she had been accustomed to throughout her childhood and was determined to reclaim for herself at all costs. And he was certainly enamoured of *her*. But then came the slow-burn realization — very slow, but very burning — that Richguy was a dullard, and also a bit of a dick. Like many lawyers, he was obsessed with work: it was the only thing that he and his social circles could talk about. He would make snide remarks, often couched in jest, about those who didn't work — and not just the homeless or unemployed, but also artists and mums at the park. He didn't seem to care about anything beyond his own ambition. He certainly didn't read books, and was dismissive of Grace's dream to one day write some of her own. The moment she decided to tear off the Band-Aid of their relationship came in 2002 when Richguy confessed to being taken with the brash young Conservative leader of the opposition,

Stephen Harper, and would vote for him at his earliest opportunity. That, for Grace, was the last straw. Alas, a complication: Grace had also fallen accidentally pregnant with Simone around that time. What to do. Get an abortion? Just marry Richguy and have it over with? Or could she, if she were brave enough, find a third way? *L'avenir dure longtemps.*

Find a third way. Be brave. Dare to reach for the life you really want. These were her mantras, and that's what Grace did. Five years of struggle, of hard work and pitching herself and setbacks and poverty and more setbacks, and then she made it. A *published* author. And then she met me. Me, the shaggy, shambolic philosopher-about-town. A man who appeared to have read *everything*. Who thought about things, deeply. Who held passions that someone like Richguy couldn't even begin to grasp. As far as Grace was concerned, I was lit from within — *You are lit from within, Philip Sharpe* — and she knew inside a month that I was the man she wanted to build her life with.

Still. There was the issue, the inevitability, of me meeting little Simone. I was downright nauseous at the thought. I always assumed that I hated children; I mean, I hated them even when I *was* one. But Grace assured me. She said, You're going to love her. She said, You're going to love her. She said, You are absolutely going to love her. And I did. By the end of our first outing together, Simone Beauvoir Daly had me rapt by her little smile. Grace had borrowed her parents' Prius and taken us out to the African Lion Safari in Hamilton on one of the last days before it closed for the season. That place was off the fucking chain: the giraffes and zebras that were just a stone's throw from the car; the ostrich that *yawp-yawp-yawped* right at our window; the monkeys who damn near tore off one of the Prius' mirrors. At one point, Simone climbed into my lap to get a better look out my side of the car, and when a lion in the distance turned its sombrely dangerous, mane-haloed face in our direction, she squealed with delight and pythoned her little arms around my neck. Then, with the maturity of someone three times her age, she asked me, cheek pressed to mine, "Is this okay?" And I thought, *Yes, this is okay. This is very okay.* And Grace looked on in gleeful victory.

The months passed. By Christmas Eve, Grace was introducing me to her parents — high-ranking civil servant dad, librarian mum, good, pleasant NDP-voting people both — in their huge house up in the north end of Toronto. The Dalys proved as warm and clever and generous as Grace had promised. Offered us holiday cocktails mere minutes after we came in the door. As Roland assembled the elaborate concoctions at his bar area (man after my own heart!) he mentioned with modesty that he'd already read two of the six books I had published by that point, even *before* he knew I was dating his daughter. (Indeed, both he and Sharon treated me — and continue to treat me — like a minor celebrity in their house. We see eye-to-eye on so many things, to the point where they take my side whenever Grace gripes to them about one of our squabbles.) Later, Sharon showed off pictures she had taken of Grace's appearance at the library branch where she worked to read from *Rapunzel Saves the Day!* to a group of gathered kiddies. While Grace got Simone down for the night, her parents and I talked about everything from the two-state solution to the genius that was Nina Simone. God, we got on like a house on fire. And the evening was sealed when they insisted that Grace and I kiss under their mistletoe.

During the week between Christmas and New Year's, Grace and I experimented with having Simone stay with us for a night at my place. The child was not used to sleeping anywhere other than her own bedroom or the ones set up for her at her grandparents' or at Richguy's, but we were delighted when she made herself perfectly at home in my book-lined bachelor loft. We spent the afternoon listening to Christmas carols and reading storybooks. We ate an early supper of chicken fingers and fries. Then we put on *Finding Nemo*, a film Simone had seen seven times before and one that surprised me with its various nuances. After that, Grace got Simone ready for bed, taking her into the bathroom to change into her PJs and brush her teeth. While they were in there, my land line rang. I picked it up and looked at the call display. It took a moment, but then the name and number appeared: it was the BBC in London.

I blinked. My heart seized up. I smiled a little. I answered.

"Rani? Is that you?"

"Hey, Sharpe." Her voice was unsteady.

"Are you calling me from *work*? It's got to be like," and I looked at my watch, "nearly one in the morning over there."

"I've been here since *yesterday* morning," she said. "I haven't left. This situation is insane. It's totally fucking insane."

"What situation?"

"Are you taking the piss, Sharpe?" It was then that I realized she was crying. "Have you not seen a newspaper today, or listened to the news on the radio?"

"No, no," I stumbled, thinking of all the fun and frivolity Grace and I'd been having over the last several days. "It's Christmas — I've been under a bit of a rock this week. Why? What's going on?"

There was a long pause, and then she said, "They killed her."

"Who?"

"What do you mean, *who*?" She sniffed angrily. "Benazir. They killed her, Sharpe. They *fucking* killed her."

"Oh, Rani, I'm so sorry." As mentioned, Bhutto had been an idol, a role model, of Rani's for years. It had been her dream to someday interview the woman, one-on-one. Like so many, Rani had high hopes that Bhutto would bring some peace and civility back to Pakistan, if she got elected.

"What happened?" I asked, and she told me. "Jesus," I said. "Jesus Christ."

"I'm still in shock," Rani said. "I mean, you know me, Sharpe, I'm not normally an emotional person. And maybe it's because I've been in this fucking newsroom for seventeen hours, but ..." And she paused again. "But this means they win, right? This means it's all over. If they can just catch her coming out of a campaign rally like that and kill her, it means the fucking savages win."

"Oh, Rani, don't say that."

"Why? It's true. They're savages, Sharpe. You know that as well as I do."

"I think you should go home," I said. "Try and get some sleep."

She took a long breath. "Yeah, I know. We're just waiting for a couple more items to come in off the wire and then they're gonna send us home." She sniffed again. "Home — to my empty flat. God. It's the *last* place I want to be right now." Then, apropos of this, she said, "Listen, I know it's been a while but I would really like to see you, Sharpe. When are you coming to the U.K. next?"

"Um, well. I'm giving a talk at the University of Edinburgh in April."

"April," she said. "Maybe I could come up on the train and see you. Just like old times."

Just then, Simone came bursting out of my bathroom and ran over to where I stood with the phone. She hugged my legs just above the knees, then leaned back and opened her mouth as wide as wide can be, to show me the fantastic job she did brushing her teeth.

"Rani, I don't think that's such a good idea," I said, tousling Simone's hair.

"Oh," she replied. "Oh, okay."

"Look, I have some company here so I should probably let you go."

"Oh, *sorry*, Sharpe." And she chuckled sarcastically. "I didn't realize you were — *entertaining*."

I chuckled back, and then grew serious. "Listen, Rani, everything is going to be okay. Okay?"

"Nope," she replied. "Nope, I don't think it is. But I appreciate you saying so. Anyway. Enjoy your 'company,' Sharpe." And then she added, perhaps as an olive branch, "Merry Christmas."

"Merry Christmas, Rani."

And then we hung up.

From behind the closed bathroom door, the toilet flushed, and then Grace came out. "Hey," she said, coming over. "Who was on the phone?"

"A friend of mine at the BBC in London," I replied. "She's pretty upset."

"Why? What's going on?"

I sighed deeply. "Benazir Bhutto was assassinated yesterday."

Grace tilted her head. "*Who*?"

I just looked at her. "It — you know what, it doesn't matter."

"Hey, Philip," Simone called as she climbed onto my couch. I went over and sat next to her. "Where am I sleeping tonight?" she asked.

"Why, you're going to sleep right here," I said, patting the couch cushion. "We're going to get you a pillow and blankets and everything."

She furrowed her little brow. "But where is *Mommy* gonna sleep?"

Grace and I looked at each other, smiled.

"Oh, *I* know," Simone said. "*She's* gonna sleep in *your* room."

Grace and I burst out laughing. We couldn't help it. Then Simone joined in, too, hooting along maniacally, though she had no idea over what.

And just like that, we became a family. *L'Avenir dure longtemps.*

The SLIP

* * *

By the following May, Grace and I were engaged, and we set a date for the summer of 2009. We went about the work of amalgamating our lives, which meant — God help me — shopping for a house. The experience proved just as soul-destroying as I always imagined it would be. We looked at everything from overpriced dumps on the Danforth to prefabricated cubes in the soulless suburbs of Markham. Grace, to my alarm, spoke to our real estate agent with well-honed authority. Her four years in a Parkdale shoebox notwithstanding, she knew exactly what she wanted in a proper home — based mostly on the North Toronto house she grew up in. Her must-have list was quite extensive. We saw a few places that I thought were passable, but she'd grow glum when they weren't "quite there." (That's the phrase she used with each: *Nah, it's not quite there.*)

And then, on a wintry day about six months before our wedding, we stumbled upon 4 Metcalfe Street — that three-storey, red-brick palace right in the heart of tony Cabbagetown. We'd been looking at something much cheaper in neighbouring St. James Town, but when it didn't suit, our real estate agent led us like pigeons a few blocks southeast to our future home's open house. As soon as Grace saw it, her eyes welled with tears. "That's my house," she said before we even stepped inside. "Oh my God, *that's* my house." The tour confirmed it. The place had everything that we — *she* — wanted (save a finished basement), and at the end of our supervised wander through its chambers and cubbies and alcoves, Grace spun around to face me with a grin that said, My life *begins* the minute we move in here. But I was already in a paroxysm of sticker shock, which I did a good job of concealing from Grace. I didn't even want to *think* about how old I would be when we — *I*

— paid off the mortgage. This house was far too expensive for a philosopher, even one with tenure, and book deals, and speaking engagements. It didn't help matters that the economy had all but collapsed the previous September, and Grace's freelance work was rapidly drying up. But what can you say to the woman you love — a woman who has brought such incomparable joy, such vigour and vitality to your hitherto frumpy, lonely life — when she arrives at the threshold of a dream you're pretty sure you can't afford to give her? What do you say when this is the *only* woman who has shown any interest in building a life with you, after meeting her at the graceless age of forty-two? Well, I was no longer Grace-less, and I was determined to make it work. I would've given Grace anything.

Still. I fell into a pit of despair when that first massive mortgage payment came out of my bank account. Don't laugh at me. When you grow up poor, you always worry about money, no matter how much you have as an adult. This, too, I hid from Grace. It was an aspect of my personality I feared she wouldn't understand, or would perhaps judge. Summer 2009 came and we enjoyed our elaborate Toronto wedding; we even made the society pages in the *Toronto Times*. By that fall, I decided to buck up and get over myself: I'd just publish more, do more speaking engagements. I *lived* to work, after all; I was hard-wired for prolificacy. Grace and I developed our "arrangement," some of it spoken and much of it unspoken. If I was going to be the primary breadwinner, there were certain trajectories to my behaviour that would need to go unobstructed: the long hours at the writing desk, the swaths of afternoons lost in the library; the full teaching loads and constant public appearances; and, most important, a steady diet of Bloody Josephs to provide me with the creative nourishment I needed to keep up my polymathic output.

Grace had no qualms. Within the first year of our marriage, her life achieved a kind of nirvanic self-affirmation: she had finally squared the circle of her feminism, trading in financial independence for the adoption of motherhood as her full and all-consuming vocation. She built strong networks among other stay-at-home mommy feminists — many of them in person and many in the online agora of Facebook and Twitter. These women supported and encouraged and nurtured each other, seemingly hourly. But Facebook and Twitter had a dark side, and so did Grace. She soon encountered other feminists who flat-out argued that, by God, a woman couldn't stay home *and* be a feminist, what kind of hypocrite were you, and her flame wars with these women made Grace tetchy and caused dishes to go unwashed. She never took her own version of feminism for granted, and was constantly re-justifying it to herself and others — especially when a nemesis made some passive-aggressive remark about Grace's "dependence on a man." And what *sort* of man? My own public persona, decidedly centrist, made regular appearances in these online spaces. If someone on the Left, for example, lobbed the occasional charge of misogyny at me — the receiving of which was just part of my job description as a high-minded humanist, as far as I was concerned — Grace would make a few desultory manoeuvres to defend me. If, on the other hand, an article of mine skewered some dirtbag on the Right, she praised me to the rafters and shared it online as widely as she could — partly because she loved me and partly because it signalled to her rivals that her spousal choice had, in fact, been sound.

While all this was a fair if precarious balance, there was still the issue of money. *Gawd.* Why do I keep harping on it? In 2010, after little Simone had been in elementary school a couple of years, I began a subtle, delicate lobbying to convince Grace to take at least some part-time work. But then she finished another children's book (*Dana Plays Hockey*; need I describe the plot?), which Tuxedo Kids rejected, and another, smaller press accepted on the proviso of heavy revision. These rewrites were, apparently, so involved and taxing that they precluded Grace from going out and getting a real job. Meanwhile, our basement stayed unfinished, our bathroom faucets began their shenanigans, and a mid-winter replacement of both roof *and* furnace bled me dry. Even when Grace landed her Motherlode column in a national women's magazine and began bringing in some money (750 words x $1/word x 10 issues a year = diddly-squat), I remained silently unimpressed. When *Dana Plays Hockey* was finally published and then promptly slipped beneath the waves, unsold and unread, I thought: *NOW will you please just fucking help me?*

But then, in 2011, Grace fell pregnant with Naomi. She literally spun around in euphoria at the news, her arms airplaned out. I was happy, too, don't get me wrong, but my stress and resentment also grew. Maybe I had adopted some of Grace's now haywire hormones through transference. Or maybe I'm just an awful fucking human being. But sometimes I would look at her during the height of this prenatal jubilation and think: Oh my God, you're *never* going to work again, are you?

Of course, dear reader, you don't *say* that to your pregnant wife. You don't.

You just gotta bottle that shit up.

Friday, November 6

Did I forget to mention that I'm also teaching a graduate seminar this term?

It's not surprising it slipped my mind. Unlike undergrad courses, with their propaedeutic expansiveness, a graduate seminar is focused, concentrated, and brutal — like a punch to the kidneys. On the one hand, they are less work for me than an undergrad class: only twelve students, we sit around at desks in a circle, and I lecture for a bit, and then they take a turn each week delivering a paper and leading a discussion. It's not really a class at all, but more like an intellectual seance. On the other hand, these three-hour gatherings cripple me with an inanition that requires a spirited Friday lunch to recover from. I don't mean to make sweeping generalizations, but I can say with certitude that philosophy graduate students are the most exhausting people in the world. Sebastian's company excluded, of course. He and I, at least until yesterday, would have been friends regardless. Grad school has not managed to beat the natural curiosity and open-mindedness out of the boy.

But what of the rest of them? I can barely stand to be in their presence under official circumstances; I can't even imagine trying to socialize with them. Do they even socialize? These M.A. and Ph.D. candidates arrive in my seminar room an inevitably grim and humourless lot, year after year. What annoys me about them? It's not just the long, dull, tendentious, and grammatically suspect essays they write for my class, the sentences that loop and baffle with cataphoric and anaphoric bungling. It's not just the *odium theologicum* I see settling into their DNA: the intense sanctimony over their chosen theoretical framework, the eagerness to denounce not only anyone who disagrees with them but anyone who chooses to talk about something else. They will take these biases and calcified beliefs, what Freud called the narcissism of minor differences, into other Philosophy departments upon graduation — or at least they *would*, if there were any jobs out there for them — and the ecosystem of academic backbiting will continue. No, it's not just that. It's really the theses and dissertations they will go on to write that bother me most. This is especially true of those Ph.D. candidates who take seven, or eight, or even ten years to finish their projects. Watching them lose themselves in the convoluted corridors of a dissertation topic is rather like watching our family cat, Constance, play with the laser pointer. The cat is *certain* that there is something there, certain that the red dot *exists*, and thinks that it will take just one more leap, one last frantic flail of its paws to subdue that crimson circle. Well, grad students do enough of their own leaping and flailing when it comes to their torturously long-winded projects. As their thesis advisor, I'm the one who holds the laser pointer, and am not above teasing them with it. I send the more obnoxious students on various wild goose chases, partly in the hopes that they'll have an unexpected breakthrough, but mostly in the hopes that they will arrive, through sheer frustration, at a revelatory moment about their life decisions. These students eventually graduate — or don't — and then disappear. What happens to them? In this economy, most drift into the semi-employment of sessional teaching.

Anyway. I host my graduate seminar every Friday morning from nine until noon. The ungodly start time helps to weed out the uncommitted. What course am I teaching this term? You won't believe, dear reader, the coincidence of it. I mean, I can't *make* this shit up. It's called "Rousseau's *Social Contract* and Its Impact on Modern Justice." After Monday's catastrophic slip with Cheryl Sneed on *Power Today*, I had of course lost all credibility in this subject area. So I was not surprised when I arrived a few minutes before class to find the seminar room empty. (Usually there was at least a keener or two in there, reading studiously at their desks.) I came in and sat, arranged my lecture notes in front of me, then stared up at the clock on the wall. The top of the hour came, but no students did. I harrumphed. Nine ten came, and still no students. I harrumphed again. By 9:20, it was clear that there had been a mass boycott of the seminar, and yet like a sap I continued sitting there, with November's grey light coming through the window, for another ten minutes. At 9:30, I stood and gathered my notes, then sulked out the door like a beaten dog.

I crossed the campus to University College. Huffing and burping up the college's ornate staircase, I arrived at my office door and was not shocked to find a note taped to it. How old school. It dangled just above my SAPERE AUDE driftwood plank. I tore the note down and opened it.

> Dr. Sharpe,
> As you have no doubt deduced by now, we are staging a collective boycott of your graduate seminar. We will not return to class until you have publicly condemned the remarks you made this week.
>
> Sincerely,
> The students of PHL1814F

I crumpled the note with one hand and unlocked my office door with the other. Stepping inside, I tossed the paper into the trash bin, then went over and flopped into the chair at my desk. Looking up, I could see the red message light on my phone was flashing once more. I picked up the receiver and dialled into the voicemail. The first message was, quite evidently, from an undergrad student whom I'd never met. Oddly enough, this young woman left her full name and student ID number, and then proceeded to term me a balding cocksucker. I hung up without listening to the rest.

I checked email. Seventeen new notifications from Facebook. I batch-deleted them, then leaned back and sighed. *How is this even happening?* I thought. It was as if a schism, a tear in the space-time continuum of my philosophical life, my self-image, had opened up. I was not in denial, dear reader. I realized how poisonous my statements were about ODS's executives, how completely unforgivable. But the public reaction, this stake-burning, seemed so out of proportion. I guess I could understand it among the PHL1814 group: we had been grappling with these very ideas all term, the notions of justice, of equality for all before the law, and how Rousseau's seminal work informed these ideas. I could see how my remarks on television had more or less undermined everything I had postulated this term. But what of everyone else? How could flippant comments about a bunch of corporate assholes draw such rage out of the populace? It didn't make sense — especially considering that I and my ideals, I readily admit, seemed quaint in 2015. The Enlightenment was out of vogue. Humanism was out of vogue. Hell, the privileging of reason over emotion was out of vogue. On my best day I was, like the note taped to my door, so old school as to be subversive. So when I betrayed my values in a moment of weakness, when I did let emotion trump reason, why didn't the unwashed masses stand up and cheer? *Yes — Sharpe's right! Throw the greedy bastards in jail! We'll figure out their crime later!*

I would need to do something about this. And like Grace said, it would have to be huge.

In the meantime, with class cancelled, I had an unexpected surfeit of free time. My usual Friday routine was to teach the graduate seminar from nine till noon, then grab a streetcar and slip back to Cabbagetown, to my local, Stout Irish Pub, for a hearty Friday lunch. The daytime barman there, whose name was also Phillip (though spelt with two *l*s) could set his watch by my Friday ritual: I came in promptly at 12:30 and climbed enthusiastically onto a bar stool, ready to order pints and food. Today, thanks to grad student rebelliousness, I could arrive a full hour early — i.e., right when the pub opened. This would put me ahead of schedule going out to Raj's place on the Danforth, as I had promised. I certainly didn't want to use this extra time to go back to 4 Metcalfe Street, as I was now a *persona non grata* in my own house. So instead, I decided to get a bit of work done there in my office — catching up on some reading, prepping for an upcoming thesis defence, *gawd* — and then I left campus. I walked south to College Street, grabbed the Carlton streetcar, and rode it to Parliament, where it deposited me at Stout's door.

I came in and climbed the stairs to the upper level. "Hello, Phillip!" I called out as I approached the bar.

"Hello, Philip," he said back, somewhat more flatly, through the peacefulness of the empty, just-opened pub. "You're early today."

"My grad students decided to cancel class, so I'm getting a jump on lunch."

He nodded without comment, then pumped me a small sample of the day's cask ale, and put it before me. The name of this craft brew was — perhaps fittingly — Pompous Ass, and I downed it, deemed it worthy, and ordered a pint. "I'll get you a menu," he said, but did so without making eye contact.

Let me tell you what I know about Phillip. While barman-ship is how he pays the bills, he is completely committed to his true vocation — that of a "dedicated father." He rises at 5:30 every morning to work with his wife to get their three small children dressed, fed, and out the door. He makes it all sound like a game of roller derby. He then comes here promptly for nine to prep the pub for the day. He serves customers all afternoon, and often pulls evening shifts if needed. Unlike most barmen, he gets his weekends off, but when I ask how he's spending his Saturday and Sunday, he inevitably says the same thing: "Oh, you know, raising children." He says this with a touch of fatigue, but also joyful anticipation. He makes my own attempts at parenthood look like loutish indolence. Despite Phillip's busy schedule, I am always impressed by how well-informed he is of current events, and he and I will have invigorating chats across the bar about everything from City Hall buffoonery to American imperialism in the Middle East.

"You want to pull the trigger on anything?" he asked, nodding at the menu, and I ordered what for me was a standard Friday lunch at Stout. Today: soup of the day (chicken minestrone), followed by a blue cheese burger and fries, followed by a brownie-and-whipped-cream sundae for dessert. All washed down, of course, with three proud pints of the cask ale. A lunch like that is going to knock your average man on his arse, but not me. No, sir. After a lunch like that I want to go out and *accomplish* things. I do some of my best, most inspired writing on Friday afternoons.

As I worked my way through today's meal, I tried to engage Phillip, as I typically do, about various things going on in the news, but he seemed reluctant to return fire in kind. This was unlike him. At first I thought it was because I had come so early and the pub wasn't quite ready to serve customers: Phillip was still doing a lot of his prep. But then I noticed again that he was hesitating to make eye contact with me. And that's when I clued in: Oh, right — I *am* the news today.

As if to confirm this, something odd and coincidental happened during dessert. My face appeared on the muted TV above the bar, which was tuned to Toronto's CityNews channel. I was just spooning some brownie out of the bottom of the sundae dish when Phillip and I glanced up at the screen together. There it was, a still photo of my furry and dishevelled countenance, with my name and position at U of T underneath. Phillip and I looked at each other, our eyes widening in unison.

I swallowed. "Any chance," I said, "that we could get some sound on that thing?"

He scrambled over to the small laptop that was supplying the pub with music (Coffee House Alternative was the name of the feed — very tasteful) and killed it. Then he fumbled briefly with the remote as he tried to unmute the television. But by the time he did, the segment was over and CityTV had switched back to its pretty, ethnically ambiguous anchor.

"Shit," I said. "I really wish I'd caught that."

"It'll cycle back around," Phillip said, "eventually." He turned to go with diffidence, once more not looking me in the eye. So I just called over to him outright: "What do *you* make of all this?"

He turned and gave me one of his timid barman shrugs. Deep down, Phillip knew I was a good man, and an even better tipper, so he chose his words carefully. "I have to admit," he said, "reading the paper on my way in this morning, I was surprised. I didn't think *that* was going to be your response to the media."

"Look, that reporter caught me in a rage," I blundered. "Some Internet troll had just attacked my stepdaughter online. And, you know, I … I …" I gave him a pleading look. *You understand, don't you, Phillip? One father to another? You don't go after a man's daughter* like that, no matter how mad you are. You just don't. I sighed. "I should have just kept my mouth shut."

He shrugged again. "That's not really an option anymore, is it? But you know, Philip, it's never too late to start doing the right thing." He nodded at my nearly finished sundae and empty pint glass. "Did you want anything else?"

"No, just the bill," I replied. He printed it off and brought it over in its little leather holder, and I paid him. Tipped him well.

"Take care, Phillip."

"Take care, Philip."

And for the first time in all the years I'd been coming to Stout Irish Pub, I left without a spring in my step.

A half hour later, I came potting out of Donlands Station on the Danforth, turning left to head north and toward the address that Raj had provided me. As I set out, I came upon a small, hole-in-the-wall barbershop, one of those narrow east-end shacks. Through its window, just below the stencilled barber's pole, I could see a long wooden shelf and, upon it, amidst old magazines and the day's papers, a box of poppies for sale. I paused. Eyed it up. Went in.

"Haircut, sir?" asked the geriatric barber as he rose from his barber's chair, the middle one in a row of three.

"No, sorry," I said, going to the shelf, "I just came in to buy a poppy." I dug my sole piece of change, a toonie, out of my hip pocket and pushed it through the box's slot. I selected a poppy, pinching it by its pin, and headed for the door.

"Well, come on back if you want me to do something about that hair."

I gave him a queer glance as I stumbled back out to the street. I looked at the poppy, the *third* I had bought in the last week, fucking greedy veterans, and began manoeuvring it onto my lapel as I set off again. This was my mistake: one should never attempt to pin a poppy while walking after three pints at lunch. My fingers fumbled just as a stiff squall of wind came up, and the poppy leaped from my grasp and took to the air like a tiny red kite. I watched it descend to the ground, scuttle like a crab across the sidewalk, and then — *ploonk!* — disappear down an open sewer grate.

"Oh, god*damn* it!"

Needless to say, my mood was pretty sour by the time I arrived at Raj's apartment. The place was as he had described it: the bottom half of a ramshackle house with an open porch, a rarity in Toronto's east end. I climbed up and rang the bell. As I waited, I looked over at his gleaming SUV in the driveway, what he no doubt used to lug his videography equipment around.

Raj threw open the door with great drama, as was his wont. "You whiskey-soaked so-and-so," he started in, "you herring-choked cock-knocker! You made it — and *early*, too."

"Class got cancelled," I muttered as I shuffled inside.

Raj gave me the once-over. "Jesus, Sharpe, you look like hell."

He was one to talk. He was dressed in a shabby bathrobe over a tank top and a pair of board shorts, his peanut-coloured feet squeezed into a set of ancient flip-flops. The archetypal ensemble of the freshly unemployed.

"It's been a rough week," I told him.

"Tell me about it."

We came in to the apartment's living room, the air of which was profuse with the loamy scent of marijuana. "The man of the hour has *arrived*," Raj announced, and introduced me to the two other members of the CBC precariat: a black kid in dark-rimmed glasses and LA Lakers cap named Jerome; and a kid of perhaps Chinese descent named Walter, whose ponytailed hair and tiny moustache made him look like a two-bit villain from a seventies kung fu movie.

"Let's get you a drink," Raj said with hospitality, and fetched a half-empty bottle of Grant's blended off the heavily painted windowsill. Grant's blended? Jeez, Raj, why don't you just serve me toilet water? Gawd, my mood *was* foul. He came over and poured some of the whiskey into — yes, you guessed it, readers — a small Mason jar, and then handed it to me. I took a sip and tried not to make a face.

"Would you like some merry-joo-wanna?" groaned Walter from his place on the couch, his eyes like two pissholes in the snow, and extended the roach to me.

"Thank you, no," I replied. "I never touch the stuff." It was true. While the science on Mary Jane's carcinogenic properties remained inconclusive, one thing was consistent across everything I had read: regular users experienced what clinicians referred to as "reduced life achievement." This did not wash with a compulsively Type A like me, and so I abstained. I watched as Walter took another blow on his J, then handed it gingerly to Jerome. *It's disturbing*, I thought as I raised the Mason jar once more to my lips, *what some people will put in their bodies.*

The four of us chewed the fat for a while as I took in Raj's bachelor paradise. Indeed, it was the kind of place you kept if you had no one to think about other than yourself: the unwashed dinner plates on his coffee table, the crowded ashtray, the towering stack of car magazines. But the more I gawked around Raj's living room, the more I realized that this wasn't a room for living at all. He had, rather, set it up like a television studio. There was a giant mixing board and editing equipment laid out on a long desk below the enormous flat-screen TV on his wall. He had no fewer than three video cameras on a shelf in one corner, their tripods collapsed and stacked neatly below. In the opposite corners stood two studio lights, each wearing a bonnet-like nylon screen atop its thin stand. And I counted at least four different types of microphones unplugged and scattered around the room. In fact, Raj had enough equipment here to film an entire TV show. I creased my brow at that. Thought about it. Felt the tickle of an idea emerge in my mind.

But before I could voice it, he addressed me about the real reason I was here, and I zoned back in. "Okay, Dr. Economy," he said, "give it to us straight. Are these boys fucked or what?"

"Yeah, you're pretty fucked," I said. "I mean, *I* certainly wouldn't want to be unemployed right now." This didn't exactly engender a positive response, and so I leaped in with a quick caveat. "Look, it's not rocket science, boys. The ticket to survival — especially if you work in anything creative — is adaptability. I mean, you know this, right? Raj mentioned you both have massive student loans, so I'll assume you're well-educated. What do you have, can I ask?"

I was mortified by their responses, which were nearly identical. Both had done about two years of an undergraduate degree — commerce for Jerome, marketing for Walter — before dropping out and moving back into their parents' basements, where they spent the next couple years smoking pot and playing video games. They finally emerged and enrolled in a program for studio production at a high-priced vocational college. Their subsequent stint at the CBC was the only real job experience they had.

Wow. It was worse than I thought. To have your undergrad background in the two areas of study *designed* to make you stupider, and then to limit yourself with a technical diploma so early in your career. No wonder they felt doomed. Someone like me should have intervened in their lives earlier, letting them know that if they had any aptitude for creativity at all, they should have done a broad-based liberal arts degree instead, which would have opened doors for these boys rather than closed them, via the simple fact that it would have taught them how to open a door in their minds. Gawd, commerce and marketing — what were their parents *thinking*? But I was too late. This sort of *cri de cœur* was not going to penetrate the haze of their pot smoke now.

"Look," I said, "the key here is the ability to switch gears on the fly, okay. I mean the idea that one institution is going to provide you with thirty-five years of employment is an anachronism from the last century."

"So says the guy with tenure at U of T," Raj smirked.

"I was *lucky*," I replied, choking down the last dribble of Grant's before Raj refilled my Mason jar. "The world was a different place in 1993. The public still believed — just barely — in funding public institutions. People still wanted to be engaged citizens and not just taxpayers looking to save a buck." This led me into my standard rant against neo-liberalism, and how the ideology of privatization had laid ruin to all manner of public institutions — everything from universities and our alleged public broadcaster to libraries and hospitals. I went on and on about it. I could see I was starting to lose the boys, so I threw in a reference to popular culture to reel them back in. "Neo-liberalism is like the Borg on *Star Trek*," I said, "assimilating and homogenizing everything in its path." I told them if they wanted to stop being a cog in a ruthlessly efficient machine, they needed to stand up for themselves. Convince people to stop voting for pro-business scumbags and start believing in the value — the *categorical* value — of robust and well-funded institutions again.

"Look, *man*," Jerome cut in, "that's all well and good, but I need money *now*, man. If I don't make, like, seven hundred dollars before the end of the next week, I'll have to move back in with my parents — *again*."

"Well, that actually brings up an idea for me," I said. I looked at the three of them. "You all know I'm in a bit of hot water with the general public, right?"

"Yeah, *dude*," Walter replied, squeezing out his words as if through a straw, "you're the one who's *fucked*."

"Yes, I am," I said, "quite. Fucked. So I have a proposition for you." I turned to Raj. "Raj, do you need some kind of special permit to upload a video to YouTube?" Of course, I knew the answer the instant these words left my lips, and the three of them laughed at me. "Okay, okay. Here's my thinking. I need a bit of a soapbox to explain what happened on Monday. To tell people that I realize what I said was wrong, and to say what I *really* believe, in my heart of hearts, about this whole issue. But I don't just want to sit in front of a webcam to do that. As my wife and others have pointed out, I need to pull off something big to fix all this." I took another glance around the room. "I noticed you have quite a bit of TV equipment here. So maybe I could hire the three of you to make a professional production of it."

Raj mulled on this, but then nodded. "Could work."

"How long should something like that run for?"

"I dunno, Sharpe — attention spans on the web are pretty short." He shrugged. "I'd say eight, maybe nine minutes, max."

"So what's that?" I did a quick calculation based on delivering conference papers. "About 1,500 words, right?"

"Yeah, give or take."

"Fifteen hundred," I said. "I could definitely articulate what I want to say in fifteen hundred words. And how much would you guys charge to produce something like that?"

He shrugged again. "We talking just you in front of a camera?"

"Well, I may want to incorporate some graphics, to illustrate my points. Maybe a bit of music for the intro and outro."

So the three of them discussed it briefly, and then came up with a number.

"That's entirely reasonable," I said, and grew excited. "So we can do this?"

"Yeah, Sharpe, we can do it." He chortled. "We're happy to take your money, if this is what you want to do."

"It is," I said. "I mean, I realize a lot of people are upset by what I said during that debate, and I just want to make amends. You know?"

"Yeah, no, absolutely."

"Okay — so *when* can we do this?"

Raj scratched his cheek. "Well, I'm actually heading up to Barrie tomorrow morning. I gotta help my worthless brother move out of his flophouse and into *another* flophouse — plus handle some assorted family bullshit with my ex and her brats while I'm there. Anyway. I'm not back until Tuesday night."

"So Wednesday," I said. "Wait — that's Remembrance Day." I turned to Walter and Jerome. "Is that going to be a problem for you boys?"

They both made little farting noises of sarcasm. "Dude, I got *nuthin'* on," said Walter.

"Me either," said Jerome.

"Lovely," I told them. "So, Raj, I'll write up the script over the weekend and email it to you. You can send me some thoughts on how we might film it when you get a chance, and then we'll all reconvene here on, say, Wednesday afternoon?"

"Works for me."

So I got up then and went to my satchel. Pulled out my chequebook and cut them each a deposit for their time. The boys' eyes swelled at the sight of the money, and Raj refilled my Mason jar once more. They invited me to stick around: they were going to put on *The Big Lebowski*, which seemed to be everyone's favourite film. I took them up on their offer, even though I had seen the movie twice and didn't care for it. Indeed, I got up and left halfway through, wishing the three of them well. I really needed to get back to the house, and besides, the end of that movie just made no fucking sense.

Dusk fell as I doddered up the steps of 4 Metcalfe Street and in the door. I expected, and found, the same chilly aura that had been there when I'd left, a fug of execration, a castrating chill clinging to every corner. Simone was at the dining-room table engaging with her phone, and didn't look up when we exchanged greetings. Naomi was staging a slumber party among her dolls on the living-room floor. Grace was in the kitchen, spreading pizza dough onto two round pans, our Friday night tradition. I asked what I could do to help, and she gestured to the vegetables on the counter. So I chopped peppers and mushrooms while she grated the mozzarella and painted the dough with tomato sauce, and then we decorated the pizzas together.

"Do you want wine with dinner?"

"I'm breathing, aren't I?"

Forty-five minutes later, the four of us sat in relative silence at the dinner table over our pizza. Even Naomi, normally chatty during suppertime, seemed to know not to say too much right now. When we finished, Simone and I cleared the table and then I asked if she would take her sister upstairs for her bath. "Be *very* careful with the faucet," I said. "It's still scalding." When they were gone, I looked at Grace as she sat there, sipping her wine like a bored queen at court.

"I wanted to let you know," I began, "that I've decided to make a public statement, next week, about this situation." Her emerald eyes flickered my way, a brief blast of curiosity. I went on: "My friend Raj — you know, the videography guy? — is going to film me on Wednesday, and we're going to put it up on YouTube."

I anticipated a flurry of questions. Like: *What kind of statement, Philip? Are you going to apologize outright for what you said about those ODS executives?* Or maybe: *How are you going to share this video around, Mr. Forty-Six Friends? I suppose you'll want me to put it on* my *Facebook page.* Or even: *Raj? Really? God, I* hate *that guy.* (Which was true. Grace always considered him a bit of a sleaze. *He's essentially a deadbeat dad, right?* she'd ask with revulsion whenever I brought him up. *I mean, does he even* see *his kids? Does he ever talk to them?*) Instead, she just said to me:

"You'll do what you need to do, Philip. I have no doubt about that." And she went back to absently drinking her wine.

"Grace —"

But then the pipes in the walls filled with the sound of flowing water, and she burst from her chair. Worried — rightly so — that her girls might still harm themselves via that goddamn tub.

I stayed behind to do the dishes — there were more than a day's worth — and by the time I finished, Grace was calling from the stairs. "Are you coming up for storytime?" Almost an accusation. I obeyed, and the two of us read, rote-like, three short books to Naomi. After we got her settled, we returned to the living room. Simone was already there, inhaling *Life of Pi.* She was making excellent progress: I could see that she was more than a third of the way through. Grace took up her own book — something by Margaret Drabble — and I took up mine, a history of working-class education in Britain. The three of us read in silence, with Simone and Grace stopping occasionally to check in with their phones. At one point, Simone's face flew up from her book and she turned to me. "Wait — he *kills* the orangutan?" She gave me a look of abject horror, of little-girl grief. "Philip, why didn't you *warn* me?" With that, she got up and went to bed. Grace and I continued on in the quietude of her absence, perpetuating our testy charade, both of us sharpening a thousand unspoken barbs in our minds. I soon got absorbed in an erudite passage of my book, and by the time I looked up Grace had slinked off to bed. She hadn't even said good night.

I read for a while longer, alone, and then slipped upstairs to my office. Waiting in my email were six more notifications from Facebook. I deleted them, then looked at the list of real emails.

There, sitting atop department memos and Tom's summons and all the rest, was yet another note from Rani.

I stared at it. My heart trembled like a tuning fork. I opened it.

> Sharpe,
> Are you going to respond to me? Or are you just going to leave me here, watching and re-watching this clip of you? I suppose you're thinking turnaround is fair play, eh? Wink wink.
>
> Love and rockets,
> Rani

Oh cheeky fucking cheeky fucking cheek. I knew *exactly* what she was referring to. She was alluding to something that I had done years ago. It was the early aughts, and the BBC had assigned Rani a couple of her own radio pieces in the wake of 9/11. Online audio was just becoming mainstream then, and I stumbled upon one of these stories archived on the Beeb's website. I remember sitting in my office at University College, the door closed, the computer speakers cranked up, and listening to that clip, over and over again. Listening to Rani's voice, that chiming East Indian/East London mash-up — and missing her terribly. This had been during a particularly lonely period in my life, and the sound of her voice coming through my speakers from far-off England conjured all manner of memory from our time together at Oxford. I even found myself getting aroused — an unbendable, instinctive perking up — as I replayed that four-minute clip, over and over.

A couple years later, when Rani and I had the last of our hookups during one of my trips to the U.K., I confessed all this to her, and she mocked me appropriately. *Wow, what an image, Sharpe,* she'd said, *you sitting there in your book-lined office, getting a big old boner listening to me on the radio.*

Shaddap-shaddap-shaddap, I replied.

And now, was she pleading guilty to a similar stirring, in that email? Had she been sitting at some desk somewhere, replaying that abhorrent CBC clip of me, and thinking the same thoughts?

I hit REPLY.

> Rani,
> Sorry it's taken me so long to respond. Things are catastrophic here, as you can imagine. This bilious outcry against me is unprecedented. Anyway, I'm glad to hear you're enjoying the clip. Hope you're not, erm, getting off on my misery.
>
> Sincerely,
> Philip

After I hit SEND, I went about moving aside the pages and notes from my new book on Christianity to make room for the video script I would start writing tomorrow. But just as I turned back to shut my computer down, a new email appeared in the inbox. Rani, forever the night owl, was up and had replied already.

I opened her message.

> You really should give me a call. 07870 663 926.

And it amazed me, then, how quickly it could return — that springboard of longing, that sudden gas-fire flame. I felt it rise and stiffen within me. A thought, then, of the cordless phone downstairs, within easy reach, and the wife and kiddies already in bed. I wondered: Is this how it begins, for most men?

I swallowed. I blinked at the screen. Then I shut my computer down.

Scant minutes later, I arrived at the marital bed in a cloud of lust. I climbed in and moved upon my sleeping wife, whose back was to me. I was prepared to beg, to *plead* for whatever shred of forgiveness might still be possible. If I apologized enough, and abundantly enough, would she turn to me then? Turn and help me rid myself of this sour, awful yearning?

I touched her, and she pulled harshly away from me.

I thought about it for a while, all that I had done. All that I *failed* to do, to make things right. I was ready to skewer myself, if necessary.

I touched her again.

"Philip — *fuck off.*"

Her words hung there in the darkness. I rolled away, onto my back. We lay there in silence, with her fury pulsing between us in the bed. She was thinking her thoughts. And me? I was thinking about something — some*one* — else.

What did this remind me of? Hadn't we been here once before?

Oh, right. Of course. How could I forget?

Victoria-by-the-Sea

Grace seemed more interested in the Confederation Bridge than she did in Prince Edward Island itself. Its figure had loomed in the long view of our GPS, which we occasionally flipped to as we made our two-day trek down from Toronto, the bridge's shape like a thin, blunt pinky stretched out across a digital blue sea. Now, that massive, concrete wave appeared in front of us as we made our final approach at Cape Jourimain, no longer a pixelated abstraction but a spectacularly real and terrifying marvel of modern engineering. I could sense the excitement swell in my wife. She actually raised her bum off the driver's seat of her little red Yaris (my wedding gift to her) as we entered the bridge's maw, her knuckles squeezed white around the wheel, her green eyes wide and enthusiastic. "This is *exciting*," she said as she tried to get a gander over the bridge's tall cement sides, and I replied with a fretful, "Watch the *road*, Grace." But then I, too, indulged, standing tall in my seat belt, looking out the passenger's side at the wide, glittering expanse of the Northumberland Strait. We climbed above it, as if on a plane, sailing up and up, and then descended toward that long, red-soiled monolith, the island of my birth. It was anticlimactic, almost anti-*orgasmic*, coming down off the bridge and passing the plastic, touristy structures of Gateway Village. Grace, now flush, gave a soft, unsatiated sigh, then grew businesslike once more behind the wheel. There were still forty-five minutes between us and Charlottetown.

This trip happened in the summer of 2010, a year after our wedding, and was a kind of belated honeymoon. As such, Grace's parents offered to take little Simone off our hands while we were gone, promising to run her to swim lessons and library visits and her weekend with Richguy. At first Grace was obdurately opposed: how could a mother spend ten days — *ten days* — apart from her eight-year-old daughter? But indulgence and possibility won out, and by the time we wrapped up a long, mithering goodbye to Simone and hit the road, it was as if Grace had unstrapped an invisible girdle and was now liberated to embrace some grown-up adventure. "Can't *wait* to see that bridge," she said as we raced eastward on the 401.

Still, I feared tiny Charlottetown might prove a disappointment to Grace. Being a native Torontonian, she couldn't help but sense what other urban areas lacked. She put up a front of intrigue, I'll give her that, during the two days we stayed in the city. (Even that term warranted a comment. "Wow," she said, "it's called the *city* of Charlotte*town*.) We visited the farmers' market, sauntered the stone-piled boardwalk at Victoria Park, gorged on mussels and local beer at a patio restaurant on Victoria Row.

There were only two places I felt I *needed* to take Grace. One was out to the large cemetery across from the airport, where my father was buried. We stood together in front of Little Frankie's gravestone and she held my hand as I had my little moment with him. "I did it, Pop," I told his gravestone, my Island accent gurgling back up. "I got *married*. 'Magine that!" And Grace put her head on my shoulder and said, "I wish I could have met him." The second place was the dog park downtown that had been the site of my father's pub before it was demolished. As we stood on the grass, sun beaming, I told Grace about the Jugglers Arms and pointed at the place in the sky where Frankie's signage had been. I said how the egregiously absent apostrophe in the pub's name had driven me to distraction as a teenager, and she laughed and said, "You know, that's not such a big deal," and I replied with, "You are not my wife." We wandered the neighbourhood after that, the streets of my childhood. It had been a number of years since I'd been back to Charlottetown, and I was jarred by the changes. On this stroll, I spotted a gastropub, an indie art gallery, a telephone pole advertising a Beckett play, no doubt staged as counterbalance to the tourism season's corny musicals. I thought, *Wow, this place is almost liveable now.*

Still, two days were enough and we soon moved on to where we'd spend the bulk of our visit: the village of Victoria-by-the-Sea, on PEI's south shore. This was what we really wanted: a cottage overlooking the water, an uncrowded red-mud beach, a quaint community to wander during the day, and the tide's slow, sloshy pulse lulling us at night. From our Adirondack chairs on the cottage's front lawn, we could see the bridge in the distance, a long, thin lifeline to the mainland out on the water's hazy horizon. Grace was kicked back in full relaxation and plowing through a stack of books written by women novelists. Meanwhile, in my own chair, I sat hunched over the page proofs of my Stephen Harper biography, due out that November, maniacally hunting for typos that may have escaped the proofreader. Grace would look at me from beneath her sun hat and shades and say, "When are you going to start unwinding?" and I'd reply, "I am unwound," before pounding the page with my fisted pen and cursing.

On our first full day in Victoria, we visited all of the village's little landmarks: the long wharf at the small marina, the quaint bookshop, the store that sold chocolates handmade on site, and a shed-like structure that peddled a hodgepodge of artisanal knick-knacks. It was in that shed, among the dangling wind chimes and sheet-metal sculptures, where I found the driftwood plank that now hangs on my office door at University College. The shed was not crowded: besides us, there was an unsupervised preteen inspecting a box of handmade bracelets, and a man about my age browsing tie-dye vases with a woman in her early twenties who was clearly his girlfriend. I manoeuvred gingerly through the narrow aisles to show Grace the plank.

"Isn't this grand?" I said. "Feel how *smooth* it is."

"You should buy it," she replied.

And that's what I did. The clerk at the desk asked if I would like it embossed. "I can write pretty much anything on it," she informed me.

I thought it over. "Yes, a Latin phrase, please," I said. "*Sapere aude.*"

"Okay, you're gonna have to spell that for me."

At the sound of this axiom, the man at the tie-dye vases perked up. "*Sapere aude,*" he called over. "'Dare to be wise.'" I turned, grinned, and we gave each other a knowing nod. After spelling the phrase for the clerk, who wrote it methodically onto a sticky note, I wandered over to the man.

"You know Latin," I said.

"I do," he replied. He gave a modest shrug. "What can I say? It comes with my job."

"Oh, really? Which is?"

"I'm a classics prof at UT Austin, in Texas. And you?"

"Philosophy prof at the University of Toronto. Philip."

"I'm Jacob," he said, and extended his hand to me. Yes, he was about my age, and roughly my height, though much thinner. He had a short, wiry beard and thick, sandy hair, a pronounced Semitic nose, brown eyes under browner eyebrows. "This is Hilary," he said. She came over with a sashay of confidence. Tall girl, taller than us, with long honey-blond hair and bright blue eyes. She wore a turquoise tank top that revealed angular collarbones.

"Yes, I'm his girlfriend," she said, pre-empting a question I wasn't about to ask. "And yes, I was his student. We're a horrible cliché."

"This is my wife, Grace," I said, outstretching my arm, and she came over.

"I was *not* one of his students," she grinned, and the four of us laughed. We chatted friendly-like for a couple of minutes, and then were interrupted when the clerk yelled, "Excuse me, please don't touch those," to the preteen, who was now molesting a display of blown glass ornaments, and the kid scampered out the door in her cut-offs. "Sir, your plank is ready."

I collected my purchase and then Jacob and Hilary invited us to join them for tea at a tea room a couple blocks up the street, near the Orient Hotel where they were staying. We agreed, and the four of us spent a sunny hour together on the deck out front. To my surprise, Jacob knew PEI well: he'd been coming here every other summer for years to escape the Texas heat. "Couldn't wait to bring Hilary up after we started dating two years ago," he said, and she added, "I was skeptical at first, but I *love* PEI now." Grace jumped in with "Philip grew up here!" and Jacob asked, "What was *that* like?" and I said something noncommittal about the Island being okay provided you weren't here during winter. This led Jacob and me to talk about our educational trajectories, which then brought us back to the Latin phrase now scorched onto my plank. He, of course, knew of its Horacian origins ("*Dimidium facti, qui coepit, habet; sapere aude, incipe*"), and I chimed in about how pivotal the expression had been to Kant and the Enlightenment as a whole. The girls drifted away then, into a conversation about domesticity, and Grace took no time to praise the charms and existence of little Simone. Hilary said, "Oh, I would love to have a girl someday, even if," and here nudged Jacob's shoulder, "her dad would be an *old fogey* by then." Grace smiled, glanced at me and said, "You know it's not so terrible, having a fogey be a father to your child." Meanwhile, I was telling Jacob about my Stephen Harper biography, and Hilary jumped in. "Oh my God, I read about that guy — he's like your version of Bush!" She then dazzled us with an array of information she had retained from a profile of Harper she'd read in some magazine. It took me a few moments to clue in. "Oh, wait," I said, "I *wrote* that article." And she said, "Oh my God!" and the four of us cheered as if we'd scored a touchdown. Shortly thereafter, Jacob looked at his watch and said, "Shit, we have to be off. We've got reservations for deep-sea fishing up in Rustico." We paid our bills and then shook hands, agreeing how delightful it was to meet. Too bad we didn't have more time together.

I was convinced we wouldn't see them again. But then we did, two days later, on the beach not far from our cottage. We had spent an unhurried morning reading in our Adirondack chairs and were now soodling hand-in-hand across the coppery mudscape of low tide. I was shirtless and basted in sunscreen and Grace was in a floppy hat and sarong, her wrap opened at the front to reveal the gusset of her bathing suit. We had enjoyed these two days of solitude — the sex and the sleeping in, the long, slow meals cooked in our cabin's kitchenette, the wine, and the endless, endless reading — but had reached that point in a vacation where Grace wanted some outside contact. Sure enough, about fifty yards ahead of us, we could see what were clearly Jacob and Hilary descending a wooden, wind-scorched stairway from the shore to the beach. Weirdly, Hilary was lugging what appeared to be a large silver briefcase, its corporate presence so incongruous against the lazy, fishboat-dotted vista spread out before us. The second Grace spotted the couple she let out a "Woo-oo!" and they looked up and waved. We walked toward each other and met in the middle.

"Oh, wow, we wondered if we were going to run into you again," Jacob said.

"Us, too," exclaimed Grace, though I had no recollection of discussing it.

I grew self-conscious, then, of my pale, doughy torso exposed to their eyes. Jacob, too, had gone topless, and I could see now what his shirt had hidden before: he was in good shape for a guy my age — his shoulders broad, his pecs pronounced, his belly flat. Meanwhile, Hilary's lithe, twentysomething body looked perfectly at ease in its two-piece polka-dot bathing suit and flip-flops that revealed dainty toes painted green.

"Okay, I have to ask," I said to her, trying not to gawk, "what's in the briefcase?"

"Oh, wait till you see," she said with childlike exuberance, and set the case down on the sand. She squatted before it and undid the brass latches. The case popped open to reveal itself to be — oh dear reader! — a portable bar. When she raised the large lid, a mechanized sideboard came up and out. On the case's inner top half, strapped down with leather, were 500 ml bottles of gin, vodka, whiskey, and vermouth, plus juices and simple syrup. On the bottom half, encased in grey foam, were martini and shot glasses, a shaker, little jars of cherries and olives and cocktail onions.

"Girl after my own heart!" I cried out.

She looked back at us over her shoulder, grinning. "You guys want a drink?"

So the four of us sipped Gibsons there on the red mud, watching the tide come in and chatting about all manner of amiable topics. Grace mentioned what a "good drinker" I was, and I described for them the marvel that was the Bloody Joseph. "It really is my signature cocktail," I said. When we finished our drinks, Jacob dug a foam football out of his beach bag and suggested we play catch in the water. We ditched our footwear and other accessories and waded out into the sea, arranging ourselves into a spread-out square. With the hand-eye coordination of an inebriated chimp, I managed to fumble or outright miss each toss that sailed my way. At one point, the ball slammed into my temple like the bullet that killed JFK, sending my comb-over flying off my head like a shattered skull and knocking me into the water. "Sorry, Philip!" Hilary called over after I re-emerged. At another point, the ball slipped as I gave it a toss, and it wobbled through the air and landed weakly on the water between Jacob and Grace. They both dashed and leaped for it, and Jacob got there first by a split second, and Grace went tumbling into the foam. I watched as Jacob laughed and apologized, then extended a hand to my wife, hauling her out of the sea with a sturdy tug. His muscular shoulders then pivoted as he threw the ball with perfect precision toward my waiting hands, but I still managed to drop it.

We came in after a bit, bodies chilled and sinuses burning from the salt water, and flopped down around Hilary's briefcase. She made us another cocktail — Manhattans this time — and we drank to our good health. Jacob asked if Grace and I were interested in joining them for their activity this evening. "There's a cèilidh at the village playhouse," he said. "I think there are still tickets. Do you guys want to come?" And Grace said, "Absolutely," and I said, "Sure, let's do it," even though I had planned to spend at least part of the night proofreading. But we beamed over this brilliant idea and did another cheers, our martini glasses tinkling in the open air.

A few hours later, now dressed for a rapidly cooling PEI night, the four of us met up outside the playhouse, located right in the middle of the village, an old white-painted church now renovated for plays. We went in, bought tickets, and found some seats in the middle of the theatre. The place was soon packed, the chatter of eager tourists filling the air. Before long a seven-man band took to the stage with instruments — guitar, accordion, fiddle, mandolin, Celtic drum, bass, tin flute — and lined up in a straight row in front of us. The lead singer, behind his guitar, welcomed us all and then mentioned that the theatre's aisles were open for dancing. They then broke into their first song, a jaunty little Irish number, and a few people clapped along. After the song wrapped up, the leader once again reminded us of the open aisles; and during the second tune, equally brisk, a few people did get up to jig and flail around. By the third song, even more people headed for the aisles, but not enough for the band's liking. During a long instrumental section, the Celtic drummer, a short, snouty man, yelled out, "Get up and dance, ye sissies!" and that seemed to shake our group from its bashfulness. Grace, Jacob, and Hilary took to their feet. Grace motioned for me to join them, but I demurred. I was happy to just sit and listen — and besides, *nobody* wanted to see Philip Sharpe try to dance. I instead watched as my wife and our two new friends rushed to the aisle and then threw their arms into the air and bounced around each other in tight, joyous orbits. During a fiery fiddle solo, the three of them linked hands and began jumping up and down, their six feet pounding at the floor.

By song five, the other shy types and I, encamped in our theatre seats, were in the minority, and Hilary had had enough. Youthful face glowing, hips swinging in her summer dress, she danced back through our row to grab me by the wrists and pull me to my feet. "*Please* join us, Philip!" she yelled over the music, and I was powerless to resist her. So there I was, stiffly reunited with them and "dancing" — a kind of shuffle that looked like an attempt to scrape gum off the soles of my Payless. Don't get me wrong, reader: I *was* having a blast. When the music got manic, I did my best to join the jig. During a slower, more contemplative folk song, the four of us linked arms and swayed like teenagers. At one point, Jacob pulled out his phone to take our picture, and the girls encroached on my face and kissed my bearded cheeks just as the flash danced in our eyes.

When the cèilidh wrapped up, we poured with the crowd into the lobby, and there was vague, fragmented talk of what the four of us might do next. Was there a pub nearby? Did they want to come back to our cottage for a nightcap? But we emerged outside to discover a pluvial torrent pounding the street. When had *this* come on? We screamed a little as our heads and clothes got soaked. The downpour was so harsh it couldn't help but quash any undeveloped plans we had and drive us apart. There was a quick, desperate exchange between the girls. "Afternoon … tomorrow … the beach!" exclaimed Hilary. "Yeah, yeah," Grace replied. Jacob and Hilary then linked arms and darted through the sheets of rain back to the Orient Hotel while we cowered under a small umbrella that Grace pulled from her handbag and hustled back to our own shoreline cottage.

The next afternoon, the pathway to the beach was still pock-marked with large puddles of the previous night's rain, and low tide had brought with it a feral and not entirely unpleasant funk from the sea. Grace and I were walking hand-in-hand and soon spotted Hilary's silver briefcase resting on a red macadam of sediment. We looked out over the water and, sure enough, there they were, playing catch among the waves once more. They saw us and beckoned, and we stripped down to our bathing suits and waded out to be with them. But as we did, Hilary broke away and came sploshing through the water toward us in large, animated strides. She seized me by the arm and said, "Grace, take my place. Philip — come with me. I've got something for you!" So Grace waded out excitedly toward Jacob while Hilary brought me in and led me to her briefcase. We squatted in the sand and she began digging through their beach bag. To my delight, she brought up a bottle of tomato juice, a stalk of celery, some Tabasco.

"I went shopping for you this morning," she said, popping open her portable bar to get at the whiskey. "I figured you might want to have your usual."

"Oh, wow, you're sweet," I replied.

I watched as she intently mixed us a couple of competent Bloody Josephs, her blond hair hanging in wet, tangled ropes around the sides of her face. She handed me my drink, and we reclined together on the sand to watch Grace and Jacob play catch in the distance, their tosses growing short as they drifted closer together.

"So are you guys really starting back to Toronto tomorrow?" Hilary asked.

"Yeah, unfortunately." I sighed.

She nodded, equally disappointed. Then she looked at me, her chin and forehead still shining with seawater. "Can I ask you a question?"

"Sure."

"Does it bother you that I was one of Jacob's students?"

I looked away, back toward the horizon. "I don't," I said, "tend to judge."

"Have *you* ever slept with a student?" she asked. "Or thought about it?"

My ears lit up like lanterns. "Every prof *thinks* about it," I stammered. "They're lying if they say otherwise. And sometimes it *seems* like one of my young charges might be coming on to me. But in seventeen years, I've never had the ..." and here chose my word carefully, "*confidence* to confirm it."

She licked her lips. "I find that hard to believe." She looked at me, and I looked at her, and we smirked awkwardly. Then we turned back to the sea, and found that Grace and Jacob had given up on catch, and were now standing waist-deep in the water together, talking. They held the football between them — his hand on one end and hers on the other.

"Hey, guys — come in for drinks!" Hilary yelled, and in a way that reminded me of how young, and possibly immature, she was. But the two obeyed, and before long Hilary had mixed the four of us a round of very stiff Gibsons. We downed them quickly as we chatted. She mixed up a second round, and we downed those fast, too. The alcohol must have gone to Jacob's head, because he burst out then with:

"I don't mean to get all 'frat boy' on you guys, but I think it's high time the four of us had a chicken fight."

"Oh God, yes!" Grace exclaimed, and climbed to her feet.

"A chicken — a chicken *what?*" I asked. But the girls were already hauling me up, one arm each, off the red mud. We all staggered into the water then, and Jacob stooped, and Hilary swung herself onto his shoulders, her legs around his ears, and up she went. Ah, I got it. I did the same, and Grace manoeuvred herself, with some difficulty, onto my narrow shoulders. Once she did, I attempted to raise us both. *Oof, dear*, I thought, *you're certainly on the south side of thirty.* Seeing me struggle, Jacob said, "Here, let's trade." He lowered himself and Hilary climbed down and splashed over to me. Grace splashed over to Jacob. He got my wife up, got her up with no effort at all. I was a bit bothered by this, but then Hilary's thighs came draping over my ears, her crotch at the back of my head. There was something seedy about it, my hands now holding her smooth, cool shins, but she was, I had to admit, quite a bit lighter than Grace. I got her in the air, and Jacob was upon me in an instant. The girls enmeshed their hands and Grace promptly pitched us into the water. "Hey, no fair — we weren't ready!" Hilary yelled once we surfaced. She climbed aboard me once more, but once more the other team sent us into the sea after a brief tussle. On the third try, I finally got a good footing, and we settled for a draw — the four of us tumbling into the surf together, the girls squealing in delight as we did. We all thrashed around in the foam briefly, and I felt someone's backside brush against the front of my trunks.

The girls decided to go for a swim, and Jacob and I returned to shore to lounge on the sand. We watched as Grace and Hilary went out and out and out, farther than we'd yet been, farther than I thought advisable. I grew nervous at that.

"Do you think they're too —" I began.

"They'll be fine," he said.

And sure enough, they soon swam back in and climbed out of the surf together, their bathing suits full of the sea. Hilary called over, "Jacob — come swim with me," and he got up to go to her. He and Grace brushed past each other for a second as Grace trotted up to be at my side. She flung herself down and nuzzled her face into my chest, and I patted her wet hair as I watched our friends swim out together.

Grace stayed like that for a bit, but then looked up at me, her eyes a touch wild, her lips pressed into an unwieldy half-grin. "So this is a bit awkward," she said.

"What is?"

Instead of answering, she pressed her face into my chest again — hid it there, really, as if she were embarrassed to go on — and laughed.

"Grace, what is it?"

Without looking at me she said, "So Hilary wants to know if we'd like to see their room up at the Orient."

"Really?" I asked, dumbly. "Why? Is there something special about their hotel room?"

"Well, that's what *I* asked," Grace replied, glancing up at me. Her cheeks were now flush. "And she said, no. No, not really. Other than its king-size bed. A huge bed, she said. A bed that's practically, you know," and here cringed her face into my shoulder. "Big enough for four people."

I gasped a little. And Grace gasped a little.

"Oh my *gawd*," I said.

"Oh my *God*," she exclaimed.

I chuckled awkwardly. "Can you *imagine*?"

She bit her lip and shrugged. "Actually, I can imagine." At first I thought she meant, *Yeah, I can imagine it — those two crazy cads, those wild Texans, suggesting such a thing.* But then I realized: No, no. What my wife meant was, *Yeah, I* can *imagine it.*

She looked up at me. Saw the expression on my face. "It's just so ridiculous," she said, backpedalling. "So *scandalous*. I mean, sure, the four of us get along really well. And yes, we'll probably never see these people again after tonight. But still. We couldn't. We *couldn't*." And she raised her face to mine. "Could we?"

I just looked at her. "Grace, it's our honeymoon."

"Oh, I know, of course," she said, wrapping an arm around my soft belly. Out on the water, we could see that Jacob and Hilary had gone out far, and were now just turning around and bobbing their way back toward us. "Except, not really," Grace went on, cautiously. "I mean, it's been over a year since our wedding. And you've spent a lot of this trip working on your book. So it's not really a honeymoon — is it?"

My mouth slackened under my rapidly widening gaze, and she lowered her head. "Grace, I am profoundly uncomfortable right now."

"No, of course. It's stupid. It's *stupid*."

"I suppose Jacob's into this idea?"

"Oh, yes, he's very into it," she said — too quickly. She went beet red then. And that's when I realized: I was not one-fourth of this discussion, this decision. I was maybe one-eighth, or one-sixteenth — a small hurdle to be overcome in an idea that the three of them had already, somehow, floated together. I thought, then, of the experimentation that Grace regularly brought to our sex life, and how I always tried to run with it. The role-playing, the gymnastical positions, her collection of *toys* — all used to create a little voyeur-exhibitionist combo, a little simulated candaulism. But this was a bridge too far.

"Anyway, I could never go through with it," she lied. "I would just freeze up. I would just *die*."

I gaped at her, silently, for a long time.

Jacob and Hilary came splashing out of the water then and walked, hand in hand, back toward us. They smiled at first but then realized the mood had changed. Realized that the conversation they knew Grace had been having with me did not go well.

"Listen," Jacob said, looking to change the subject, "we're thinking about going for an early supper. You guys want to come?"

No, get the fuck away from me, I thought.

"Sure, that would be lovely," Grace answered for us.

Jacob nodded, and then gave my wife a slight, barely perceptible shrug of resignation. Hilary, meanwhile, crouched in the sand and began gathering up the contents of her portable bar. She looked over at me, sadly, the thwarted *allumeuse*. I suppose I should have been flattered by her disappointment. But I wasn't. I was revolted.

We returned to our respective nests to get cleaned up but then reconvened at a patio restaurant near the village's playhouse. The dinner conversation was stilted, cold. I was monosyllabic for the entire meal. When it was over, we exchanged a series of bland goodbyes. Grace and Hilary promised to find each other on the Facebook, and Jacob told me to drive safely tomorrow on our trek back.

"I don't drive," I informed him. "I've never even had my licence. *She* does all the driving in this relationship."

"Ah," he replied, nodding without quite believing.

* * *

That night, in our cabin, Grace and I made love. I didn't want to, but it felt necessary to clear the air between us. It was good, industrious, missionary-position sex; and upon its detumescence I promptly rolled over and fell asleep. It was a great sleep — deep and solitary and dreamless. It was like I floated in some nowhere-place a million miles away from the unpleasantness of that afternoon.

But then I woke, later on, to a sound I mistook for the surf's arrhythmia outside our window, its pulse and squeak, its pulse and squeak. I sat up and looked over at that window, at the moonlight blazing through it. But the sound was not coming from there. So I glanced to where my wife lay, well over on her side of the bed. She was naked and on her back, her knees up, her torso arched, the sheets swirling like eddies around her ankles. She must have gotten out of bed at some point (slinked out really, while I snored on my side of the mattress), and fetched two of her silicone friends from the pocket of her suitcase. Because there they were, long and large and very lifelike. She pressed one between her legs, her wrist like a metronome beyond the crest of her raised thighs. Her other arm was curled lightly, sensuously, around her head, with the second silicone friend moving in and out and around her open mouth, her pawing tongue. Grace's eyes were squeezed shut in rapture, and she released soft, starved cries of pleasure each time the toy moved out of her mouth.

"Grace —"

She sprang bolt upright then, like a jack-in-the-box. "Philip — oh my *God!*" The two toys went rolling off the bed and thudding onto the floor. Her sexual flush turned to a flush of embarrassment.

"*Grace.*"

She let out a little gasp then, or a gasp-laugh, and waited for me to return it. I didn't. So we both hovered there, in space and time, not moving. Then she lowered herself slowly back onto her pillow, her eyes wide, her face burning. I stared down at her, own face aflame, but then settled back onto my side of the bed. We both lay there, doing an excellent job of examining the ceiling, there in the darkness above us.

"Grace, it's our *honeymoon*," I said finally.

A quick rustle of the sheets and her forehead was pressed into my shoulder, her hip hooked around mine. "Do you ... want ... want to ... *help* me out here —"

"*No.*"

So she moved back to her side and went stiff as a plank. The truth of what she'd been doing — what she'd been *fantasizing about* — draped over us like a canopy. It felt as if every cell in my body had died at once, wiped out by the images dancing in Grace's head. Images of me and Jacob — together. But mostly, probably, just Jacob. My wife had been lying next to me as I slept thinking of somebody else. And on our *honeymoon*, no less.

Oh gawd, I'd thought, naively at the time. *How do we ever recover from something like* that?

Saturday, November 7

Let us speak of weekend rituals. I will marvel, as you no doubt will, at the way children can sleep like Tut in his tomb all week long, ignoring the beseeches of parents pleading against the clock, only to swarm from their chambers on Saturday morning and fill an ungodly hour with frenetic clatter. But I'm up. I'm up and I'm there. I'm there to provide assistance at the toilet, to find a lost Dora, to pour cereal and locate cartoons on TV. I'm there in bathrobe, in eye crust, in fuzzy slippers. I am there with spatula in hand, hunched over sizzling skillet, cooking my wife a hot, proper breakfast. I'm there on the porch, hauling in fat weekend papers (though not as fat as they used to be), which I will divvy up like a whale carcass after a hunt. To Grace go sections like Style and Living and Weekend. To me go sections like Focus and Argument. The kids get the funnies. We each have our perennial favourites: Grace goes straight to *Globe* Style, which, oddly, contains recipes; I, meanwhile, grouse over an increasingly etiolated *Globe* Books and then dive-bomb the *Star*'s op-ed section. And if things are good, if things are *humming*, my wife and I will speak to each other in the idioglossia of our marriage, a nonsensical lexicon of love and domesticity. If things are good, we will cheer or heckle or debate what we read, aloud to each other, our fingers gone black with newsprint ink.

But on this Saturday, things were not good. Not good at all. Four Metcalfe Street seemed full of gloom. I had brought the papers in but not bothered to divide them up; they sat in a segmented pile on the kitchen table, portending more column inches about my unconscionable gaffe from Monday. As for breakfast, I couldn't bring myself to do much more than a couple of toasted bagels for Grace and me. The Bloody Joseph I mixed for myself tasted flat. The autumn light through our kitchen window held a faint grimness. Grace came downstairs, a Medusa of bed-head and frayed kimono, sat at the kitchen table, picked briefly at the papers, stared out the window. I sat across from her, slowly smearing my bagel with cream cheese. We said nothing. We said nothing.

Thankfully, Naomi filled the space with her incessant, three-year-old's nattering. She burst away from the TV cartoons and the cereal I'd set up for her on the coffee table to race over and leap into her mother's lap. "When I, when I, when I, when I go swimming, okay, swimming, with *you*, Mummy, where, I mean why, I mean why, why aren't there dine'sores at the *poo*-ool?"

Simone came down, eventually, pink iPad and *Life of Pi* under her arm. I got up and fixed her a bowl of cereal, and she sat with us to read a while in silence. She would look up at me, at Grace, noting, I'm sure, the Cuban Missile Crisis–esque tension between us, the vast, tetchy DMZ of the breakfast table, before returning to her book.

"But I did, Mummy, I did, I did, I did one time, I did see a dine'sore at the *poo*-ool. One time."

"Hey, Naomi, what were you watching?" Simone asked.

"*Veggie Tales*," she sang back.

"Wanna go watch some more?"

"'Kay."

So Simone led her sister by the hand back to the TV, granting us a blessed moment alone. Grace looked up and took the opportunity to speak.

"I'm going to cancel tomorrow's brunch, by the way."

"What?" I asked. "Why?"

"Why do you *think*?" she jangled with incredulity, then glared at me as if I might answer. "Two couples have cancelled already. We're down to just eight of us. Nobody, Philip, wants to be around you right now. *I* don't want to be around you."

"Did Jane Elton cancel?"

"Philip —"

"No, I'm asking. Did Jane Elton cancel?"

Grace turned, sulking off into space. "No. She and her husband are still coming."

"Well then."

"Look, I can't just —"

"No, that's *my* dolly — *my dolly*!"

"Naomi, I don't even want your stupid doll."

"Guys — guys!" Grace called over to the TV. "No fighting!" Then she turned back to me, her face a cauldron of fury. I had never seen my wife this upset before.

"I just want all this to be over," she muttered.

"Look, don't cancel the brunch," I said. "You wanted to get your manuscript in front of Jane, so let's do it. I mean, that was the whole *point* of this brunch." That only seemed to upset her more. "Look," I went on, "people will probably be too polite to say anything to me about what happened on Monday. I mean, that's pretty much been the case all week." I gave her a half-smile. "The slip that dare not speak its name?"

But Grace wasn't buying it. She looked up at me then, the corners of her mouth twitching in suppressed rage. "We're not in a good place right now," she said. "And I'm not sure I can put up a front for our friends."

"Grace, don't cancel the brunch. It's important to you, so let's just get it over with. Okay?"

She mashed her lips together, as if contemplating another rebuttal, but then decided against it.

"Fine," she said.

"Fine," I said back.

She tilted her chin up at me. "So I got the kids booked in to see that exhibit at the museum later this morning," she said. "Are you coming with us?"

Oh gawd. Something *else* that had completely gotten away from me. How does this keep happening? I took a pull on my Bloody Joseph. "What time?" I asked.

"Eleven thirty."

I looked at the clock on the wall.

Grace gaped at me. "Wow. You're *not* coming with us."

"Well, I have *work* to do," I told her. "I really need to take a crack at this YouTube script for Raj."

Grace sighed then, a ventilating gasp of despair, and shook her head at me as if to say, *I can't* believe *you.*

"It's important, Grace. Okay? It's important." This did not convince her, so I offered an olive branch. "Listen, come up and check in with me right before you guys go. If I've made good headway, I'll come. All right?"

But this was not all right. She got up from the table without saying another word to me, and headed toward the kids at the TV. "Simone, did you feed the cat yet? You didn't, did you? And you really need to do her litter box, okay. We have *company* coming tomorrow. I'm not going to ask you again."

And so our household rolled on as I sat there. Sat there with our unread newspapers and uneaten bagels. Our thwarted Saturday sacraments.

Squeeze, dash, shake-shake-shake, pour. I headed upstairs to the solitary bliss of my office, closed its door and settled in at my crowded desk. The tomato-juice-stained notes and manuscript pages of "Christianity and Its Dissidents" sat in a towering lump on the desk's far right-hand corner. I suppose I had Christian-like forgiveness on the brain as I opened a fresh Word doc and got down to writing my script, my YouTube *mea culpa*. I would plead for forgiveness, beg for it from those who had lacerated me so savagely, so perplexingly, over what I had said about those ODS executives. I would ask for mercy; but do so, paradoxically, by arguing why *we* should forgive them for what *they* did. Yes, their despicable acts would wreak havoc in the Canadian economy for years to come, but they still deserved to be treated well inside the boundaries of our judicial system. I acknowledged outright that what I had said about ODS was wrong, that I *knew* it was wrong, and that it had just come spurting out from some dark place inside my lizard brain. I then proceeded to *prove* that I knew it was wrong by going back through history to show how our notions of fairness, justice, and proportionality had developed over centuries, and how each milestone could be applied to the awful acts those corporate executives had committed.

It all went really well. The words just piled up, and I soon disappeared into the loops and spirals of my argument, my swelling verbiage. The script format tripped me up in the beginning, but I soon got the hang of it, leaving parenthetical instructions for Raj along the way, such as "<Show still image here of Solon, the ancient Greek legislator and politician>" and "<Can we blow up this quote from Thomas Hobbes' *Leviathan*?>" Time moved untraceably as I worked, and before I knew it I was done — 1,509 words on the button. They had just flowed out of me. I printed off the script and read it over a couple of times, making a few typographical corrections along the way. Then I emailed it off to Raj with a note:

> Hey Raj: Here's the script. I'm curious to see how you'll bring your videographical eye to these ideas. Let me know what you think. — Philip

Then I began to delete the trickle of Facebook notifications that had come in overnight, and was surprised when a response from Raj came back right away.

> Hey buddy,
>
> Just on the road here in Barrie. I'll download your Word doc when I get a chance. In the meantime, I had another idea. I'd really love to introduce that cocktail of yours, the Bloody Joseph, to the boys when you're all over on Wednesday. If you email me the recipe, I can pick up the ingredients on my way back into Toronto, and we can inhale a few while we're filming. I noticed you didn't really care for my windowsill whisky yesterday. ;)
>
> Raj

This struck me as a corking idea, so I quickly hammered out my recipe for the Bloody Joseph and sent it off to him, wondering if Raj might blanch at the various inclusions and modifications I had made to the traditional formula. When I finished, I leaned back in my chair and was filled with a sudden glow of satisfaction. It felt great to get that script off my chest, to apologize unmitigatedly to the world, and to have something to look forward to on Wednesday.

I sat up, and for the first time in more than an hour, my eyes flickered to the little clock in the corner of my computer screen.

I jarred. 11:17. What the hell? Where the *fuck* did the morning go?

I turned toward my closed office door, to the hush of 4 Metcalfe Street beyond it. Shouldn't Grace have popped up by now to let me know they were leaving for the museum, and to see if I still wanted to come? I got up and went to the door, opened it and stuck my head out to the landing.

"Grace?" I called down. "Grace, are you there?" The house was a catacomb of silence. "Grace, I finished my script. I can join you guys now."

No answer. I went down the stairs to the second level and checked our bedroom, calling her name. When I didn't find her, I moved to the ground floor. "Simone, Naomi, where's Mum?" Again, no answer. Was the house empty? Had they just … just *left* without checking in with me? Constance the cat strolled by my ankle. "Constance, where *is* everybody?"

But I already knew the answer. I went to the living-room window and looked out over the street parking in front of our house. Sure enough: Grace's little red Yaris was nowhere to be found. I stood there gawping, a rage ascending in my throat like dyspepsia. I shook my head. Un. Fucking. Believable. She *knew* I still wanted to come. She *knew* I wanted her to check in with me. How — how could they just leave me behind?

My rage intensified. I couldn't believe it. *What am I even* doing *here?* I thought. *What* am *I to these people, my supposed "family"? How do they even see me? How can I be, as Grace put it, "plugged in" to what's happening in my own house when I'm not even a presence in this house? When I don't count. When I'm just — a thing. I am just a thing. I'm a sounding board. I am a paycheque. I am a cock, a dildo with a dental plan. I am just the thing around here that does the things that make all this possible.*

A moment later I was back up at my desk, staring at my computer screen and feeling thoroughly sorry for myself. A couple of fresh Facebook notifications appeared then — more rancour from cyberspace, no doubt — but I ignored them. Instead, I stared at the message that had come in last night. The message from Rani.

I reopened it.

> You really should give me a call. 07870 663 926.

I got up from my desk. Went downstairs, to the living-room end table where the cordless phone sat in its docking station. I picked it up, brought it with jittery haste back upstairs. Closed my office door. Sat back at my desk, my shoulders tightened, my bowels watery, my stomach thrumming with nervousness.

I dialled.

There was a lengthy, transatlantic pause. But then it rang. And rang. And then she picked up.

"Hello?"

"Hey, Rani," I said, my voice a deep, husky timbre.

"Oh," she replied, "my God."

"Hi."

"Is that *you* inside my mobile, Philip Sharpe?"

"Yep."

"You called me. You actually *called* me."

"I did."

"You did."

"How are you?"

"I'm fine," she replied. "Just fine. How are *you*?"

"I'm a mess." My voice cracked like a teenager's. "What can I say? I am a total fucking mess."

"Ah, Sharpe." She chuckled sympathetically. "Here, hang on a sec." I heard her move out of the chattering BBC newsroom, to another room and close the door behind her. "How bad is it there?"

"You have no idea," I said.

"Tell me."

Such an inviting plea. Such a warm, worldly accent in her voice. I hesitated. It felt unseemly to share such intimacies with a woman I hadn't seen in nearly a decade. But then, buttressed by the house empty all around me, I went for it. "It's just … it's just unravelling everything. This situation. There are no words. My colleagues at the university … my students … my *marriage*, gawd. It's been like … like a punch to the solar plexus of my marriage, Rani."

"Huh," she said. "Hmm."

"Yeah. Exactly. It's just, it's just — awful."

"Ah, Sharpe," she repeated. "You sound like you need a hug."

I need a lot more than a hug, I nearly said, but bit my tongue. "It's just so bad here. I can barely describe it."

"Well, *that* doesn't sound like you," she replied, a sly curlicue on her words. "You're usually pretty good at, you know, articulating yourself."

"Yeah."

"So what are you going to do?"

I released a long, slow sigh. "Well, I've just finished scripting a comprehensive apology. A videographer friend of mine is going to film me delivering it — do a whole professional production — and we're going to put it up on YouTube."

"That's good," she said. "No, that's really good."

"Anyway. I don't know if it's going to help at all. But I have to do something."

"No, of course," she replied. Then she added, "Look, for what it's worth, I think the response to your gaffe has been wildly out of proportion. I mean, come *on*. Sex slaves in Iraq, kidnapped girls in Nigeria, but no, no, this — *this* is what people choose to get upset about."

I felt some tears trickle into the fur on my cheeks. "You have no idea," I told her, "how much I've wanted someone to say exactly that to me all week." I took a deep, snotty swallow. "Thank you."

"You're welcome," she said with cheer.

"Anyway. Blah blah blah. Enough about me. What's new with you?"

"Well, funny you should ask," she said. "I have some amazing news myself."

"Oh? What's going on?"

"Well, I've just received a promotion," she replied. "As of January 4, I'll be the BBC's new bureau chief in Mumbai."

"Oh my God — that's *amazing*," I exclaimed. "Wow. You — you must be just over the moon."

"I am," she said.

"Oh, Rani, congratulations. This is so well deserved. You've worked incredibly hard for this."

"Thanks, Sharpe. It's really exciting. I mean, I've been back to India tons of times but I haven't lived there since I was a kid. And my parents are back there now, retired. They're getting on in years, so being closer to them will be great. It's just an incredible opportunity all around."

"That's so wonderful," I said.

"Thanks." And then, with a flirty little snicker, she added, "So — any chance you want to ditch your life in Toronto and run away to India with me?"

"Ha, ha," I laughed. "That's funny."

"Ha, ha," she replied. And then there was — yes, you guessed it — a long awkward pause. "So …?" she added.

"So … what?" I asked.

"So …?" Another pause. "You wanna run away to India with me?"

My bowels went watery again. "You aren't serious."

"Actually, I think I kinda am."

"Rani —"

"No, just listen to me." And so I did. "I've been sitting at my desk all week, Sharpe, watching and re-watching that clip of you on the CBC. I mean, on the one hand you're at your least attractive in it. You're fumbling around with that toadstool of a woman, letting her wipe the floor with you. And you look like hell. I mean, I don't know *what* you think that comb-over is accomplishing but you really should reconsider it."

"Rani —"

"Just *listen* to me. But despite all that, I'm looking at you in that clip and I can still see the man I met twenty-five years ago. I can see that guy, Sharpe. The guy I was so crazy about but afraid to love back then. It's true. I really loved you, Sharpe. I did. But I …" She sighed like a furnace. "I just loved my career more. What can I say? I sacrificed a lot for it, and still do. I mean, it's Saturday afternoon and I'm here in this newsroom after already putting in a seventy-hour week. But I have nowhere to go; I have no one to see. I'm forty-eight years old, I've never been married, I can't seem to stay in a relationship longer than six months these days, and I'm … I'm alone, Sharpe. I've never been able to follow through on things with guys. Lord knows I couldn't follow through with you."

"Rani, you really should stop talking."

"No. You're going to listen to me. Do you know when I started petitioning for this promotion?" she asked. "Five or six years ago, when you got *married*. I thought: well that'll be it. That'll be the end of our international hookups. I mean, I *lived* for those, Sharpe. I thought, What's the point of being one airplane ride away from you, now? But … but I look at my parents, retired and living out their last days in India together, and I think …" There was another long stillness on the line. Was she crying? "… I think, I don't want to die alone. I want to die with someone I can love. And I know that's you. And maybe this cock-up you've caused, this body blow to your life over there, has created that opportunity. So I'm asking you, Sharpe. I'm putting myself out on a limb over here. I'm a middle-aged woman asking you to be with her."

I had to make a joke. How could I not? "You've been watching *Notting Hill* again, haven't you?"

"*Shut up*. Be serious. I'm asking. Come to India in the new year. Come be with me."

"Rani, I — I *can't*."

"Why not?"

I did a quick prioritization in my mind. "I have a job here," I said. "I have tenure at a major North American university."

"Oh, Sharpe, you hate your job," she replied. "You said as much to me, years ago. How did you put it? The gormless undergrads; the backbiting colleagues; the uptight, cynical grad students. You hate it all. I *know* you — you'd love nothing more than to give all that up and just write full time. And I'd be happy to offer you that chance. With this job, I can take care of us. And you — you can just lie around all day, reading books and writing." And then she added, "You know, like your wife does now."

"Rani, knock it off."

"Hey — your words, not mine."

"I *never* said that about Grace."

"Oh, I suppose you didn't," she said. "I suppose I just inferred it from other stuff you told me in emails, about your set-up there. And from reading her column online."

"Rani, I —" It had to be said. "I love Grace."

"Do you? Then how come you're calling me? And how come you went all week without hearing what you needed to hear, about the reaction to your slip being so wildly out of proportion? How come she didn't — or wouldn't — reassure you of that?"

"Rani …"

"I mean I know she's, like, twenty years your junior —"

"*Fourteen* years —"

"— and I'm sure she's cute as a button. But come on. When you first described her to me, and after I read a few of her columns, I thought — *really*? *This* is who the inimitable Philip Sharpe has ended up with? She's what — thirty-six years old? — and she sounds like she's still a child."

That word triggered something in me, and I was about to speak, but Rani wasn't quite done.

"Sharpe, I'm asking you. Walk away. Walk away from that mess you made in Toronto and come be with me."

"Rani, I have a daughter," I said sternly. "I have a daughter, now." *Actually,* I thought, *I have two daughters.*

There was another stretch of silence on the line.

"Arrangements can be made," she said, finally. "We could work something out. I mean," and here she chuckled, "how long could the flight between Mumbai and Toronto be? Twenty, maybe twenty-five hours?"

"Rani, I'm going to go. I can't even think about what you're proposing right now."

"Well, think about it," she said. "Go get your apology to the world online, and then think about it. You know we're very good together, Sharpe. We always were."

"Goodbye, Rani."

"Think about it."

"Goodbye."

And then I sat there with the extinguished cordless in my lap. I wouldn't think about it. Nope. I wouldn't. I had a daughter. I had *two* daughters. I wouldn't think about it. I wouldn't think about it at all.

* * *

Oh, but how could the rest of the day go, the rest of the evening, after that? Grace came home with the kids and we did not speak. Fury hung between us like a sheet. She announced to the house that she needed to get some writing done, and so settled in at her little alcove while I took the kids. Naomi and I escorted Simone over to her friend Sarah's house, and then walked back, with me dutifully humouring the three-year-old's unremitting queries. *Why do trees have leaves, Daddy? When will chipmunks fly? Can I can I can I?* Back home, I tried to get Naomi down for a nap, but she would not have it. We read some storybooks; we had a tea party in the living room. *Would you like some ceeeem? Why, yes I would. Okay, but Piggy gets some furrrst. That is fine.* While Naomi coloured in her colouring book on the kitchen floor (more dine'sores; always more dine'sores), I did a bit of prep for tomorrow's brunch. I vivisected a cantaloupe; I mixed up a couple pitchers' worth of pancake batter, saran-wrapping the tops and finding room for them in our fridge. At one point, I walked by Grace's alcove and saw her screen, saw the little red bubbles along Facebook's blue border. As the supper hour approached, Naomi and I went out to fetch Simone while Grace got up to throw some chicken tits on the George Foreman and make a salad. When we got home, I ventured a question. *How did it go?* The answer came back as predicted: in three hours, she had managed about a sentence and a half.

During dinner, we did not speak. Then came bath time. Then came PJs. Then came more storybooks after we sidled Naomi into bed. But oh God. Oh *God*, Naomi. Why tonight? *Why?* You went down so easily on Wednesday. Don't you realize we're hosting a very important brunch tomorrow? But no, no. One story would not do; nor three, nor five. A pee. Sippy cup of water. Another pee. Okay, okay, time for sleep. Right? Wrong. Wrong! This was the World Series, this was the *Olympics* of Not-Going-to-Sleep, and it was as if she had trained for it her whole life. *Stop jumping on the bed and get under those sheets — right now!* But no, no. Oh gawd — *gawd!* Go to sleep, you little terrorist. If you get out of that bed one more time! *Gawd!* No, we ALREADY READ THAT ONE!

When a child refuses to sleep, it can make your evening feel like it's trapped inside a very bad prose poem — all jarring transitions and fragmented narrative arcs.

At 9:10, she wandered downstairs clutching blankey and claiming a nightmare. I picked her up and put her back to bed. Another storybook.

9:45: Grace and I were reading in the living room when Naomi started roaring like a camel upstairs. Grace bounded out of her chair to go investigate.

10:50: We were in the ensuite flossing for bed when Naomi wandered in to our room (a HUGE no-no!) holding Constance by the throat in a kind of half nelson. Grace led her away just as the child began to roam a bit too close to Mummy's "special drawer" in the bureau.

11:10: The sound of frantic tears from Naomi's room. I got out of bed and went to her. I informed the child, in no uncertain terms, that she needed to go to sleep — right now. But she screamed at me that she wasn't tired. Only, she pronounced it in her three-year-old's way, putting stress on the wrong syllable: "I'm not tie-red!" she pleaded in despair. "I'm not TIE-RED!" Oh, Daddy, why are you being so obtuse on this point?

12:20: I got her down, finally. I thought then of slipping up to my office and dossing on the futon there, leaving the rest of the night to Grace. But no, no. I am a plugged-in dad, damn it.

1:00: Grace got up and went to her.

2:20: I got up and went to her.

4:05: Grace shook me awake. "Philip? Philip, you need to get up right now. Naomi has *literally* shit the bed."

Oh God.

So there we were, in the pre-dawn hours (how long before our guests start arriving?), yanking sheets off and finding something to wipe those jaundiced smears of turd off the mattress. Simone, all cloudy-eyed from sleep, wandered in to the pestiferous stench of Naomi's room and looked at us as if to say, *What is* wrong *with you people?*

Yes. A very good question, Simone. What *is* wrong with us? Whoever thought that procreation was a good idea? Maybe my dad was right all long. Why would any man *choose* to subject himself to family life? Why put ourselves through it? Why not just be blissfully alone, all the time? Do *you* know, Naomi? Tell me. Why do we put ourselves through this? Remind me again, my love — why are you even *here*?

The Midwife

I was at Stout when Grace went into labour. A February Friday in 2012, the sky a silver canopy, the air holding a belated bite of winter after an unusually warm season. As per my Friday routine, I had fled campus after whatever soul-sucking graduate seminar I'd been teaching that term to hide away in the bricky warmth of my local. I was halfway through my third pint of the gorgeous black beer that Phillip, the daytime barman, had pumped me after clearing my lunch plate — pulled-pork sandwich and a salad — when the pub's land line rang. Phillip gave a Just-a-sec gesture and went to answer.

"Stout Irish Pub."

He turned to me then, his eyes brightening, his lips curling into a grin. He extended the cordless. "It's for *you*."

So I left my pint half finished on the bar and went bounding out to Carlton and Parliament, over the scabby death traps of ice, and across the two blocks to 4 Metcalfe Street. I came in the house to find Grace mopping the front entry's tiled floor.

"Oh, sweetie, I thought you were —"

"Just watch you step," she said. "My water broke over there."

We summoned the Midwife Sterne, announcing the labour via a text message. We then called Grace's parents. Roland and

Sharon, according to plan, would come over to intercept Simone when she got home from school and keep her entertained while we brought her baby sister into the world upstairs in our bedroom.

Yes, yes. This was to be a "home birth." I had my reservations but Grace was adamant. She did not want a repeat from ten years earlier when she had given birth — three weeks *before* her due date — to Simone. She held near-perfect recall of the entire harrowing experience: Roland and Sharon absent due to an ill-timed conference for Roland's work; Richguy, still smarting from the breakup, nowhere to be found; the hospital's anonymizing assembly lines; the anomic cadre of nurses; the extraterrestrial lights; and, worst of all, the doctor's cold, strange-smelling hands on her body. *A birth canal was all I was to him*, she would say later. He had been unsympathetic to her screams and anguishes, her loneliness, and insisted on treating Grace as exactly what she was: a piece of meat expelling another, smaller, piece of meat.

Well. Not this time. This time, she would be ensconced in the familiarity of her own nest, of her own home, of everything she had worked so hard to build for herself, and surrounded by those she loved most. I would be a doting accoucheur, doing everything I could to ensure that little Naomi Woolf Sharpe-Daly came into this world exactly as Grace had wanted.

Her parents arrived first. Roland and Sharon helped me get their panting, sweating daughter upstairs and propped on the bed, and stayed with her when the doorbell rang and I dashed back down to answer it. The Midwife Sterne — a soft, stocky woman with a gently freckled face and a bun of hair piled high on her head — made her *coo coo cooing* greeting as she came in the house and hugged me with the arm that wasn't lugging her tote bag of birthing implements. I followed her wide, swaying rump up the stairs as she asked about contractions. "About four minutes apart," I told her, and she replied with a cryptic "Ohh, ohh."

She came in to the bedroom and took immediate charge, stripping off her winter wear and stating that we needed to initiate Grace's "Birthing Plan" at once. She greeted my wife with smiley effusion and then took her blood pressure, ensuring to make lots of eye contact as she Velcroed and pumped. I, meanwhile, set the room to its planned mood: threw closed our bedroom window's nacreous curtains; dimmed the lights; steered into position a framed photo of Simone on the bookshelf — Grace's pre-chosen focal point for when the pain got really bad. The Midwife Sterne suggested that Roland and Sharon head back downstairs, since Simone was due home from school any minute. "Don't worry," she said. "There'll be chances to visit in the coming hours." When they were gone, she measured Grace's cervix for the first time. "Three centimetres," she reported. "Okay, honey, the real fun has just begun."

Through her long, languorous breathing, Grace said, "Philip, the music?" and I replied with "Oh, right!" How could I forget? I went to the iPod in its speaker station on Grace's bureau and deployed her "birthing playlist" — a curious bricolage of bands she had listened to in high school and university: Indigo Girls and Nirvana, Sarah Harmer and Hole, the Smiths and Alanis Morissette. The assemblage of songs was, artistically, a nonsensical mess, but it seemed to soothe her.

From the hallway stairs: "Mommy! Mommy!" A moment later, Simone came flouncing into the room and onto the bed.

"Hey, Baby," Grace said, gasping and sweating. Sharon and Roland stood framed in the doorway.

"Is little Naomi really *coming*?" Simone asked.

Grace would've answered, except a tremendous contraction roared up within her then.

"Okay, maybe," the Midwife Sterne cut in, "we could have a quick hello and a quick goodbye, and then you can head back downstairs with your grandparents. I'll send Philip when she's ready for another visit."

The hours passed. The curtained window grew dark. The room filled with strange hormonal scents. At one point, Grace and I climbed atop the bed and waltzed awkwardly to "Basement Apartment." At another point, during one of their visits, her parents and Simone brought up the rolling pin that had belonged to Grace's grandmother — a profoundly sentimental object that Grace turned to in her baking — and I used it to massage her aching back to the knuckle-dragging rhythms of "Lithium."

Around hour five or six, Grace's cervix dilated to seven centimetres, and the Midwife Sterne let out another cluck of concern. "Okay, honey," she said, "things get more painful from here on in. This is where you get to be your *bravest.*" As if to confirm it, a debilitating contraction squeezed Grace then, and I clutched her hand as she coiled forward and gave out a loud, weepy scream. This happened right in the middle of "Closer to Fine" by the Indigo Girls, and when Grace emerged from her pain she looked at me with desperate eyes and said, "Philip, play that song again!"

The Midwife Sterne and I shrugged at each other and I got up to hit the BACK button on the iPod before returning to bed. A moment later another contraction slammed into Grace, worse than before. "… *closer I am to fi-iine,*" she sang along tunelessly as she came out the other side of it, then looked at me again. "Christsake, just put that song on repeat, would you."

I did what I was told. And so, for the next three hours, we listened to "Closer to Fine" over and over — and *over* — again. We listened to it as Grace bore down on the picture of Simone on the bookshelf, a cherubic reminder of what awaited her at the other end of this pain. We listened to it when the real Simone popped by, now in her jammies, for one last visit before Roland and Sharon put her to bed. "We'll wake you after the baby comes,"

Grace promised from her sweating delirium, then kissed her good-bye. The song played as Grace declared the need for a crap, but was too weak to get out of bed. The Midwife Sterne handed me a bedpan, which I tucked under Grace's backside, and then our marriage achieved a whole new level of intimacy. "... *closer I am to fi-iine,*" Grace serenaded me as I took the turd-filled pan away to the bathroom.

Somehow, finally, we attained ten centimetres. "Here we go," beamed the Midwife Sterne, and made warm, joyful eye contact with my wife. "Grace, honey, this is where Baby Naomi needs the best of what you've got." So she began to push, and the real pain came then, pain that rose and curled and frothed like a Bondi Beach wave, and I encouraged Grace to get up onto the surfboard of her breathing and ride each crest all the way to the shore. "... *closer I am to fi-iine,*" she sang weakly between each spasm.

And then another sensation came. Grace would describe it later as like vomitous urges emanating from the wrong end of her body. A sense of inevitability, of achieving the point of no return. Like vomiting. Or like an orgasm. Yes, there was a certain orgasmic quality to my wife's screams then, and I stood by like a hapless wittol as some imaginary paramour ravished her there on our bed. The Midwife Sterne snapped me from this absurd anxiety when her face rose over the top of Grace's knee and glowed like the moon. "Philip, do you want to come see this?"

I did. I went around Grace's spread legs and looked. Her perineum had inflated like a balloon, like it might give itself an episiotomy. I stared into Grace's great labial yawn and saw what looked like a shiny, oversized walnut appear there. I mistook it for the grooves of a brain. *Good God!* I thought. *My baby's born without a skull!* But no. It was merely the arrangement of tiny black hairs atop her wet mauve head. "One more push!" the Midwife Sterne yelled. Grace obliged, and her vagina spread like a smile. Naomi emerged then in a great gush of water, her umbilical cord slung over her shoulder like the strap of a satchel. The Midwife Sterne moved it out of the way as she pulled the baby free.

Naomi was greyish-purple — the colour of a good blueberry crumble — and I briefly panicked. *Oh no, she's dead!* I nearly hollered aloud. But the Midwife Sterne bopped her on the butt and wiped the vernix from her face, and the baby gave out a loud, lusty cry. The Midwife Sterne set her on Grace's stomach. Time — and the placenta — passed in due course. Our madam went to her tote bag to fetch a pair of scissors. "Do you want to do the honours?" she asked, and passed them to me. The umbilical cord was slipperier than I imagined, and I fumbled with it. "Don't snip it gently," she said. "Give it a good, decisive shear." And that did the trick.

She manoeuvred the baby onto Grace's heaving chest — skin to skin — and I brought over the blanket to cover them both. I petted Grace's brow while the Midwife Sterne prepared the room for visitors. Before long, Sharon and Roland entered, the latter piggybacking a groggy, plucked-from-sleep Simone. They approached our bed — first as if it were a car-crash scene, then as if it were a banquet. Roland set Simone on her feet, and the child climbed in with us. "She's really here!" she cried out. We all cuddled round this twitchy, burbling stranger — now sporting an adorable beanie cap — at my wife's breast, and the camera phones came out. Meanwhile, the Indigo Girls sang on. Grace looked at me. "I think I've heard enough of that tune," she said with a warped and weathered smile.

So I went to the bureau and took the iPod off repeat. Just as I was coming back, ready to climb in and rejoin my overjoyed family, the next track came on — "Smells Like Teen Spirit," by Nirvana. The opening riff, followed by thunderous drumming, blared through the room. The six of us jolted. Roland gave out an *Ack!* Baby Naomi started to fuss. The women looked at me as if this egregious turn of events was *my* fault. I hustled back to the iPod and killed the song before Kurt Cobain's angsty wailing could completely spoil the room's atmosphere.

When I came back, Grace was already doing her first hand-off. She passed the baby to Simone, and she held the child carefully while the camera phones flashed and flashed. Then Sharon got a turn. Then — and I admit this stung me a little — the Midwife Sterne. I just stood there, watching as this (at best) stranger-turned-family-acquaintance mewed possessively at my baby. I don't know if other men, other husbands, feel this way, but I sometimes think that when women turn the world into a gurgling aquarium of "feelings," we get excluded. We get boxed out. We drift to the periphery of things. It was as if a Charlie Brown cloud had arrived abruptly above my head. This should have been a moment of unadulterated happiness for me, but I caught a sudden gust of hate as I looked upon these people. Why hate? What is *wrong* with me? In an instant, I was reminded of — and frightened by — how quickly my mood could blacken, and at the most inappropriate of times.

The Midwife Sterne, perhaps sensing this, turned to me. "Philip, come hold your daughter."

So I took one fatherly step forward, and she handed me that tangle of limbs, that tiny fagot of life. She manoeuvred my arms where they needed to be, and then left me to it.

I looked down, and oh God.

Oh *God*.

Everything was forgiven. Surely I am the only human being in the history of human beings to experience this, right? To fall completely in love with another person in one, singular instant. She was perfect. She was perfect.

Then Naomi gave me a gift: she opened her eyes for the very first time. They were the deepest galaxies of blue, and already held that sly slant I would come to know. And I thought that whatever happened from here on in, however much I might fuck this up, whatever she might *endure* by having me as a father, at least we could say that I was the first person she ever laid eyes on.

She looked at me. And I looked at her.

Here I am now, her stare said. *Entertain me.*

Sunday, November 8

W here *did* that child get her energy?

Naomi had, as far as we could figure, slept all of two hours through the night — and yet possessed enough vim to jump around and scream on the living-room couch as Grace tried to coax her upstairs for a bath. It was unequivocal: our daughter stank, and with company arriving in less than an hour, we needed to deal with Naomi's eye-watering night-bourne B.O. By "we" I, of course, mean Grace, as this was the morning's grumpily agreed to division of labour. With puffy eyebags and the stooped posture of exhaustion, Grace took on the chore of dragging Naomi upstairs to our dysfunctional bathroom. The child resisted like an Occupy protester, now wedging herself between couch and coffee table and hollering, "No bath! No bath!" her screams echoing over the suck and grind of the vacuum cleaner that Simone shoved around the front entry, hoovering up tumbleweeds of cat hair and other assorted household crud. I, meanwhile, was blessedly alone in the kitchen, watching these proceedings through the archway as I did the last bit of prep on the bounty we would offer our — excuse me, *Grace's* — guests for brunch.

"Naomi, *enough!*" I heard her plead. "I mean it! You need to come with me — right now!"

And what a bounty it was: Great collops of ham adorned with juicy wheels of pineapple; jugs of pancake batter ready for the griddle; sliced bagels ready for the toaster; Grace's homemade scones; the vivisected cantaloupe. There was a pot of coffee for the coffee drinkers, tea for the tea drinkers, a pitcher each of Bloody Joseph and mimosa, complemented by a carton of straight-up OJ, in case it turned out to be one of *those* parties. Like Grace, I, too, was knackered beyond belief, and was dismayed that the two Collins' worth of Bloody Joseph I had already consumed did not invigorate me. My eyelids were stones. My muscles ached. My mouth felt loose and gummy. As I went about setting our long dining-room table, I fantasized about ditching the party outright and stealing upstairs to flop cruciform onto our bed for the remainder of the day. I had never been this tired.

Indeed, I must have zoned out then, or fallen briefly asleep on my feet, because when I came back I was chopping fresh mint at the cutting board (for what, I have *no* idea) and Grace was hovering over me. Time had clearly passed, because she appeared presentable now — her henna-dyed hair damp and braided back in a ponytail, her face lightly dusted with makeup, a poppy pinned to her sweater. I must say, despite the lingering eyebags and brow crumpled by fatigue, she looked *yummy* — and I would have told her so, too, except she threw me a glare of utter contempt. At first I thought it was because of the mint I was wasting, but then she jabbed a finger toward the half-depleted jug of Bloody Joseph.

"Sorry, *how* many cocktails have you had this morning?"

I stared at the pitcher, a bit surprised, but then sneered at her. "Oh, fuck off," I shot back, scraping the inexplicable mint into the compost. "I'm doing this for *you.*"

* * *

And so, brunch.

As mentioned, we were down to four couples — plus kiddies, for a total of seventeen people. The first to arrive was Grace's best friend, the one she'd had tea with last Tuesday: Stacey Howard, corncob-blond authoress with two albums of gently wry short stories under her belt, towing along her tall, black, handsome, breadwinning cardiologist husband, Ian, and their three — there is no politically correct adjective to describe them — children, who were playmates with ours. I remained surprised that they were one of the families who *hadn't* cancelled, since Stacey loathed me on principle and barely acknowledged my existence at the best of times. It was clear that my gaffe on the CBC still billowed in the firmament of her mind, because she once again refused to even look at me while making herself at home in my house. I nonetheless offered them something to drink. "Maybe a bit of coffee," Ian said with an apologetic whisper, as if someone had died. The children, meanwhile, ran off noisily to play.

Next came the guest of honour — Jane Elton, along with her husband, Joel, whom I had never met. An impressive mound of a man (four hundred pounds if he was an ounce!), he was one of those people so obese that his earlobes jutted out perpendicular from his head, and an unkempt goatee sprouted out of the moonscape of his face. Both he and Jane had poppies pinned on their fall coats, and seeing them there, I once again felt the acute absence of the three I had already lost throughout the week. Joel wrapped a meaty hand around mine and shook it, but his eyes wouldn't meet mine. *So there you are, in the flesh*, his expression seemed to say, *the guy who thinks we should send business people to jail without a trial.* "Sure, I'll have a drink-drink," he said when I offered him one, but Jane gave him a look over her oversized eyewear.

"Joel, honey, blood pressure."

"Ah," he replied. "Maybe just some orange juice, then."

"And tea for me," Jane said.

When I brought their drinks, Jane touched my arm and asked, "How are you holding up, Philip?" It was the first time she had made reference to what had happened on Monday. Neither she nor any of my editors or publishers had written or called, choosing — perhaps wisely — to maintain radio silence until things blew over.

"It's been a hell of a week," I sighed. "We're all just really, really tired."

"Sorry to hear that," she said with a solemn nod. I half-expected her to say more, to reassure me that as revolting as my slip was, as philosophically inconsistent with everything I had said and done and published up until now, she would still stand with me. But no. Jane seemed unwilling to raise the particulars of my gaffe while in my home. "And the book on Christianity?" she asked instead.

"Oh, the book is fine," I assured her. "I'll still hit my deadline, no worries there."

"That's good," she said. "No, that's good."

Grace insinuated herself. "Yes, it's been a real challenge — having *two* writers in the house, trying to finish books — during all this craziness. I can't speak for Philip, but I certainly feel that *my* boo —"

Our door popped open then, and a female face appeared around it. "Hell-ooo, Sharpe-Dalys," sang the head of our last family to come, another close friend of Grace's. Virginia Steinway was arguably Toronto's best-known and most prolific mommy blogger: I read somewhere that she averaged five posts a day last year, despite having a litter of small children. The oldest three came loudly rushing into our house and went tearing up the stairs in search of their youthful brethren. "No running!" Virginia yelled, an instruction they duly ignored. The fourth, a finger-sucking newborn, dangled face-out in a Snugli strapped to the chest of Virginia's silent, breadwinning husband, Ramon, a software engineer. He gave us all a single, wordless wave.

With everyone now arrived, we migrated to various positions on the ground floor. I donned one of Grace's aprons and took up my place at the stove, where I decanted circles of pancake batter onto the now-heated griddle. Joel sat behind me, wedged into the kitchen table, his glass of orange juice looking very small in his hand, while Virginia and Ramon arranged the various food people had brought — fruit salads and muffins and such — onto the counter. "You can put that one in the fridge," she ordered him, "and then give me the baby." He obeyed, and she went off with the newborn to chat up Jane Elton, who stood alone in the living room admiring our overflowing bookshelves. Grace, Stacey, and Ian, meanwhile, formed themselves into a cozy threesome near Grace's writing nook.

"Did you *see* what Felicity Sanders wrote in yesterday's *Globe*?" Stacey asked.

"I *know*," Grace replied. "And then she called whatshername a *bitch* on Twitter."

I poured myself another Bloody Joseph and then offered some to Ramon, but he shook his head. "Got tea?" he asked, so I fetched him some. The three of us hung out silently there while the women, and Ian, gabbed and gossiped. "So, Joel," I asked to break the quiet as I manoeuvred pancakes onto a cookie sheet, which in turn went into the oven to keep warm until the rest were ready, "what do *you* do for a living?"

What he did was security at Toronto's Pearson Airport, which was pretty much what I imagined him doing. He must have intuited my lack of surprise, because he hastily pointed out that, despite the shift work and endless repetitiveness, it really was a fantastic job, unionized and all that, and one he had held for the last seventeen years. "Janey's essentially self-employed, and her income is real feast or famine," he said, "so it's good that *one* of us has a steady paycheque coming in." Ramon and I nodded, our shared plight.

I then made the mistake of asking Joel if he could remember how much his job had changed in the wake of 9/11. This precipitated a long, convoluted relaying of the minutiae of airport screening, of metal detectors and pat-downs, of liquid and gel allowances, of body scans. Ramon listened politely but I zoned out, shaking and flipping pancakes in the griddle, my exhaustion wanting to drag me to the centre of the Earth. As Joel droned on, my eyes and ears drifted once more to where Grace stood with Stacey and Ian. The girls seemed to have ended their "writing community" bashing and were now speaking to each other *sotto voce*, their heads leaned in at an intimate tilt. My ears burned and my stomach clenched, for I got it into my mind that they were now talking about *me*, about how uncomfortable it was to be here with so much animus over my gaffe still floating in the air, and how *brave* Grace was for not cancelling this brunch outright. Part of me wanted to go bounding over there to defend myself, though I knew that nothing I could say would confute Stacey's low opinion of me.

But then Ian — tall, chiselled, perfect-teethed Nubian Adonis, Ian; he could've been in an Old Spice ad — whispered something, and the girls tittered. Once more the three of them leaned in conspiratorially, and I watched as my wife touched Ian's muscular forearm with affection and said something that might have been, "I would certainly *like* to, believe me." Then she turned and looked upon me at the stove — me, with grotesque comb-over and frilly apron, holding a batter-crusted spatula and looking half-asleep on my feet — and released a brief but pronounced shrug-sigh.

Oh, reader! Just imagine the thoughts that went corkscrewing through my imagination then, what the three of them — the *three of them!* — would get up to, the unspeakable venery, the shadowy midday indulgences with blinds pulled, if only *I* wasn't in the picture. Grace's every treacherous fantasy danced before my eyes. A smell of burning filled my nostrils then, and I turned with the spatula to raise up the pancakes, saw that their underbellies had gone black as a starless night. I flapjacked them onto the cookie sheet anyway, and poured more batter-patties onto the griddle. I then transferred the last of the Bloody Joseph into my Collins glass. Downing the contents in two large gulps, I then went to the kitchen table, to the jug of untouched mimosa. I filled my glass, not caring about the film of tomato juice that clung there.

"— want kids?" Ramon was asking Joel.

"Nah. I mean, yeah. *I* do. I *did*. But, you know." Joel shrugged. I noticed for the first time his loud, stertorous breathing — no doubt a by-product of his obesity, each lungful a Darth Vader snore, even while awake. "It's fine. Janey wanted to concentrate on her career. And we can't really *afford* them now, anyway. We moved back downtown last year — you know, for her work; all the publishers are down here anyway — and it's bloody expensive, let me tell ya."

"God, your commute must be a killer," Ramon said.

"Oh, it's a real killer. But you know," and he twisted that goatee into his best happy-wife-happy-life smile, "you make adjustments."

Never had I wanted so much to beat a person to death with a frying pan. And I might have, too, except Naomi — small, inexhaustible Naomi — came sliding into the kitchen then and hugged me around my aproned legs. "Daddy, I'm honngry. Can I have a strawwwwwwberrrrry?"

Fuck, pancakes take forever.

I was pretty much out on my feet by this point (Naomi's sleepless night becoming mythic inside my addled brain) and trapped in a delirium of rage that felt sourceless. I was again reminded of how uncomfortable everyone seemed around me, as if my slip and its fallout had placed a cloak of unapproachability around my shoulders. Indeed, I was alone in the kitchen now, finishing up the last of the pancakes as the party reshuffled itself. The children had streamed back downstairs, and Stacey and Virginia were now attempting to lead them in a game of charades. Meanwhile, Ramon, Joel, and Ian began transporting food onto our dining-room table and arranging it with modern-husband industriousness. This left Grace to do what she had been waiting to do all along — button-hole Jane Elton near her writing alcove and bring up, once again, the topic of her new children's book.

Ah, yes, Grace. My rage was not so sourceless. I watched as she, nervous and awkward, leaned her bum against the back of her writing chair as Jane stood at her desk. I could see Grace struggling to create a contrivance in which she would ask Jane if she was interested in reading the manuscript, and perhaps representing her. It was all very cryptic and casual at first, but then Grace just went for it. I watched with no small delight as Jane gave her that wonderfully neutral literary agent's smile — no teeth, just the slightest upward squeeze of her cheek muscles — as she waited for her to finish.

Grace explained how far along she was, and how much more time she might need to finish — nine months, maybe a year at most. She then went on to describe the plot of "Sally and the Kitchen Sink," such as it was. Jane's dispassionate face expressed volumes, at least to me. It spoke the unspoken words that I had seen Jane unspeak to dozens of writers at dozens of parties: *Tell me something I haven't heard before. Because if you can tell me something, anything, I haven't heard before, I might just get to eat.*

"Anyway," Grace said, showing hints of deflation, "it's sort of Judy Blume meets Karen Sampstra."

"Oh, I represent Karen," Jane said, suddenly cheery. "A great writer. And a great mum. Did you know she has *five* kids?" She sent her thumb flipping over the small stack of Grace's manuscript pages. "And she still cranks out about three of these a year for me."

And then I could see it in Grace's profile — the abrupt onset of despair. She tried to hide it behind a hostess's pleasant facade, but it conspired with the enervation from our night with Naomi to wink out the small candle of hope she still held for this party. I could tell Grace was reaching for words, looking to speak before Jane did again. And failed.

"Yeah, no, listen. I liked your first two books. I did. They were very *interesting*. But I just think it would be problematic to represent a husband and wife writing team. You know?"

I could tell that Grace's smiling face wanted so much to cry, right then and there. I suppose if the conversation had gone the other way I would have been happy for her, would have glowed in a spouse's mandatory *mudita*. But I'll admit it: the sight of her getting shot down, of that brief moment of powerlessless, filled me with a wild and wholly inappropriate joy. It's petty, I realize, but it felt like I had just captured a large swath of territory in the war we'd been waging all week.

The pancakes were done. I donned oven mitts and then pulled out the now mountainous cookie sheet. I carried it in two hands to the kitchen's archway and, with my biggest shit-eating grin, declared to the house, "Brunch is *served*, everybody!"

Eight adults and Virginia's youngest at the dining-room table — Grace at one end, me at the other — with the rest of the kiddies scattered hither and yon in the living room with their meals on their laps. I indulged in a brief toast, acknowledging the benison of "good friends in troubled times," which caused everyone to stare awkwardly at their plates. Then we resumed the eating and gabbing. As I filled my Collins glass with more mimosa, I noticed with dismay that this brunch — like every other brunch we hosted — was not elevating to the drunken bacchanalia that I always imagined it would. Coffee-drinking Ian discussed the latest action movie — something involving racing cars and guns — with tea-sipping Ramon. Joel with his OJ was still talking about the ins and outs of his airport job in my general direction. Grace and Stacey had resumed their literary gossiping, while Virginia whipped out a breast and began nursing her baby right at the table. Children occasionally popped by to refill their plates or humour our incessant grown-ups' questions.

"Simone, honey, your mum says you're reading *Life of Pi*."

"I am. I'm nearly done."

"This pancake is burn-ed!"

"Well, Naomi, sweetie, don't just put it back."

"Stuart, Cole — coasters please!"

This was my life. I had a vision, then, of my long-dead father and what he would have made of all this. Little Frankie, during my harsh PEI upbringing, had no patience for idle, phatic chit-chat, especially during meals. Meals were a time for serious conversations about serious issues, an opportunity to be engaged citizens. He would have been mortified that we weren't talking about the one thing that every adult around this table was *dying* to talk about — my indefensible rant on the CBC, and what an awful person I was. He'd be mortified that we didn't just clear the air and get it out of the way.

"— make another sequel to it?"

"Well, $280 million at the box office. What do *you* think?"

I poured more mimosa into my Collins glass.

And forgive me here, reader, for our talk turned, as it inevitably does at every Toronto social gathering, to the most phantasmagorically dull topic of all phantasmagorically dull topics — real estate. I was ready to swallow my own tongue in boredom.

"And then they went and paid seven eighty — for that *shoebox* on Lansdowne."

"I know! It's just, it's just *incredible*."

Yes, yes. We all nodded at the incredibility of it. The inflationary nightmare and budgetary strangleholds, the spatial compromises, the bubble that just wouldn't burst. Even cardiologist Ian (via massive student-loan debts and a wife who didn't work) gestured in the affirmative at the recurrent term "house poor." He then said as much. "And to think: my father, who managed a small pharmacy, had a house down here *and* a cottage in the Kawarthas."

Oh gawd. The dreaded *C*-word. I watched Grace, at the other end of the table, perk up right away. This remained a long-standing division in our marriage, whether we (that is, I) could afford to buy us a small family cottage in the Kawarthas. Grace, who had grown up with cottage culture, now longed to return to it as an adult — bright, summery days of unstructured time, with her daughters diving joyously off a lakefront wharf or frolicking in a garden. Grace showed an almost Pavlovian response whenever she heard the *C*-word, and would make her case to me at least once a year. But the fancy math that "proved" our budget could handle it, the sly temptations over having more wall space for our books, the goading promises of how much work I could get done in the cottage-country quietude (as if I weren't prolific enough here at 4 Metcalfe Street) failed to convince me. I obfuscated, delayed, changed the subject, put my foot down, et cetera, et cetera, each time the topic came up.

She was now, across this crowded table, giving me a look, a *well-well-well* tilt of her head.

Thankfully, the matter seemed to be sputtering out. "— could in no way swing it," Ian was saying, "at least until all my loans are paid off."

"Yeah, seriously," Joel wheezed and gasped. "I mean, we can barely afford the house we have. A cottage is completely unrealistic."

"Well, actually …"

We all turned, then, to look at Virginia. She gave a sort of bashful shoulder-bob as she moved the baby off her breast and tucked herself back in. She glanced at Ramon, and Ramon glanced at her, and they did that same self-conscious shrug, together.

"I was going to say something earlier," she went on, "but yeah, no, Ramon and I just bought a cottage — up in Gravenhurst."

"Oh?!" Grace said. Her throat went flush.

"Yeah, yeah. No. Ramon finally settled his parents' estate *and* got his loans paid off this fall. So we looked at the numbers, and we can *just* swing it. Mind you, the place is *tiny* — the kids will have to double up — and it's a bit of a hike to the water. But still. It'll be so nice to have a place of our own to retreat to during the smoggy summer months in the city."

"No, absolutely," Grace said. "Oh, sweetie, I'm so *happy* for you."

"Thanks," Virginia replied, and Ramon gave a nod. "You guys will have to come up and see it. I mean, Grace, I know it's been your *dream* for years to own something up there."

Shut up. Shut up shut up shut up shutupshutupshutup.

"Oh, definitely," Grace said, and then she gave me another of those looks — one that everybody at the table caught. "But *we're* not convinced we could afford it."

Great emphasis, Grace. *We're* not convinced. I felt utterly defenceless, in my exhausted stupor, and totally incapable of building a case in front of these people, the case I often built against this absurd wish of Grace's. I scoured for something, anything, I could say — a mercilessly succinct sentence — to put an end to this conversation.

I reached for the now-empty pitcher. What happened to all the mimosa?

"Of course, it would be great for the kids," Grace went on, "and it's a really good investment."

"Yeah, it's a great investment," Ramon sighed with the tenor of a man forced to believe in magic crystals against his will.

"But we ... well ..." A hush dangled over the table. "We're not sure our budget could take it. I mean, money would probably be tight." Then Grace raised up a cunning, vicious chin to me. "Isn't that right, Philip?" she called over. And once more everyone stared in my direction.

I sneered back at her. "Oh, I know, Grace," I said. "I mean, God — *you'd* have to get a *job*."

I'd like to say, dear reader, that what happened next did not follow that awful Hollywood cliché — the cliché of clinking silverware put on pause, followed by a bone-numbingly uncomfortable silence. I'd *like* to say that, but I can't. All conversation vaporized in the mushroom cloud of my remark. Our guests lowered their heads, as if in prayer. Then Virginia ventured a glance at Grace's gobsmacked face — she looked like she'd been whacked with a paddle — and took her hand in concern. Jane Elton continued staring into her syrup-sticky plate. Stacey Howard, usually so insipidly pretty, now appeared hideous as she looked upon me with unmitigated hate. No one made a sound, save for the metronomic rasp of Joel's breathing.

I gazed into Grace's shocked face. Shocked, and immeasurably hurt. It felt as if an ominous chunk of our marriage's polar ice cap had broken off, and our relationship's very environment would never be the same again. Was I regretful? In that moment, no. I had been dying to say those exact words to Grace all day, all week, all *marriage*. And I felt leavened to have them off my chest now. I threw her a cruel, toothy grimace across the table.

The party broke up pretty quickly after that. We blew through the cantaloupe course and then people motioned to help clear the table.

"No, just leave it," Grace said. "Just, just leave it."

"Okay, we're gonna … we're gonna *go*."

And then people went. As I stood at the dining-room table, stacking plates and gathering cutlery, I could see Grace give each family a quick, perfunctory goodbye at the front door. When it was Stacey and Ian's turn, I watched as Ian leaned down to hug my wife, to rub the side of her arm lovingly, and whisper something in her ear. She nodded when he let her go, touching his sculpted chest with one hand while twining Stacey's fingers with the other. I watched this and seethed.

When everyone was gone, Grace turned back to the house and immediately called over her children.

"Simone, I want you to take Naomi upstairs to your bedroom," she said. "Take her to your bedroom, and close the door."

When she did, Grace came back — ran in, really — to the dining room, and let me have it.

How much are you interested, dear reader, in what transpired next? In one sense, it was a fairly typical domestic row, a bile-spewing stichomythia that orated the inanities of our marriage. On the other hand, you should probably know that Grace and I once again ignored the true catalyst of our fissure — that abominable slip of mine from Monday. Once again we didn't mention it, and ergo mentioned pretty much *everything* else.

Anyway. Here's an abridged transcript to give you a taste.

> … to *humiliate* me like that in front of my friends?!?
>
> *I* humiliated *you*? You're the one airing our money issues in front of company.
>
> We don't *have* money issues, Philip. <WEEPING ANGRILY NOW> Why, oh God … *why* are you so hung up on thinking otherwise? With your cheap loafers and ratty tweed coats, your refusal to get a haircut, and your dismissal of *every penny* my writing brings in …

Why? Because I carry the bulk of the financial burden for this household, Grace, so you can stay home all day and play with the kids and hang out on Facebook ...

Oh my *God!* <UNINTELLIGBLE>

And it's a lot of pressure, okay. It's a lot of responsibility. And if we have money, it's only because I *pulled myself up from NOTHING.* So show me some respect!

You don't deserve respect. I work hard, Philip. I work *damn hard* to raise those girls right and keep this household running while you go off to be a "public figure." So fuck off! You don't deserve respect ... the way you speak to me ...

I only speak the truth, Grace. As I did at the table today. If *you* want a fucking cottage in the fucking Kawarthas, then you'd need to get a fucking job to help pay for it.

You want me to get a "job," Philip? You want to give up all this free child care

You couldn't *get* a job, Grace. You haven't had a *real* job in years. In this economy, you couldn't compete for a secretary's position.

<SLOBBERY WEEPING> Oh my God ... Oh my God ...

I only speak the truth.

Really? Do you say these things because they're true or because you're always drunk?

Oh, is *that* what we're talking about now?

Yes, it is ... yes, it is.

Well, Grace, before you open your trap about

it, you should think long and hard about *why* I feel compelled to always drink.

<UNINTELLIGBLE> … Stacey says I should leave you. She says you're a drunk and I should just fucking leave you.

Well then, why don't you? You could move in with her and Ian. Then you guys could have the *threesome* you've always dreamed about.

What?!? Are you fucking insane??

I see the way you look at each other.

Philip, I can't even begin to imagine how …

<UNINTELLIGBLE, BUT POSSIBLY INTIMATING ABOUT THE SIZE AND GRANDEUR OF A CERTAIN PART OF IAN'S ANATOMY> … and I know you're not satisfied with me. Up there. In our bedroom.

<MORE WEEPING> You're so pathetic, Philip. And also a little racist.

You said as much to me on Monday.

Okay, we *really* need to talk about your drinking. Because you wouldn't even think these things if you weren't <UNINTELLIGBLE> at *EVERY POSSIBLE FUCKING* …

See? You don't really care about this. It's all sort of boring. But what you *might* care about is that after our row reached its expletive-rich crescendo, Grace went tearing up the stairs and, a few minutes later, came back down again clutching an inconsolable Naomi in one arm and an overnight bag in the other. Grace said she was fleeing with our daughter to her parents' place because she couldn't stand to be in the same house with me right now; and no, she didn't know when she'd be back. Simone couldn't come, because Simone had school in the morning, and I damn well better get her out the door on time. I would get a taste of solo child-rearing, if I thought it was so damn easy.

And then Grace and Naomi were gone, leaving me with the wreckage of our — Grace's — brunch to clean up.

So how *would* it work, exactly?

I thought about this as I loaded and unloaded our dishwasher, and loaded it again, stacking the innumerable plates and cups and cutlery we used during the party. I thought about it as I scoured pans and pots and then dried them. I thought about it as I gathered garbage and wiped down counters and tables. I thought about it as I swept the floors. How *would* it work, exactly?

So I leave Grace. I leave Grace for Rani. Figure we should've just been together this whole time anyway, and I get on a plane in January and meet her in Mumbai. I quit my job at U of T and go full-time author, leaving everything back here in Toronto to Grace. She sells 4 Metcalfe Street, buys something cheaper, and lives off the difference until she can upgrade her skills and get a job-job. I send back a full half of whatever income my work generates in alimony and child-support payments. I make a couple trips home a year to spend time with Naomi, and when she's old enough (how old would she have to be?) maybe she'd get on a plane and visit me sometimes. Meanwhile, I become Rani's kept man: I write and read all day in the Indian heat while she works at the BBC, and then we spend our evenings discussing important World Issues and fucking like we used to, back at Oxford. And perhaps Grace will one day meet a man who *wants* to be the malleable Stepford husband she's always wanted. Or maybe she can get into some kind of polyamorous arrangement with Stacey and Ian. He *is* a cardiologist, after all, albeit at the beginning of his career. He'll soon be able to afford two wives. Everybody wins!

Except. Except birthdays. Except graduations. Except watching Naomi grow up. Except walking the girls down their wedding aisles. Except Simone — brainy, compassionate, whimsical, grown-up Simone — whom Grace would ban from my life forever. Except except except.

Also: What if Rani's not the same? We haven't actually seen each other in years. What if we're not really attracted to one another anymore? Or what if she *is* the same, and whatever indifference kept us from committing to each other back at Oxford still lingers? What if that indifference comes roaring back once the novelty of being together has worn off?

And except — what if, despite everything, I still love Grace?

These thoughts made me pretty sad throughout the cleanup. Just as I was finishing, Simone came back downstairs with *Life of Pi* under her arm. She went to the living-room bookshelves, put the tome back in its place, and then came nervously into the kitchen.

"Hey," I said, then nodded at the shelf from whence she came. "Finished?"

"Yep."

"And?"

She rolled her eyes. "Silly cop-out, at the end," she said. "All that — for *that*?"

"Yeah, I know," I agreed. "It basically asks you to believe that two versions of a reality could exist simultaneously, or something. Pretty improbable, if you think about it." A silence hung between us for a moment. "So," I said, and shrugged. "You heard your mum and me fighting?"

She folded her arms over her chest and looked off, a defiant stance. Wow, she really was Grace's little mini-me. "Yep."

"Did Naomi?"

"Yep."

"Was she scared?"

"She was," Simone replied, and then looked up at me. "We both were."

"Believe me, we didn't want you to hear all that," I said. "We really didn't want to scare you."

"I know."

"It's just — there are no words, Simone." I tried to laugh; I tried to make light of it. "I mean, who knew that my off-colour comments about a bunch of corporate jerks would dredge up so much stuff between your mum and me." I realized then that this was the first time I'd actually alluded aloud to the particulars of my slip in this house. It felt pretty good. It felt like getting something off my chest.

Simone raised an eyebrow in confusion. "I don't know anything about that."

But I plugged on. "I mean, I shouldn't have said what I said about those executives, okay. I *get* that. But still. Everybody hates those guys, and yet because *I* said what I said about them, I think people are projecting their anger onto me. Everybody's doing it — including your mother. It's not fair. It's just not fair."

Simone looked even more confused. "I don't *know* anything about that," she repeated. "All I know is that she wishes you'd just hurry up and apologize for threatening to rape that woman on TV."

"When I —" I jarred. "When I — *what?*" I blinked at her. "Simone, what the *fuck* are you talking about?"

"What the fuck are *you* talking about?" replied my thirteen-year-old stepdaughter. Then she looked at me like I was a complete idiot. "Philip, this is what *everybody's* talking about."

I blinked at her again. "No," I said, shaking my head slowly. "No, that's … that's not right."

She gaped at me with both bemusement and a deep concern over my well-being. "Are you trying to make a *joke* or something?"

"Simone …"

"Come with me," she said. "No, come with me."

She led me by the wrist upstairs and into her bedroom. On her nightstand sat her pink iPad, and she brought it over as we settled onto the edge of her bed. She set the thing up on our thighs and quickly found the YouTube clip of my TV appearance on Monday.

"Simone, I can't even bear to —"

"Would you just," she said. "Would you just."

So I watched the clip. I watched it for the very first time. At the beginning I merely harrumphed over the strand of comb-over standing at attention off my skull. *Why hadn't that producer, Lori, I* thought, *done something about it before we went live?*

But then I heard those words. Those fateful, awful words.

"*Well, Cheryl, I would love nothing more than to* penetrate *you with these ideas, but I worry you wouldn't* enjoy *it enough.*"

"And here are the comments," Simone said, sweeping down to them.

And then, for the first time, I read some of them. I mean, I really read them. All of the anger and obloquy, the conversations lapping and overlapping with one another. I read a bunch of them for the first time.

When I finished, I raised my hands. I raised my hands, reader, and then I buried my face into them.

I stayed like that for a long, long time.

"Are you crying?" Simone asked after a while.

"*No,*" I moaned from behind my hands. And then, without lowering them, said, "Simone, I would *really* like to be alone right now."

"This is *my* room."

Then I did look at her, through my spreading fingers. "Right enough," I said, putting my hands down. She moved the iPad out

of the way, and I stood up. I stood up and walked out to the hallway. I walked there, reader, but by the time I reached the stairs
leading to my third-floor office, I wasn't walking anymore.

By the time I got to those stairs, I was running.

Don't say it, dear reader. You don't have to speak a word.

I know what you're thinking. You're thinking: How is this, this
ignoble and implausibly delayed anagnorisis, even possible? How
could all this have really happened? How could I have gone *six days*
without knowing what people were really so upset about? Am I
trying to pull a fast one? Do I think you're all fools?

I don't know what to tell you.

This is what I'll tell you.

The situation requires some context, and I will provide it using
an analogy. The analogy involves that *Globe and Mail* reporter,
Roberta Rosenbaum. I mentioned to you that she and I had dated
briefly in the late 1990s, but I never said how our romance came
to fizzle out. It involved one of the biggest movies to be released in
the summer of 1999: *The Sixth Sense*. We went to see it a couple of
weeks after it arrived in theatres, and scuttlebutt had it that there
was some wild twist, some earth-shattering surprise we should
expect at the end of that film. As we settled into our seats, munch-
ing on popcorn and Twizzler sticks, with the rest of the anxious
audience all around us, we wondered what this purported shocker
might be. Well. I don't think it's bragging to say that I had the
movie's conceit figured out after the very first scene. I mean, *come
on*. I looked around the darkened theatre to see if anyone else had
deduced it. But, it seemed, no one else had. So while the rest of the
audience — including Roberta — lapped it up, I sat there, arms
folded over my chest, tutting and huffing at each elision and near
miss designed to mask the true nature of Bruce Willis's character.

I thought, *What? During the entire course of these events, does he not take a shit? Does he not go for pints with his buddies? Come on!*

After the movie let out and we were walking back to the subway, Roberta went on and on — and *on* — about how brilliant she thought the ending's twist was. "I mean, I was just shocked!" she said. "Were you shocked?" *No!* I frothed. I told her I had figured out the gag after the first scene and found the movie to be the most transparent and manipulative drivel I'd ever sat through. I couldn't believe it had played people for saps. When she got defensive I tore a strip off her, mocking her gullibility and lack of observational skills. "And you're supposed to be a *journalist*," I said. Well. That pretty much spelt the end of us. Roberta, perhaps already doubting my reservoirs of tact, decided that this was a haughtiness too far. Within days, she was letting me know that we'd be better off as "just friends."

But now I get it. Life is full of elisions and near-misses. I could now understand, sort of, what Bruce Willis's character was going through. Like a ghost, you sometimes wander through life trying to do the right thing — or at least the thing that you've always done — by rote, and then just get crushed by a sudden realization, a new, harsh reality that was always there — *it was always there* — and yet you couldn't see it. I thought of my interactions with Sebastian, with dean Tom Howardson, with Phillip at Stout, with — oh *gawd* — Roberta when she finally got me on the phone. Life is full of elisions and near-misses.

But what about *you*, dear reader? Do you believe any of this? Or do you think I've pulled a fast one, played you for a sap, pushed the boundaries of narrative credibility? If so, then go back and reread these pages. Go on. And if you *still* feel that way, then can I ask: Why are you still here? Why didn't you throw this book across the room long ago?

* * *

The SLIP

I hurried to my desk to write a hasty email.

Dear Raj,

Please disregard the script I sent you yesterday. (I'm
only now — duh! — getting caught up with everybody
else.) Obviously I need to write a new one. I'll get it to
you in the next day or so.

Best,
Philip

To my relief, he wrote back right away.

Hey Sharpe,

No worries. I was wondering why you were still going
on about that other stuff. I look forward to seeing
what you come up with.

Raj

Monday, November 9

That's it, reader. No more flashbacks. No more *stalling*. I had work to do.

I had work to do. It became paramount to get down onto paper a *new* script for Raj, what I now called my Proper Apology. I meant all last night to begin it. But the presence of that need was overwhelmed by the absence of something — some*one* — else. Grace. Oh God, the state I was in. I made several drunky attempts to reach her on her cellphone, but she was not answering, she was not answering, she was not answering. Each time her chipper little voicemail greeting — and not her voice — kicked in, it felt as if this very house, and, perhaps, our entire marriage, grew more permanently empty. I eventually declared defeat and crawled into bed on my hands and knees. It was still *early* — Simone hadn't even retired for the night yet — and what I'd hoped for was a brief, refreshing blackout before starting work on my new script. But instead I awoke hours later, and feeling as if someone had broken into 4 Metcalfe Street and beaten me up in my sleep. My temples ached; my muscles throbbed; my stomach churned with nausea. But these maladies soon paled in comparison to the shame, my humiliating and disgraceful conduct from the previous day, the previous *week*, that came dredging back to my mind as I lay on my half of the marital bed. The ignominy of it all spread over me like a bloodstain. I decided to force myself vertical and get to work. It was 4:30 in the morning.

I went upstairs to my office, flopped down at the desk, and turned on my laptop. The bookshelves along the wall stood crammed with the weight of Western thought. The little attic window facing the street still cupped the night's darkness. Launching a fresh Word document, I lay my fingers on the keys, determined to unleash an unbridled *mea culpa*, a colourful cavalcade of penitence, onto that white phantom page. But did I? Of course not. What kind of moron tries to write something coherent at 4:30 in the morning? I sat staring at the cursor's slow, steady heartbeat, its rhythmic blink. I stretched my shoulders. I pinched my nose. I leaned in. I leaned back. I twiddled my fingers.

I checked email. For once, there were no new messages; not a single ping from the Facebook. I felt almost jilted. *Should I go back*, I thought, *and try to wade through what social media's Greek chorus had been saying about me all week*? Yes, yes, that seemed like the reasonable thing to do. I clicked on my DELETED folder and began trawling through the notifications I'd been batch-removing from my inbox. *Oof!* How could I have been this reckless? The scandal's entire trajectory, my public knouting, was laid out there in black and white. At first, the participants were focused on me, but then quickly shifted as they turned on each other. It was amazing how people who had roughly the same world view and specific agreements on what a shitbag I was could go hammer and tongs at each other over the most minute of points. "*No, Raymond, I already KNOW the legal definition of assault YOU'RE the one who could use a dictionary okay*," howled someone. "*Suzie, did you even read my comment above? Scroll back up and just READ it, okay?*" howled someone else. The arguments got pretty heated;

the comments grew increasingly lengthy, increasingly essay-like, as each contributor meticulously split the hairs of a previous split hair. As I worked my way through the days, a few commenters dropped links to news stories about my slip, and I clicked on them. These pointed to articles, columns really, written by frosty feminists (so many of them seemed to have their own columns now), their cross-looking thumbnail headshots parked above their words of wisdom. And what wisdom! Yes, yes, yes. These gals laid bare exactly why my dig at Cheryl Sneed had been indicative of larger issues in our culture, and why such a gaffe had been so unsettling, so vicious, so … *exhausting*. Yes, yes, yes. It was like I read these insights with a brain I hadn't even possessed twenty-four hours earlier.

When I finished, I returned to my blank Word doc. *Okay — here we go here we go here we go.* I clenched my fingers into talons over the keys. I grit my teeth. I hummed. But still. Nothing came. Nothing came. Eventually, I glanced up at the computer's clock. Wow. More than two hours had passed. I thought I should maybe go then and get Simone up for the day. But then I heard movement through the house below me.

"Hey, Philip?" Simone called from the landing. "Philip, are you there? Have you seen my *math book*?"

The morning rolled on. I brought the newspapers in from the porch while Simone poured us a couple bowls of cereal. These rituals seemed to exacerbate the absence we both no doubt felt in the house. At this point in the morning, Grace would have been passing judgment on Simone's choice of wardrobe or asking about activities upcoming in the week; Naomi would have been filling the air with her playful three-year-old's banter. Instead, the kitchen seemed stuffed with silence as Simone and I moved through our respective tasks. Each time her cellphone buzzed, I felt my heart strum like a guitar string. *Was that your mother?* I wanted to ask.

We ate together and I checked her homework. I must have looked like shit, reader, because when I finished Simone touched my hand and asked, "Are you okay?" I experienced a small spark of anger at her abbreviated politeness. It was that sort of thing that had helped keep me in the dark all week. *Don't say "Are you okay?"* I thought. *Say "Are you okay that you've now discovered you verbally assaulted a woman on national television?"*

But I just nodded.

She nodded back. "Okay. I have to go now."

So we got up, and she went to the closet and put on her coat, and I helped her don her bookbag. She reached for the doorknob but then spun on her heels. "Oh shoot — I don't have a *lunch.*"

I promptly dug my wallet out and slipped her three twenties. "Is that enough?" I asked.

Simone's eyes bloomed at this offering, but — ever the miniature adult — she passed two of them back to me. "I'll be fine," she replied.

And then she was gone.

I turned back to the empty house, the empty day spread out before me, a wide and vague terrain of unlimited freedom. *Wow,* I thought, *so this is what it feels like for Grace after she's shooed us out the door.* But I wasn't creatively charged by all the unstructured time. In fact, I felt somewhat oppressed by it — like there was a looseness, a bagginess to the hours ahead that would stifle my return to the aberration up in my office, that blank Word document. There was nothing standing between me and my Proper Apology, and thus it felt as if *everything* stood between us.

I returned to the kitchen to read the newspapers. Now that I'd gotten a taste of what people had been saying about me all week, I was keen to catch any mention of my slip, a residual article about it from seven days on. I started with the *Toronto Times*, flipping through news stories of earthquakes and budget reports, ISIS executions and the unravelling Canadian economy. Had I missed the boat? Were all the printed palavers about Philip Sharpe's behaviour already over?

But then I reached the op-ed section and saw my name — *my name!* — in the headline of one of the columns. Whose column? Come now, reader. Who do you think? Yes, it was *her*. Of course it was. Her column ran on Mondays, Thursdays, and Saturdays, a reliable deluge of down-home conservatism. I stared at her thumbnail headshot, thinking what I always thought whenever I saw her thumbnail headshot: *Oh, wow, dear, you do not look like* that *anymore.* I settled in to read the words below her incendiary headline.

Get over yourselves, ladies: Philip Sharpe did not threaten to "rape" me
By Cheryl Sneed

Here's how you know our "culture wars" have jumped the shark: when feminists come racing to *my* defence.

I've waited a full week to write about what happened last Monday during my appearance on CBC-TV's *Power Today*. I wanted to take full stock of what has been an explosive public reaction before I waded into the fray. For those of you living under a porch these last seven days, here's what happened: Last Monday I was on that show to discuss the collapse of ODS Financial Group with University of Toronto professor and prominent left-wing intellectual Philip Sharpe, a man I've been having a low-level feud with for about 10 years now. Truth is, I've always had a grudging admiration for Philip

— he's a cunning thinker and seems to have the entire canon of Western thought at his fingertips at all times — and I knew that, with the ODS failure being such big news, our "discussion" would quickly turn into a "debate."

And it did. Things got very heated very quickly, but for some reason Philip seemed frazzled and not at all himself. One thing led to another, and just before we went off the air, he made some comment (more nonsensical than horrific) about wanting to "penetrate" me with a bunch of the wishy-washy ideas he'd been spouting.

Naturally, the feminist media erupted into indignation. The usual clique of sensitivity queens began howling for his blood and pointing to his slip as further evidence of our so-called "rape culture." The mandarins running U of T promptly sent out press releases throwing their star professor under the bus, and they set up a "safe space" for any students who had even *heard* about the incident. Parents demanded Philip be fired. Anyone who dared defend him or downplay his comment was promptly skewered on Facebook and Twitter. The public shaming industrial complex shifted into high gear.

Philip, to his credit, has not gone grovelling for forgiveness (unlike so many other men who have fallen victim to this kind of overblown witch hunt). He has stayed wisely silent, save for one ill-phrased "statement" to my colleague, journalist Roberta Rosenbaum — a comment I am convinced could not have possibly been on the record.

Well. Here's what *I* think.

I think feminists have once again taken a minor idiotic remark by a man and amplified it to promote themselves and their sanctimonious ideology. What's most galling is that these women have come racing to *my* defence. It's as if pigs have started enlisting in the Air Force! Well, get over yourselves, ladies. I am not a "victim." Philip Sharpe did not threaten to "rape" me. And I *don't* need your indignation. The only reason I didn't deal with his blunder in the moment was because it came right at the end of our segment and the host was desperate to go to commercial. Had there been even 20 seconds left, I would've shot Philip down for saying something so tasteless to me.

Why? Because in my day, that's how you dealt with males who did stupid things. If a man made an off-colour joke at you, you chewed him out right away. If he said something inappropriate about your clothes, you gave it right back to him. If he tried to grab a boob in the photocopy room, you elbowed him in the ribs and told him to knock it off. Today's young feminists don't want to hear this, but men are hard-wired for high-risk behaviour, and it's our job to correct them when they go out of bounds with us. It's called having agency, a term that today's feminists don't even know the meaning of.

I guess what I find so infuriating about this situation is how predictable the fallout has been. It's always the same young feminists who kick-start the fracas. These women, who have so many platforms now to spew their misguided beliefs, spend their whole day, their whole *careers*, snivelling about sexism and chasing the chimera of so-called "gender equality." I guess this is what happens when we hand over our media and arts coverage to teenagers.

Philip Sharpe is by no means perfect, but he didn't deserve the vitriol and ad hominem attacks he suffered last week. I don't see eye to eye with Philip on many things, but I consider him a worthy adversary and someone who has earned our respect. His comment at me was inappropriate, but it wasn't *literal*. It had no violent or sexual intention behind it.

In the end, it was a slip, ladies. It was only a slip. And it's incredibly irresponsible of you to preach otherwise to your choirs.

I closed the newspaper over and stood up from the kitchen table. Un.

Speakable.

CUNT!

But then I stopped myself. I thought: *No, no. We're not reacting that way to things anymore.* If you can't help thoughts like that from travelling over the transom of your brain, then you need to *keep your fucking mouth shut.*

It all seemed pretty simple, really.

I nonetheless felt armed to tackle what I wanted to say in my Proper Apology. I went to my bar fridge and mixed myself an extra stiff — *very* stiff — Bloody Joseph and then trudged back upstairs to my office. I roosted at my desk, opened my laptop, and returned to my blank Word document. Oh, Ms. Sneed, you have *no idea* the grovelling I'm about to exact onto this page. Just watch me!

My mouth gawped. My fingers curled. I leaned in.

I leaned back.

I sipped my Bloody Joseph. The cursor slowly tick-tocked atop that endless white page.

I gulped my Bloody Joseph. The whole tomatoey mess slid down my throat.

I leaned in. I tapped the side of my laptop, lazily, with my spread fingers.

I leaned back.

Oh, for fuck's sake!

I checked email. What else could I do? When you become engulfed in hesitancy, when you actually feel terror rather than ambition at the sight of a page's taunting blankness, you'll look for anything to distract yourself from your fears. Email's great because email is a living thing: at any moment, another polyp of inquiry can sprout up in your inbox, demanding your attention.

And that was exactly what had happened. There was a new message waiting for me there. It had, according to its time-stamp, come in while I'd been eating breakfast with Simone.

It was from Sebastian.

Oh Jesus.

His subject line, so ominous in its simplicity, so precise in its foreshadowing, pierced me right through my sternum. It read:

Grad school

Oh Jesus. Oh Jesus Christ. With my mind coiling backward to last Thursday's class, I knew exactly what Sebastian was going to say, what he was going to *do*.

I didn't want to open his message. But I opened it anyway.

The SLIP

Dr. Sharpe,

This letter is to inform you that I'm dropping out of the Ph.D. program. This may come as a surprise, but please know that I didn't reach this decision lightly or in haste. I've been grappling with it for a long time now, and I suppose the events of last week have helped snap into focus why this is the right decision.

There are many things that you taught me that I'll never forget. I still remember that incredible rant you went on at the beginning of your David Hume seminar five years ago, when you reminded us all — a roomful of neurotic grad students in desperate need of reminding — why a liberal arts education was so important. You said that a liberal arts education taught the most important skill that anyone with any kind of imagination can have: to spot patterns in disparate bits of information so that we might create something new. You kept repeating that, like a mantra we needed to hear as we set out on our own intellectual journeys: *Spot the pattern, create something ... Spot the pattern, create something new.*

But you said something else that day. You said that studying the Humanities not only taught us what it meant to be human, but also what it meant to be humane. That's what you said: that by the time you were through with us, we'd be "masters and doctors of humaneness." Well, I think it's fair to say that you have fallen down on that role, on that obligation, over the last week. I don't care what your excuses were for not coming to that protest; and I can't even fathom why you would make such a repugnant statement about your actions to that *Globe and Mail* reporter. Rape jokes, Dr. Sharpe, are not jokes. Women deal with this shit every day of their lives. They do. And it just crushes me that you — you, of all people — couldn't spot *that* pattern in order to create something new, to make amends for your fuck-up on TV. Your failure to do that undermines pretty much everything you taught us. What's more, it exposes your ideas for the peacock-like posturing that they are.

Of course, you are not the sole reason I'm dropping out. I'm going to be thirty in a couple of months. I've been in university for the last eleven years. I have no real job experience; I have no real practical skills. But clearly I need some: every day I read another article about how the academy is dying, how cohort after cohort of Ph.D. graduates are finding nothing but adjunct positions or sessional work at serf-labour wages. Meanwhile, I have friends and relatives my own age who have started their grown-up lives — kids and a house and all the rest — and I'm scared shitless that I'll miss out on all that. So I'm cutting my losses now. I can't devote any more of my youth to what is clearly a bill of goods. I can't dedicate my life to what is clearly a lie.

Please know that I will fulfill my TA obligations until the end of term. You will have me until January. But then I'm out.

Yours sincerely,
Sebastian

I became pretty unhinged after reading that. Getting up, I paced my office floor for a while. Then I sat down again. Then I stood up again. Then I sat down again. Then I clicked REPLY.

Dear Sebastian,

I can't express how gutted I feel after reading your email. Forgive the corniness, but this truly is a professor's worst nightmare, to lose a grad student in this way. I say that not just because I've invested so much time in mentoring you, but also because you're so close to the finish line and have such potential to be a great scholar and teacher. I feel deeply ashamed that my actions last week have played a role — large or small — in this very serious decision.

But you're right. I couldn't spot the pattern before. You wouldn't believe me if I told you, but I completely *missed* the pattern all last week.

I see it now. I see it, and I am utterly disgusted with myself.

While I respect your decision to leave the program, I want to ask if you would give it, and me, one last chance. I ask that you not make your *final* decision until after tomorrow's class. I'm going to do what I should've done a week ago: get all this out in the open, and talk candidly and transparently with our students about my actions. Let me do that, and if you still want to leave graduate school after I'm done, I will support your decision one hundred percent.

Yours very sincerely,
Philip

After I hit SEND, I rested my head on the edge of the desk and thought about tomorrow's class. *Gawd.* I had given myself yet another task to do.

I looked at my screen and turned back to the waiting Word doc. But I felt like an empty husk now. I couldn't bear to confront the page's emptiness. I couldn't even bring myself to put fingers onto the keys.

I went downstairs looking for something to distract me. I made an early lunch, ate it, and then washed and dried all the dishes from it and from breakfast. Then I got an idea. Our front entry closet held a floppy old copy of the Yellow Pages, one I had refused to throw out despite Grace's protestations. I took it down from the shelf and flipped to the listing for plumbers. If I was to suffer such a perplexing blockage at the word processor, I might as well use this time to do the thing I had promised Grace I would do, the thing that had caused this whole mess to begin with. I found a tradesman we hadn't used before and called to get a quote. His price was *ghastly* — I gasped at it — but then I booked him anyway to come on Friday. I would get that goddamn, motherfucking tub fixed once and for all.

Then I decided to get an early jump on dinner. Grace kept a copy of the Milk Calendar hanging inside our pantry door, and upon it I discovered this month's recipe: phyllo chicken and root vegetable pot pie. I jotted down the lengthy list of ingredients and then sallied off to our local Loblaws — a former hockey arena transmogrified into a bountiful, brightly lit mecca of yuppie consumerism. I returned home with my purchases and spent a vigorous forty-five minutes prepping this hearty autumnal meal — precooking chicken and chopping potato, carrots, parsnips, and squash, then sculpting the sheets of phyllo pastry like an artisan — before parking the dish into our overcrowded fridge for later. Then, again, I washed and dried all the dishes.

After that, I searched once more for the tug, the impulse, the gravitational lure to return to my writing desk, my as-yet-unbegun Proper Apology. But no. It was like a mental boulder was blocking the route to my third-floor office.

So what to do? What *do* you do, reader, when you "don't feel like writing"? I went up and checked the communal hamper in the bathroom, but the laundry situation was well under control. I went downstairs and gazed into our backyard from the dining-room window, but Grace had clearly done a recent job of raking up the leaves. I went into the kitchen and yanked open the oven door. That grey cauldron was a bit grimy, but not quite ready for a cleaning. I turned my attention then to the fridge, its shelves and crispers. But everything was, more or less, spotless.

Reality sunk in. I wasn't going to find anything to abet my procrastination here in Grace's domain. She had, I could tell, all her little systems and routines to keep the household and its multitudinous chores under control. What's more, as I stood there trying to find some domestic (don't say trifle, don't say trifle) task to divert me from the one thing I didn't want to do, I began to see this space, Grace's effusively chipper terrain, in a whole new light. I hadn't realized just how much of my wife's sun-kissed personality was all over this kitchen: the colourful backsplash on the wall; the daisies in their vase; the skillfully hung artwork and bunting; the corkboard arrangements; the fridge door with its effortless collage of thank-you notes and 100-percent homework assignments and a black-and-white photo-booth strip in the middle, pictures of Grace and Simone and Naomi during some midday sojourn to the mall, grinning and laughing and faux-posing in each shot, the three of them looking so carefree, so joyous, like they had just pulled off the biggest scam in history. Where was *I* that day?

I want my wife, I thought. *I want my fucking wife.*

I went to the cordless and, once more, phoned Grace's cell. It rang and rang, but she wouldn't answer. I knew she knew it was me. Who else would be calling from our land line? But she wouldn't pick up. She just wouldn't.

I want my fucking wife, I thought. *I want Grace.* I want this woman, this woman — this woman of whom, perhaps, I haven't even painted a proper portrait for you yet. Grace was, she was, she was — what? What? Oh, reader, you haven't seen anyone laugh until you've seen Grace Daly laugh. Arms wrapped around torso, body coiled inward on couch, head thrown back in uncontrolled rapture. No one allows happiness, when happy times come, to inhabit every molecule of her body the way Grace does. And that — that cocky jut of her chin. Those smooth, confident glances at the kids. The wisdom. The wild green eyes. And the *temper* — did I mention her temper? Even that seemed sexy, sometimes. And also her astuteness, her ability to cut through bullshit with one keen-eyed remark and get to the heart of a matter, of any matter that mattered. I mean, *gawd*, I just want to fuck her on the spot when she does that. And yes, yes, she was vain, so very, very vain, and deeply insecure about her writing, about being a writer, and even about her true métier, her motherwork. But you know, she felt that if you just surrounded yourself with a bunch of fat-brained feminists, if you yourself *became* a fat-brained feminist, why, then there was no telling what you could accomplish with your life, irrespective of fate. I mean it was just so, it was just so … *adorable*. And, and, and — have I ever mentioned her smells? Oh, her smells! The cottony, baby-powder scents of the flannels she'll wear to bed in winter? Or the aromas that get trapped in her hair? Or her lips? Her *lips*. Even that wet sheen they get when she's been talking for too long has a fragrance I can't get enough of. And also — she loves me? She loves me. She *loves* me. We met when I was forty-two and I had never been loved, not really, not *properly*, and she just went about the business of it, the business of loving me, and, and, and … I want my wife. I want my wife. I want my fucking —

I called Rani. Unlike Grace, she picked up — following another oceanic delay — on the third ring.

"Hello."

"Hey, Rani."

And she chuckled. Oh, reader, how she chuckled. "Philip Sharpe, are you *still* trapped inside my mobile?"

"I'm afraid I am, yes." I sniggered back. "How are you?"

"I'm okay," she replied. "How are *you*?"

I grunted, loudly, in despair. "Are you free to talk?" I asked.

"Well, I was just about to head home — it's been another *long* day here — but I've now been told to stay back. There's an update coming on that Russian passenger plane that went down in Egypt. But I have a couple of minutes."

"You know, you work too hard," I said.

"*Phwore* — look who's *talking*, Mr. Full Professor with Ten Books Published by Age Fifty." She gave a light laugh. "You and me, we're both wired for hard work. Isn't that right, Sharpe?"

"Absolutely," I replied, trying not to turn my thoughts to the blank Word doc waiting for me upstairs. "So listen," I went on. "Before I start, I wanted to ask you something. What do you think I did last week? I mean, what did I really say on TV to enrage the entire world?"

"What, are you taking the piss?" she asked in bafflement. "Sharpe, do you need me to repeat it? '*I would love nothing more than to penetrate you with these ideas ...*' Was — was there any *doubt* about that?"

"Not a gram," I said. "Not, not now." The fact that she said this cast our Saturday conversation on the phone — and Rani herself — in a whole new light. I pressed the ball of my hand into my forehead. "Anyway, the situation here has gotten far worse. My wife and I had a huge fight yesterday, and right in front of 'brunch company' no less."

"Oh *Jesus*, Sharpe."

"Yeah, I know. She stormed out of here with our kid, and I haven't seen them since. Yeah. So — yeah." I took a breath. "Anyway. I've been thinking a lot about what you said to me on Saturday. I have. And, Rani, I just, I just — can't. Okay? I mean, even if everything here goes to shit and it all falls apart, I ... I can't. I just can't. I'm sorry."

"What did I say?" she asked, kind of cheekily.

"What, are *you* taking the piss now?" I waited for her to answer but she didn't. "Rani, you asked if I'd run away with you to India."

"Oh, Sharpe," she replied, "I was just — I was just joshin' around."

"No, you weren't." I felt myself grow a touch angry. "Rani, you weren't."

There was a long, staticky pause on the line. So long, in fact, that I thought our connection had dropped and I'd lost her. But then she cut back in.

"Do you know what all this reminds me of?" she asked. "It reminds me of those articles that came out a couple of years ago, that said that scientists now believe there are 'parallel universes' existing somewhere. Did you read those articles, Sharpe? Of course you did — you read *everything*. Anyway, I saw those and found myself strangely heartened by them. You know? I thought: Maybe out there, in the vastness of space, there's another version of Earth somewhere, an alternative reality to the one we're living. And in that alternative reality, you and I decided to just take the plunge with each other, back in '93. I thought about that, and wondered if we were still together in that reality, and still happy with one another. Isn't that crazy?"

It *was* crazy, I thought. It was batshit nuts. But also not. And that felt weird.

"Rani, I have to live in the reality I'm in," I said with the definitiveness of someone yanking a plug out of the wall.

"Yeah, I know," she replied. "Me, too."

There was another pause, and then she asked:

"So I guess this is it, eh?"

"Yeah, I think so."

"Well, I realize it's the second time I've said this in twenty-two years, but it's been great knowing you, Sharpe."

"You too, Rani."

"Okay." And then she hung up, very quickly. I sighed, and then I hung up, too.

Somehow, through a tremendous act of will, a great force of fortitude, I managed to return to my upstairs office. With a fresh Bloody Joseph in hand, I manoeuvred myself behind my desk and returned to my Word document. I could sense the opening salvo of my Proper Apology, of what I'd been trying to say all day, coalesce and swell at the front of my mind. I got that familiar urge to shoehorn words onto the page with great authority and skill. I felt immense relief that it was finally going to happen.

I leaned in. Sipped my Bloody Joseph. Munched absently at its celery stick. I placed fingers on keys. Twiddled them. Waited.

And waited.

I leaned back.

Fuck. Fuck. Fuck fuck fuck fuck FUCK FUCK FUCK FUCK!

So, reader, I just sort of sat there awhile, not moving, barely even breathing. My desolation felt almost hypnotic. Would words not come? Would words *never* come again?

Before long I heard the front door of 4 Metcalfe Street pop open. "Hell-lo," Simone called out as she returned home from school, and I shot up from my desk. I came bounding down the stairs desperate to greet her and hear about every last piece of minutiae from her day. I got an immediate faceful of it, like the hot air from an oven door freshly opened. "… can't even, okay, if Caitlin thinks like that," she said in mid-sentence, in mid-thought, as she threw her bookbag on the kitchen counter. "I mean, that's what I *said*, but that's not what I *meant*. And if she's gonna act that way then she can't come when Sarah and me go to the Eaton Centre for that thing on …" Yes, yes. I understand completely. We soon talked about the evening's homework assignments, and she got down to them at the kitchen table while I put on the pot pie for dinner. I kept glancing at her bowed head, wanting to ask the questions that had been stirring in me all day: *Have you heard from your mother? Have you and Grace been texting at all? I tried calling her earlier but she wouldn't answer ...* Putting these to Simone felt like a bridge too far, like an invasion of their mother-daughter privacy, so I bit my tongue.

We set the table together and then tucked in to the pot pie. Our conversation was stilted as we ate. At one point, Simone's glitter-encrusted cellphone rumbled on the table, and she picked it up to glance at its screen. Then she looked at me and saw what I'm sure was an expectant stare on my face. All those questions, those anxieties, no doubt flaring in my eyes.

"She just needs her time," Simone said. "Philip, she just needs her time."

Ah.

Got it.

After dinner we did the dishes and then I gave Simone an hour of screen time. After that, we read books together in the living room — me returning to my bulky biography of the British working class; she rereading one of the later Harry Potter novels, which she adored — and then it was soon time for bed. Unlike Naomi, Simone was fairly self-sufficient in this regard. She passed by the living room at one point, PJ'd and teeth-brushed, to fetch a glass of water to take up to her bedroom. She did not stop by as I read my book to give me a hug or a kiss; she just tossed me one of her crook-armed, thirteen-year-old's waves before sprinting, like some pajama-clad fawn, back up the stairs. *You're growing up way too fast, young lady*, I thought.

* * *

Okay, this stopped being funny twelve hours ago.

I sat at my desk, seething — once again — at the screen's wretched whiteness. How could this be happening to me? I mean, Rani hit the proverbial nail on the proverbial head: I *am* Mr. Full Professor with Ten Books Published by Age Fifty. I do this. This is what I do. I put words on pages. Pound out books, columns, articles, essays, ephemera. I do this. This is what I do.

It was there, somewhere. I knew it. The case I wanted to make in my Proper Apology, all the things I wanted to say, about Cheryl Sneed, about women, about the world they lived in, and why I was a complete shitbag for having said what I said. It was there. It was there. It was all there — wasn't it?

Okay, Sharpe, I thought. *Just get something down. Anything. Put something on that page before you call it a night. Don't let this be a wasted day.*

So I placed fingers on the keys and typed:

The

I stared at it, that one word.

Fuck it, I thought. *Fuck it all to hell.*

Then I saved my "work," closed my laptop, and sent myself to bed.

Tuesday, November 10

Today, the Internet tells me, is Tuesday, November 10. The weather sites say Toronto will be rainy with a high of plus nine degrees. It is the kind of day, perhaps, that induces clinomania in a certain type of person. The sort of day where you think (*you* think; I certainly wouldn't) that it's better to remain in bed all day, not face the world at all, just lie there under your body-warmed sheets and receive a long, mellifluous blow job from your stay-at-home wife. Your stay-at-home wife stays at home, after all. She might as well make herself useful. (I, of course, would *never* think this. And besides, my stay-at-home wife was not at home. Day 3 and still no sign of or any word at all from Grace.) Yes, the weather sites indicate it's going to be that kind of day. Meanwhile, let's check the headlines: 25,000 Syrian refugees will be coming to Canada. The new PM says so. Come on in, boys, the water's fine. Canada has a new PM? Is Harper really gone? Ah, yes, the Sprout got himself elected last month, and via a landslide no less. In the *meshugas* of threatening to rape a woman on live TV, I must have forgotten to mention that. I like the new PM. I wasn't planning to. But then he proved himself a genuine centrist, and I ended up agreeing with every last thing he said. That's the thing about being a genuine centrist. I'm sure the Sprout feels the same way. It's like attending the most affable dinner party over and over again, every single day, all the time. I think this is why I'm a centrist. It's the only way someone like me has any hope of achieving affability. Meanwhile, the news tells me, Calgary's commercial real-estate market is in free fall thanks to dropping oil prices. The collapse of ODS Financial Group won't help matters — the firm had, like, three offices out there. Also, today is the fortieth anniversary of the sinking of the *Edmund Fitzgerald*. Well. I know the feeling, on both counts. I get your vibe, Edmund. I understand where you're coming from, Calgary. I'm down there in the depths with you both.

Indeed, for the second morning in a row, I had risen early, very early, too early, an anxiety stirring me awake like nightmares, like a fast and unshakeable terror, and I crept in the pre-dawn darkness up to the my third-floor office, closed the door, sat down, opened my laptop, opened my Word doc, and glared at that travesty, that train wreck, that abomination of the previous day's output. The future of my Proper Apology felt more uncertain than ever. What was its structure, its *skopos*, its range? How should it begin? What crescendos should it build to? What were its points of reference, its *point?* I had nothing. I had nothing.

What's more, in a few short hours I would need to face my survey course students and the promise I had made to Sebastian. The thought of it filled me with a rancid dread. If only I could get something down now, onto that limitless Word doc, it might provide me a kernel of inspiration to confront my hostile classroom. Or maybe the opposite was true: maybe engaging my students and Sebastian about my unconscionable acts last week might trigger a bit of stimulation to this lifeless endeavour, this clogged creation. I thought about that as the early morning hours passed. I rested fingers on keys, begging fate that at least an opener, a brave beginning, might now emerge.

Beyond my closed door, I could hear movement on the third-floor landing.

"Philip? Philip, are you there? I don't think this homework's right. Can you come help me?"

Gladly.

The homework was not right — assignments in column B were for Wednesday night, weirdly; assignments in columns A and C were due now — so I got Simone to fix them while I made us a breakfast of cereal and toast. As we ate I checked her work and deemed it satisfactory. She packed up her bookbag and I did the thing I forgot to do yesterday: I made her a lunch, assembling tuna sandwich with avocado, accompanied by yogurt, pear, banana, and granola bar. She deemed it satisfactory. Then I assessed her wardrobe. "Maybe a sweater today?" I asked, conjuring Grace's guidance. "That brown turtleneck you got for Christmas last year?" Simone agreed.

In the front entry, I helped her into her raincoat and then she squeezed her bookbag onto her narrow shoulders, pulling the straps tight. Perhaps I was expecting a few words of encouragement from my stepdaughter before she left. *Have a great day writing, okay. I'm sure you'll knock it out of the park.* I was, after all, almost certain that she has said those exact words to Grace during her own interminable bouts of writer's block. But Simone did not say this to me. She just grabbed our only functional umbrella out of the hall closet, yanked open our front door, and slipped out into the morning with her usual, cheery "Okay, bye!" and then was gone.

I harrumphed, there in the wake of her absence.

* * *

Squeeze, dash, shake-shake-shake, pour. The Bloody Joseph and I headed upstairs where I took a shower (gingerly dancing around the nozzle's random spurts of scalding), got dressed, then marched myself back up to my office with new-found zeal. I was done fucking around, reader. This was it. This was *it*. I didn't need morale-boosting from a child. I didn't need inspiration from a gaggle of undergraduates. This was *it*.

I sat down and settled in at my laptop. Okay. Just apologize for what you did, Sharpe. Get it out. Get it done. This is it. Be genuine. Be sincere. Make it HUGE.

Here we go here we go here we go.

I leaned in. I leaned back. I farted lustily.

Oh sweet goddamn motherfucking Jesus — *what is wrong with me?!?*

For the longest while I sat there in a haze, in a daze, in a dysthymic trance, pouring the Bloody Joseph's last gulps down my gullet with a rhythmic, mindless tilting of my hand, like I was one of those weighted drinking birds you see on office desks sometimes. I was *drooping*, reader. I was withering on the vine. I was just about ready to curl up into a fetal position there in that chair. I was just about ready to die. I *was* going to die. I was going to die right then, right there, at that desk. Goodbye, world. I'm going to die now. I'm going to *die* at this goddamn desk.

Then I had a revelation. Yes, yes. Perhaps what we needed, reader, was to get back to first principles. You know? We needed to return to some kind of pre-computer, pre-*typewriter* age where it was just us, our minds, and the most basic of chirographic implements. *Yes, yes,* I thought. A *corking* idea. The first draft of my biggest-selling book had been written by hand, after all. And so, too, would this.

I rolled over to my filing cabinet and dug out a fresh pad of canary paper, then rolled back and grabbed a pen (uni-ball Vision blue — accept no substitutes) out of the jar on the desk's corner. Then I had another thought: perhaps I needed a change of scenery, too. I mean, if you're going to apologize for threatening to rape a woman, maybe you shouldn't be surrounded by book-shelves stuffed with canonical works of Western philosophy. So I flung myself — and I mean *flung* myself — out of my office with pen and pad in hand. Oh, yes, there was a real spring to my step now. I went down and set my gear up at the kitchen table. Yes, yes, this was *perfect*.

Squeeze, dash, shake-shake-shake, pour. I sat down, uncapped the uni-ball, and sipped.

I stared at the pad for — oh God, I don't know how long. I tapped the table with the pen's end. I fluttered the pad's pages with my thumb. Was this not just like that afternoon at Oxford, all those yesterdays ago, with Rani, in post-coital cheekiness, telling me to fuck off and stop whining (no, no, not whining — whinge-ing, *whingeing*; such a great British term) and write what I damn well wanted to write? Yes, it was exactly like that. So do it, Sharpe. Stop your whingeing and write.

I stared into the canary pad's deep yellow soul. *Oh, please,* I thought. *Please release me — release my* mind. *You can do it. You can. You've done it before. So do it. Do it now. Now!*

I leaned in. I leaned back. I let out a weepy sigh.

Then I looked up at the clock on the wall.

Oh fucking Christ!

I hate being late. I am always late.

I tried to nab a Beck on Parliament Street, but no Becks came. So I stood at the bus stop, but the bus wouldn't come. So I began walking through the drizzle northward to Castle Frank Station. When I was almost exactly between my stop and the next, the bus came rumbling by, its wide rump jostling, its exhaust pipe spewing black death. I chased after it, running in that shambling way that fifty-year-old men try to run when they're late. But it was no use. I arrived at Castle Frank Station on foot, wheezing and gasping and drenched. I paid my fare and went down to the platform. Then I waited. And waited. There soon came an announcement — that cringe-inducing, robotically staccato voice — over the PA.

"Attention. Passengers. On line two. We are currently experiencing. A delay. WESTBOUND. At. BROADVIEW STATION. With a passenger assistance alarm. Activated. On board. A train. Response personnel are ..."

Oh for fuck's sake, people, I thought. *Get your shit together!*

I waited. And waited.

And waited.

Finally, another announcement boomed through the station.

"Attention, passengers. On line two. The delay we were experiencing. WESTBOUND. At. BROADVIEW STATION. Is now. Clear. Regular service. Has resu —"

The whoosh of the train arriving at the platform cut off the remaining words.

On the way to St. George Station, I wondered if I had time to stop and acquire yet another poppy, should the veteran who'd been selling them outside the station last week still be there. Remembrance Day was nearly upon us and I felt nakedly conspicuous now without that symbolic gesture poked into my chest. Indeed, as I looked around the subway car, it seemed as if everyone — all the grim, swaying masses — had a poppy on now. Like judgy red eyes, those plastic blossoms stared at me from dozens of jacket lapels. Yes, I thought. Despite being very late for class, I would stop and buy yet another poppy, if I could. I needed the dignity, this one shred of social decorum before facing my students and Sebastian.

I arrived at the station, bounded up the stairs, pushed through the turnstiles, and glided up the escalators to street level. I came out into the drizzly day and veered toward campus. As I hustled, I looked around for the veteran, that bereted, blazered old goat, but there was no veteran there. There was no veteran selling poppies. Instead, reader, in his place, hovering on the sidewalk ahead of me, was a millennial, a very eager millennial, wearing what looked like hiking boots and cradling a clipboard on her arm. She was clad in a nylon vest with BECAUSE I AM A GIRL emblazoned on the tit. She stepped right into my path as I approached.

"Hey there, fella — nice hairdo!" she said with sweet-faced phoniness. "I just *know* you want to stop and talk to me."

"No — *fuck off!*" I snarled, and barrelled past her.

But then I felt bad. Terribly bad. I doubled back and called her over. So sorry, that was incredibly rude of me. Please. Please, I want to hear your spiel. I do. So after a not-brief squint of trepidation at me, she launched into it, and we had the requisite exchange. What? Really? Little girls still not going to school, eh? Why, that's just dreadful. No, of course. Of course. Anything I can do to help. Sorry — what? Oh. Well, I might have forty dollars here in my wallet. Sorry — what? You'd like me to sign up to your — You want me to give you my credit card number, right here on the street? Well, I don't see why not.

Needless to say, by the time I dealt with all *that* I was now catastrophically late for class. I *ran*, readers — ran like the dickens, like the devil, like Forrest fucking Gump — through campus and toward the lecture hall. The day's rain misted my face. My shirt came untucked from my waistband. I felt my comb-over sprout wings and try to fly off my head. I blinked like a psychopath as brow sweat — in clear defiance of the chilly autumn day — rushed to join the Jacuzzi of rainwater pooling in my eye sockets. I arrived at the lecture hall, yanked open the doors, and hurled myself into the auditorium. A quick gander at the seats as I marched up onto the stage revealed that less than a quarter of the class was still there. Some of the stragglers sat absently lingering over their phones or laptops, their feet up on the seats in front of them. Others were clustered together as Sebastian tried to lead them in a group discussion. A few had been just getting up and were about to slink away. I cut them off.

"I threatened Cheryl Sneed!" I screamed. The room jarred. People clutched inward in a kind of terror. I was panting maniacally in my dishevelment, but I plugged on. I plugged *on*. "I threatened her, people," I said. "I did. On TV. In a most appalling, *abhorrent* way. And we didn't talk about that, last week. We didn't, but we should have. So we're going to talk about it today. We're going to get all of this out in the open — right here, right now. So everyone please sit down."

They all sort of blinked at me.

"*Sit the fuck down!*" I squawked, even though most of them were, in fact, already sitting the fuck down. Those who weren't descended back into their auditorium seats with reluctance, with great petulant chucks of their bookbags.

The room fell silent. I paced the stage like a tiger, my nostrils flaring. I could sense Sebastian's stare — wide and baffled, frightened and, most of all, angry — all over my body. My heart thudded in my chest, and I took in long laborious breaths as I summoned what I wanted to say, felt it rise and flower inside my mind.

I just let it all come pouring out. I did. Do you believe me, reader? I don't blame you if you don't, because I don't believe it either. And the *reason* I don't believe it is because I don't remember it. It's true. To this day I have no idea what I said, there on that stage. I wish I did. It certainly would've helped with the stalled project that was my Proper Apology. But by this point I was caught up in a kind of hypnosis, a delirium that made me wonder if this was what speaking in tongues was like. Apparently, I put on quite a performance. In fact, one of the students in the room, perhaps the only student who went on to do graduate work in philosophy, said later that it was the single most impassioned, persuasive, and enthralling lecture he'd ever seen me give. I wish someone had recorded it. I wish I could remember what I said.

By the time I finished, I had come down off the stage to take up a more personable position in front of them. I tried to draw everyone in to me, an intimate engagement, as if I were a folksinger. It felt like I'd been talking forever, even though just a few minutes had passed.

"... but I want to hear from you," I said. "I want to know what you think. Questions? Comments? Please. Let's just get it out. Let's just talk about this."

The silence shimmered. I looked from face to face to face: most were staring at their laps, lowered in a kind of contemplative meditation. Sebastian's was neutral, cryptic. *Please,* I thought. *Please. Please.*

Then, finally, a strawberry blonde in a denim jacket raised a hand. Oh blessed child. "Yes?" I asked, expectant.

"If you feel all that," she said, "then how come you gave that awful quote to the *Globe and Mail* on Thursday?"

I told them that some feminist firebrand had attacked my daughter's Facebook wall that morning, and I was out of my mind with rage when that reporter got a hold of me.

That seemed to get things going. A couple of hands went up; a couple of skirmishes volleyed around the room. Some pimple-faced boy at the back, referred to earlier in the term as a "gamer" (whatever *that* was), cavalierly threw out the word "feminazi," and I cut him right off. "We don't use terms like that in this room," I said. But the girls were already on it. The girls let him have it. The kid rushed to claim they were silencing him, censoring him, stifling him. But I reminded the little shit that you don't get to participate in meaningful conversations if you can't stay within the bounds of civility, if you resort to reductive terms. What about the chick on your daughter's wall? he asked. Same thing, I told him. "She used a reductive term. She called *me* a 'piece of shit'" — this earned a light laugh from the class — "so we deleted her comment. It was completely out of bounds and unwarranted, so we didn't respond. We didn't engage." This led to a tasty little chat about the term "reductive," and what counted as "in bounds" versus "out of bounds." This inevitably led back to my scrap with Cheryl Sneed and that unconscionable dig I took at her. Again, the girls were on it. They were *on it*. And I marvelled, as I stood there with my back against the stage, at how close all this was to the surface for them, how they talked as if they'd been having this conversation all along, having it with each other, having it right under our noses, well before I ever violated Cheryl Sneed on live TV. Indeed, they said, my slip had been the very essence of reductive thinking, to diminish a woman right down to her sexual bits, and to force something onto her against her will. And my remark was not horrifying because of its novelty. Far from it. It was horrifying — yes, horrifying, but also exhausting, dispiriting — because it was so *commonplace*.

"Yes, exactly," said a girl in a badly dyed Cleopatra bob. "When guys do this — and they do it *all the time*," she said in the general direction of the pimple-faced gamer, "it makes us feel like we're shut out. Shut down. Not allowed to participate in the … in the … What's that ten-dollar word you taught us at the beginning of term, the one for 'public sphere'?"

"Agora," called out another girl, an Indonesian in a hijab.

"Yeah, yeah. It makes us feel like we're shut out of the agora … the agora of ideas. Like we have no place in it. Because we're *women*."

"Yeah, I can totally see that," said a guy in porkpie hat who hadn't spoken up all term. This kid, reader, let me tell you, with his air of above-it-all nihilism, well, I had pretty much written him off as some sort of arse-picking layabout. But what he said next kind of floored me. "It's like that quote from Pericles that you gave us back in September," he stated. "How we consider people who don't share in public life not to be people who just keep to themselves, but *useless* people. And that's the crux of it. Women just don't want to feel useless when it comes to matters that have nothing to do with their sexual parts."

"That's exactly it," said Cleopatra in her bob. "And it certainly excludes us from … What did Kant call it? The 'realm of ends'?" She dug *Foundations of the Metaphysics of Morals* out of her bag and went flipping. "Like it says here: *For the esteem which is a rational being must have for it, only the word 'respect' is a suitable expression. Autonomy is thus the basis of the dignity of both human nature and every rational being.*"

Oh, reader. I could've wept.

We were soon out of time, on account of me being so late for class. As they all packed up, I tried to make eye contact with Sebastian. I could tell he was delaying it, fighting the urge to face me man to man. But as the last of the students trundled out, he did turn to me. His expression was still so cryptic, so inscrutable. His blond hair fell over one eye and his skinny-jeaned legs were crossed, one Ked-clad foot over the other. He looked deeply forlorn at the prospect of settling this big decision once and for all. To stay or to go.

I have no map to give you, I wanted to say as we stood there, not speaking. *I have no map to give you, Sebastian. I wish I did. But this is the territory we tread, for better and for worse. We are philosophers, you and I, and this is the territory we tread.*

He turned and left without speaking to me. Hustled up the aisle and out the door. *He'll have to make up his mind,* I thought. *He'll have to decide his next move, and soon.*

I returned to 4 Metcalfe Street. As I slipped off my Payless and hung up my tweed, I could see through the kitchen's archway the pad of canary paper and the capped uni-ball sitting on the table, waiting for me. You would think that, after what happened in class, I'd be ready to attack my Proper Apology with renewed keenness. But what we had talked about, my students and I, was already dissipating inside my mind, and I felt another funnel cloud of procrastination swirl up to replace it. I stared at the pad and pen for a moment, but then headed upstairs to my third-floor office to check email first.

There was a message waiting there, from Raj.

> Hey brother,
>
> Just writing to see how your new script is coming along. I'll be packing up here in a few hours to head back into the city, and I just want to give the boys an idea of what we're shooting tomorrow afternoon. So if you could fire the script off to me when you get a chance, that'd be great.
>
> Looking forward to it.
> Raj

I rubbed my temples in slow, tight circles. Puffed out my furry cheeks in a big, arduous sigh.

Okay.

I got up and headed back downstairs to the kitchen.

Squeeze, dash, shake-shake-shake, pour.

I sat at the kitchen table and stared at the blank pad.

Squeeze, dash, shake-shake-shake, pour.

I sat at the kitchen table and stared at the blank pad.

Squeeze, dash, shake-shake-shake, pour.

I sat at the kitchen table and stared at the blank pad.

And then I just started writing. Oh, reader, I have to tell you. What came out then, in my frustration, was pure unadulterated drivel. I mean, a total slurry of stream-of-consciousness bullshit. I wasn't even thinking while I wrote; my hand moved across the page as if divorced from my mind. I had tried to conjure up everything I had thought and felt over the last forty-eight hours, the realizations and the shame, what we had talked about in class, and what should have been stewing in my brainmeats since, but what flowed from my pen was the ghastliest doggerel imaginable.

It went on for five paragraphs across two pages. I stopped myself midway through paragraph six, flipped back to the beginning to read the whole thing over, that blazing blue mess. Oh God, it was garbage. This was what I thought, my PEI accent once again warping the rhotic: *Oh my gawd, it's just g'yarrbage!*

The front door opened then, and Simone appeared back in the house. What was she doing home so soon? But then I looked up at the clock on the wall. No, no, this was her usual time to come home from school. Where did the afternoon go?

She came into the kitchen. "Hey," she said.

"Hey there," I replied. "How was school? Things okay with … uh … Katie?"

"Caitlin? No, we hate each other now," she said simply, setting her bookbag on the counter and pulling her ponytail free of its scrunchy.

"Oh," I said. "Um, much homework tonight?"

"No, not much." She went to the fridge and pulled out the milk jug. After she'd poured herself a glass, she approached the table and nodded at the marked-up pad in front of me. "What are you working on?"

"Ah, it's … *Dah* …" I aspirated with great hopelessness. "It's supposed to be my apology to the world," I told her. "You know, for threatening that woman on TV last week."

"Oh?"

"Yeah. My videographer friend, Raj, is supposed to film me delivering it tomorrow, for YouTube." I pressed my lips together in grim frustration. "I'm afraid it's not going very well."

"You're working on it here?" Simone asked, sipping her milk. "Not in your office?"

"It was going even worse up there."

"Can I read it?"

I hesitated, but then motioned to the pad in a Be-my-guest gesture.

Simone leaned over the table, and I watched as her green eyes — almost identical to Grace's — strolled back and forth as she read. I wondered how much of this incoherent claptrap she was absorbing. She tucked a strand of hair behind her ear, and I watched as her thirteen-year-old face creased in concentration.

She let out a sudden kind of snort. "Well you can't say *that*," she said, pointing at the second sentence in the third paragraph.

"Why not?"

She just leaned back and gaped at me. "Because it's *sexist*."

"What? Wait. No. Where?" I read the sentence again. "No, no. That's not. I mean, what I meant was …" But then I sputtered out. I wasn't sure what I meant.

"Here, why don't you do this," Simone said, taking the seat next to me. "Why don't you get rid of this whole offensive part here," and she pointed at the first clause in the sentence, "and then take this part," and she pointed at the second clause, "and move it all the way to the top, here," and she pointed to the middle of my opening sentence.

Hhrmm. This didn't seem right. But then I just went ahead anyway, scratching out below and scribbling above. When I finished, I looked over the change.

Huh. Wow. It did read a lot better.

I looked into Simone's now proud face. "All right, smarty-pants," I said, "what else?"

"Well, I *love* this part here," she said, tapping the third sentence in the second paragraph. "It's really sweet. But Ms. Varn, in Language Arts, says that if we're going to make 'big statements,' we should always back them up with examples."

"Examples."

"Yeah. So are there girls or women in your life where *this*," and she tapped the sentence again, "would apply?"

I thought about it. "Well, there's *you*, obviously. And Naomi."

"And *Mum*," she chided.

"Yeah, and your mother, too."

So Simone took the pen from me and wrote these in the bit of space above the paragraph. As she finished, another question sailed into her head. "What about *your* mum?"

"I never knew my mother," I told her. "She walked out on my father and me while I was still in diapers." I swallowed hard. "She didn't want to be a mum."

"*Oh*," Simone said in shock, as this came as genuine news to her. She touched me on the shoulder. "That's so sad."

I just nodded my agreement, in silence. But then we had a talk about it, and she even helped me to work that into the text — and to do so without it being all self-serving and weird.

Soon we were really cooking. Oh, reader, the edits and changes just kept piling up. It became hard for the uni-ball to keep pace with our thoughts, and so I journeyed to my office to fetch my laptop. I returned with it to the kitchen table and Simone began reading the script out to me as I typed, and we polished and rejigged even more as we went along.

We were just starting on a seventh paragraph when the front entry door opened again.

Naomi came tearing into the house. "Daddy Daddy Daddy!"

I stood from my chair but then squatted, squatted to her eye level, and she came flying into my arms. I swept her up like a big twister and held her tight. Swung her madly as she pythoned her arms around my neck.

Hoh. Hoh.

"I missed you so much!" she screamed.

Hoh. Hoh. I'm so glad you're here, Naomi. I'm so happy that you've come along, that you've graced us with your existence. I am. What would I ever do without you? The fact that you exist makes me feel like I've finally joined the human race. You make me feel this. You … and Simone … and … and …

I tore my gaze away from our squeeze to see Grace there, framed in the kitchen's archway and glaring at us. I set Naomi back on the floor and she slid down my shin, sat on my foot, and wrapped her arms around my calf. "Can I have a horsey ride?"

"Not right now, sweetie," I said, stooping at the waist, picking her up, and parking her on my hip.

I took one step toward my wife. Was she still mad, reader?

Oh, you better believe she was. Grace stood there stiff as a brass statue, arms folded over chest, mouth pinched, eyes narrowed into an umlaut above her pert, sharp nose. I envisioned a brief exchange between us — *Hey there. Hey.* — but then I decided to forgo the pleasantries. There was no point, what with *that* look on her face.

"I didn't know," I told her. "I didn't know. About Cheryl Sneed. Grace, I didn't … I didn't *know.*"

"Yeah, I know," she replied, matter-of-factly. "Simone texted me about it on Sunday night." Her features very slightly softened. "I can't … I just can't *believe* it."

"I don't really believe it myself," I said.

Her face softened a bit more. "But you want to hear the strange thing? After I found out, I told my parents — and they said they always suspected that's what was going on. Based on how you were acting all week, they figured you didn't know the real reason everyone was so pissed off at you. They didn't say anything to me because the idea seemed so … so *outlandish.* But it actually was the case. They said it must have been awful for you to learn the truth, and that I should go easy on you." Her face coarsened again. "They're always taking your side of things."

God love them, Roland and Sharon. They're good people. But then something occurred to me. "Wait — you've known the truth since Sunday night? Then why are you only coming home now? And why didn't you answer your phone when I called?"

"Because I was *mad*, Philip," she replied. "I'm *still* mad. And I needed my time, okay. I needed my time with that anger. So if I wanted two days to be under my parents' roof and lie on my childhood bed and think all this through, then I was going to take them. Okay?"

Must be nice, I thought. *Must be great that I provide you with that kind of luxury.*

But then I shoved those thoughts aside. *Get the fuck out of my head*, I told those thoughts.

"You hold so much resentment toward me," she said, as if she'd read my mind. She said this as our two children studied us closely. "You hold so much resentment toward our set-up here — this house, the fact that I don't 'work,' and all the rest. It gnaws at that big brain of yours, all day long. Doesn't it?"

"It really doesn't," I retorted. "Not … not all the time, no."

"But a lot of the time," she conceded with a sarcastic tilt of her head. "It does, doesn't it? And what I want to know, Philip — what I've been struggling with for the last two days — is why would you bottle all that up? Why would you hold these feelings, this bitterness, inside you until you just couldn't hold it in anymore? I mean, we've lived in this house for *six years*. Why would you go along with a domestic arrangement, a financial set-up, that you didn't really agree with? Why would you go along with all that, and with," and here her eyes flickered, almost imperceptibly, toward the ceiling, toward our bedroom, "*other* things, if you're not really comfortable with them? Why would you do that? Why?"

"Because I love you," I said. The words came out deflated, and a bit sad. "And despite all the trouble we've been having, I know this 'arrangement' really is your dream life."

"It is," she said. "What we have here is exactly what I've always wanted."

"— and I'd do anything to give that to you, okay? I would agree, Grace, to just about anything. I would *put up* with just about any-thing," and here thought of my financial turmoil, our miscues in the boudoir, her frequent and impulsive alluding to my failures as a father, husband, homeowner, "if it meant being with you and our children."

Well. She didn't quite know how to process *that*. Her face didn't soften further, but it didn't exactly stay stern either. It sort of vacillated between two looks I couldn't read.

"And how's *that* working out for you?" she eventually asked.

"It is," I replied, "a rather unfortunate situation. But it's better than the alternative." And here, I thought of the alternative — say, a crumbling rental on the Danforth, all my work equipment set up permanently in the living room, a bottle of Grant's whisky on the windowsill, and no relationship, no relationship whatsoever, with my own offspring. "This is *my* life," I said. "I love you. I love the kids. And this," and I gestured dismissively, despairingly, disparagingly, to 4 Metcalfe Street, "is just my life now."

We fell silent for a while. Grace appeared — perhaps for the first time in our marriage — genuinely unhappy that I was unhappy. She seemed perturbed by the realization that my go-along-to-get-along attitude might obstruct rather than facilitate the life of Riley she was so desperately trying to live. Was that fair? Am I just being a soggy old martyr? And I wondered: Was she less furious at me for saying these things to her, or more? I wished, then, that I could better read that expression on her face. I wished that I had a crystal ball so I could stare deep into our future together.

"Um," Simone said from the kitchen table, breaking the silence, "did you want me and Naomi to *go*?"

It was as if Grace and I came out of a trance, together. She turned to her daughter. "No, it's fine, okay. It's fine." She nodded quizzically at the laptop and scribbled-up canary paper. "What are you two working on?"

"Well," I said, desperate to change the subject, "now that I know the truth — about what really happened last week — I'm scripting an apology, a proper one, for Raj to film. It hasn't been going very well, so I recruited Simone. She's been a tremendous help to me."

"I want to help, too!" Naomi exclaimed. "Noam *sayin*?"

"Can *I* take a look?" Grace asked.

So I set Naomi down and then resumed my place at the laptop, scrolling up to the Word doc's beginning. Grace leaned over my shoulder and began reading, tapping the keyboard's down arrow as she did.

She let out a sudden kind of snort. "Well, you can't say *that*," she said, pointing at the first sentence in the fifth paragraph.

"Why not?"

She just leaned back and gaped at me. "Because it's *sexist*."

I turned to Simone with a look that said, *How did you miss that one?*

So we all pitched in then. We did — revising sentences, crafting new ones, arguing points with each other. It all unfurled in a great collaborative swirl. If you were there, reader, you would have heard things like, "Well, if you're going to put that example *there* then you have to put it down here, too," and "Philip, this is a *YouTube* video, okay — nobody's going to know what 'eusebeia' means." All the while I typed and typed and typed.

Soon Grace's brow furrowed. "Okay, there are a lot of concepts here. We need a better way to display them." She got an idea. "Simone, do you still have —"

"I do!" she replied. "I'll go get them!" She went dashing out of the kitchen and up the stairs. A minute later she came dashing back down again, holding four sheets of bristol board — two pink, two fuchsia — left over from a school project a month ago. She and Grace set them up on the table. Out came the Magic Markers and Sharpies. I logged on to Grace's wireless printer, and we printed off family photos, pictures of women's lib icons, and a headshot of Cheryl Sneed. I typed and typed while they drew and coloured and pasted.

"Hey, Naomi," said Grace, "do you know what this sign really needs?"

"Elbow macaroni!" the child screamed in delight.

"And glitter," Simone added. "Get some glitter, too."

Okay, okay.

I typed and typed, and then we were done. Word count, reader: 1,513. Oh my.

I printed the script off so I could do a dry run. We all stood up. I held the pages in my fist while my daughters took up the bristol boards — one in each hand — and raised them aloft in great swaying animation, as if they were at a pop singer's concert. I started to read.

Nine minutes later, I finished. I turned to my wife. "What do you think?"

She stood there with arms doubled tight over her breasts. Once more, I could not parse the expression on her face. She said nothing for the longest time.

"Well," she began finally, "it's either the most adorable hara-kiri in the history of civilization, or …" And here gave a light shrug. "… or the most condescending. I don't know which. I mean, you can never be sure how people — women — are going to react to things. We're not exactly a monolith, you know."

"Yeah, I know," I replied. "But it's still the right thing to do."

"Yeah, I know," she replied.

I wanted, reader, to linger on that moment of simpatico between us. It felt so rare, so fleeting, like the most beautifully improvised set of trills on a piano. A gorgeous melody you just wish you could lock up inside your brain before it vanished forever.

Grace turned to Simone. "Okay, you can put those very carefully in the hall closet for Philip, and then take your sister up for her bath. And please, be extremely …"

"I know, I know," Simone said with a roll of her eyes. "The tub."

When they were gone, Grace and I just sort of floated before each other, there on the kitchen tile.

"I called a plumber," I ventured. "He'll be here Friday."

This news caused no discernible reaction for a moment. But then Grace lowered her eyes, as if embarrassed by something. "So while you were having your revelations over the last two days, I was having some revelations of my own," she said — very slowly, very deliberately. This was difficult for her. "This is difficult for me," she confirmed. "It's difficult to say that I was wrong. It's a hard thing to admit, because I'm usually right about things. But I shouldn't have accused you of not being a plugged-in dad before you left for the show last week. I realize that now. You *are*, Philip, a plugged-in dad, a lot of the time. You are. It happens right under my nose and I don't see it, or I refuse to. My parents, actually, pointed it out to me over the last couple days. They said, 'Now, Grace, Philip does a lot for you and those girls. You just don't see it, but he does.'" She lowered her eyes again. "They're always taking your side of things," she repeated with a sniff.

"Grace ..."

"But I know now that I refuse to see it a lot of the time. And the *reason* I refuse to see it, is because ..." And she turned her gaze to her little alcove, her little writing nook. "Because things aren't going well for me, over there," she said, nodding at her desk. "I mean, writing comes so easily for you — just *boom-boom-boom* and it's out. And it should be easy for me, too. I mean, in a lot of ways I live under the ideal conditions to be a writer. But every sentence is an agony. I ... I just ... I guess I just convince myself that the reason my books aren't a success is because I don't have a husband who's plugged in, who supports me. Even if ... even if, I see now, that isn't really true." She grit her teeth for a bit. "So I've decided that I need a change. I think we both do."

My heart tumbled. Tumbled and shrank.

But then she said: "I put a CV together yesterday. Dad knows a guy at a children's charity right around the corner, at Carlton and Parliament. He said they're looking for a new newsletter editor, so I put a resumé together and submitted an application."

"Oh, Grace," I said, with both relief and a not small amount of shame. "I ... I ... You don't have to do that. I, I ... You shouldn't feel like you have to do that." *A job like that also wouldn't pay very well,* I thought but did not say aloud.

"It's already done. And Dad's friend called me this morning. I have an interview with them on Thursday." She seemed to grow angry at the thought. "If I get the job, Mom says she can come here and look after the kids on the days you're on campus."

"Grace, you don't have to do that."

"But I *do*," she replied. "I can't have you resenting me, Philip. I can't have you thinking that there's this great imbalance around here in terms of what you contribute versus what I don't. So I'm doing it. It's done." She inhaled deeply then, flaring her nostrils. "But you're going to do something for *me*. Okay?"

"Okay …?"

"You need to cut back on your drinking. I'm serious, Philip. This is non-negotiable. I know you're a 'philosopher' and all, but you're also a fifty-year-old dad. You need to start showing some restraint."

"Consider it done," I replied, soberly. "You're right, Grace. You're absolutely right. I know … I mean, I *realize* I get a few into me and then say some pretty hurtful things. I do it all the time to people, but … but especially to you." And here, I thought of our disastrous brunch. "I don't want to do that anymore. It's not who I really am." Grace nodded, very slightly. A very slight agreement. "And thank you," I went on, "about the job thing. It … it is going to help us out a bit, financially."

She lowered her head then, and that's when I realized she wasn't angry about the job thing. Just sad. Just incredibly sad that this chapter of her life was coming to an end. "I'm still going to write," she said without looking up. "And I'm still going to be a great mum to those girls. But … but things will be harder for me now. I really hate cubicle life. I really," and here she plunged into a hitherto unchartered depth of honesty, of disclosure, with herself, "hate *working*."

Boy, I felt like a complete heel after that. I tell you. The only thing worse than losing a game-changing argument with the person you love is winning one.

Then she did look up at me, and we sort of glared at each other for a while. What to do with all these gaps, these cracks, these fissures between us? We just have to keep tamping them down, I suppose. Grace and I were very different people, but we didn't hate each other. We didn't. We just sometimes hated the fact that we loved each other. I mean, what a bloody fucking inconvenience.

We heard water rush through the pipes in the walls.

"Oh *fuck*!" Simone screamed above us.

Naomi howled like an animal.

And Grace and I, we bolted in unison. We bolted toward our children, together. We tore around each other as we ascended the stairs to get to our kids, like it was some kind of race.

Wednesday, November 11

I hate being late. I am always late.

I came wheezing and burping out of Donlands Station, trench coat over tweed, satchel over shoulder, decrepit umbrella in one fist and my bristol-board signs, tied up in black garbage bags to protect against the afternoon's threatening rain, in the other. The street shone slickly from an earlier downpour and the air seemed thick from the drizzle that still loomed. I blossomed the umbrella above my comb-over as I came out of the station, turned left, and headed northward with the blundering, lumbering air of a man already several minutes behind schedule.

It had been a frenzied morning at 4 Metcalfe Street. I had awoken to the realization that, thanks to the events of the last two days, I had done nothing, absolutely no prep at all, for either tomorrow's survey course or Friday's graduate seminar. So while Grace brought a level of normalization back to our breakfast-time routines (feeding the kids, checking Simone's homework, convincing her to wear a raincoat today and getting her out the door, stopping Naomi from drawing a giraffe on the living-room wall with one of the Sharpies left out from yesterday, et cetera), I slunk upstairs to my office earlier than usual and closed the door behind me. I soon became a veritable piazza of busyness myself, preparing lecture notes *and* Socratic queries *and* discussion topics for Thursday, then rereading a chunk of *The Social Contract* in the event that my grad students returned to Friday's class after I posted my Proper Apology on YouTube. After that, I got a hankering to work on "Christianity and Its Dissidents," so I hacked out a half chapter as morning turned to afternoon. Just as I finished that up, Grace was on the landing calling to me. "Sorry, Philip, *what* time are you going to Raj's?"

Oh shit.

By now, reader, you know what to expect. I made a jumpy, curse-laden sprint down the stairs. In the kitchen, I snuffled up a quick lunch while Grace rolled and garbage-bagged the bristol-board signs for me. As Simone had once again taken our only functional umbrella for her walk to school, I traipsed down to the dungeon of our unfinished basement on the rumour that there was another, older one down there somewhere. I eventually found it: black, faded, dusty, and with dislodged arms like broken bat wings. It would have to do. Meanwhile, Grace dug both my tweed and trench coat out of the closet to prepare me for the chill and rain of the day. Sensing my haste, she sort of dressed me there in the front entry, manoeuvring one jacket and then the other over my doughy, narrow shoulders as I shoved the printout of my YouTube script into my satchel. Then I turned to face her and dipped in for a kiss, but she leaned away with a look that said, *Nope, nope, Philip, we're not quite there yet.* But she did wish me luck as she pushed me out the door. Behind her, Naomi was just emerging from a much-needed nap.

Now, a couple minutes free of the subway station, I realized that — no, it wasn't actually raining. The air was cool but empty. I lowered my dilapidated umbrella and found myself, as if at the threshold of fate, standing outside the place I had been before, that white-bricked old hovel, that same hole-in-the-wall barbershop that I had encountered on Friday. It sat like a squat, blanched toadstool there on Donlands Avenue. I turned to face it and, oh, reader, got a good gawk at myself in the reflection of the shop's window. Jesus. Jesus Murphy. It was as if a ghost, or at least another of life's little elisions or near-misses, floated there in the space just to the left of the stencilled barber's pole. I think I saw my hair, my comb-over, as it was, as it really, *truly* was, for the first time. Jesus. Jesus Murphy. I was going to go on YouTube looking like … that?

I pushed my way into the shop.

"Haircut, sir?" asked the grey-smocked codger as he stood up from his barber's chair.

"Yes, please," I replied, all businesslike. "But let's make it snappy. I'm in a rush."

I turned away from his mirrors and gingerly set my garbage-bagged signs, satchel, and umbrella onto one of the waiting-area chairs. Then I sort of pinwheeled out of my trench coat, evaginating the sleeves, and flopping the whole thing down over my stuff. Then I dunked out of my tweed and tossed it onto the pile without even a look, as I was already turning back toward the barber. I took one brave step forward, like a man facing his execution, and climbed into his chair.

"So, so," he said in a kind of old-man singsongy voice. He fastened a paper strip around my throat before draping me in his nylon cape and securing it at the back of my neck. "What are we doing today?"

"Everything."

His wrinkled face sort of dippy-dooped in surprise. "Sorry?"

"Take it off," I said. "Just, just take the whole thing off."

"You mean, like, with the clippers?"

"Sure … sure …"

"Well, okay. How short would you like it? The number two guard, the number three?"

"Which is shorter?"

"The number two."

"Then let's do that."

"Okay, but …" And here he raised one of the limp, carrot-coloured tentacles off my skull, "once I do this, you can't ever really go back."

"It's fine, it's fine. Just do it." I closed my eyes. "Hurry up, before I change my mind."

So *buuuuuu-zzzzzz* went the clipper as he made long, looping half-orbits around my cranium. I felt/heard my hair fall away in soft, feathery tuffs over the cape and onto the floor. *Buuuuuu-zzzzzz …* *buuuuuu-zzzzzz.*

"And the beard, too," I said with eyes still shut, as if talking in my sleep. "Give it a nice, good trim."

Bzz-bzz-bzz went the clipper as he stroked it along my furry face in short, quick snaps of his wrist.

I knew he was finished when he undid the Velcro fasten at the back of my neck. I opened my eyes just as he swept the cape away. There, in the mirror, I got my first gander at the new me.

Huh. Wow. My head, reader, now looked taut, sleek, aerodynamic — but also *tough*, like you might want to think twice before picking a fight with me. The beard was neat, neater than it had been in fifteen years. It molded itself attractively along the contours of my jawline.

"Excellent," I said to the barber. "How much?"

So I paid him, and tipped him well, and then returned to my piled belongings in the waiting-area chair. As I absently donned my tweed, I looked out his large window and up at the sky. Not only was it not raining, but the sun was peeping between the clouds a bit. As a result, I decided not to put my trench coat back on, but rather drape it over my arm. I gathered up the rest of my stuff and then headed out his door.

I felt so light, so free, so *new* as I headed north on Donlands and then turned left onto Raj's street. It was as if there had been a change in the very chemistry of the world, a sweetness added to the air. The ground's damp, gutter-choking foliage did not reek of death — it reeked of *life*, of vitality, of endless possibilities. I swelled with a great sense of renewal. I felt capable of just about anything.

As I approached Raj's place, I saw him out on his open front porch, smoking a cigarette. He looked deep in thought, a bit per-turbed, a bit *taxed* by whatever anxieties dangled in his brain.

He turned to see me coming, and I waved at him with one of my garbage bags of rolled-up bristol board. "Hello there!"

"Sharpe, you douchebag," he said, and pointed at my chest with his cigarette. "You were supposed to leave that thing on the cenotaph at eleven o'clock."

"What ...?"

I halted on the sidewalk and looked down at my tweed. There, high up on its left lapel, beyond the periphery of my peripheral vision, sat an expertly fastened poppy. It was parked there, *planted* there, looking permanent and immovable, a crimson kiss over my collarbone. What the ...? How the ...? Somehow it had survived all my fumbling on the subway and at the barbershop as it hid under my trench coat. It lay unnoticed as I hiked my way up this street. But how? I mean, in the first place. How the hell did it ... did it ... end up on ... me?

Grace.

Grace.

I imagined her then, from earlier, preparing my jackets in the front entry as I searched our basement for the umbrella.

And I glowed, reader. I glowed with an indescribable gratitude.

I climbed onto Raj's porch, and he sized me up.

"Holy haircuts, Batman," he said. "Fuck, Sharpe, you look fantastic. You look, like, ten years younger."

"I've had a Come to Jesus moment," I told him.

"That's hilarious — especially coming from *you*."

"How was Barrie?"

"Don't ask," he said darkly, and flicked his cigarette into the street. Then he nodded toward the door. "Come on. You're late. The boys are waiting for you."

We entered his apartment and I took in the living room's immediate, noticeable transformation. The furniture had been shoved to the sidelines, and in the space the move created stood two angled video cameras on tripods and, about six feet in front of them, a director's chair. Behind the cameras, large, expensive-looking lights hovered on tall, thin stands. Behind the director's chair, a soft, sepia-coloured backdrop had been erected. Black cords crawled all around the floor. Through the doorway that led to Raj's large, galley-style kitchen, I could see the ingredients for the Bloody Joseph — bottle of Jameson, bottle of tomato juice, light-bright lemons, a verdant, esculent stalk of celery — lined up on his countertop.

Walter and Jerome were sitting on the pushed-aside couch, smoking marijuana and reading motorcycle magazines. Next to them, on the couch's arm, I could see a printout of my Proper Apology, which I had emailed to Raj the night before. The boys greeted me as they set aside their dope and their mags, and stood up to get to work. I watched as they went around turning on the cameras and the lights. Jerome lowered his face to one of the viewfinders while Walter fiddled with a monitor set up on a kitchen chair. I must admit it was heartening to see these boys in professional mode, doing what they had trained to do. They were just so matter of fact about it all, this technology and what it was capable of. *I really hope somebody gives them a job*, I thought.

"All righty then," said Raj, nodding at my garbage bags. "Let's see what you got."

I untied the bags and pulled free the bristol boards as I took them over to his desk. Laying them on the desktop, I began walking Raj through the sequence of pictures and quotes and gnomic little platitudes, this grand visual arc. "And when we get to *this* part of the script," I said, moving my hand crabwise along the bristol board, and looked up at him, "what we'll want to do is —"

But then I stopped. I stopped and gazed into Raj's face as he stared intensely at the images in front of him. His expression, reader, hadn't changed, not really. It remained the same cocky, dopey, stiff-lipped, slightly sleazy visage it always was. Except. Except his eyes, reader. His eyes were now lightly glossed with tears.

"Raj?"

"Your kids make these for you?" he asked.

"Yeah. Yeah, they did. I mean, they helped me with them."

He pressed his wrist to his nose, held it there a moment. "You're a lucky man, Sharpe," he said, his voice quavering slightly. "You're a fucking incredibly lucky man."

"Don't I know it."

A pall fell over us both then. I don't think I could put into words what I felt, there in the spume of Raj's sadness, but let me try. Pride and thankfulness, maybe, a slight delicate skein of entitlement. But also shame and unworthiness, ignorance of the sheer magnitude of my fortune. Sort of like you're somebody who jaywalks all the time and yet, miraculously, never gets hit by a bus. Looking over Grace and the kids' bristol-board work, I felt as if all of this, my whole life, had grown extraordinarily fragile, and I dare not extend myself too far lest I puncture reality's thin skin. Glancing back into Raj's face, I sensed that *his* reality had already been punctured. That his life had been torn to shreds long ago.

But just as quickly as he entered it, Raj pulled himself out of this emotional tailspin. "All right, boys," he said, "let's stop fucking around and get down to some real work." He went to his shelf and grabbed an expensive-looking camera, one with a huge, complicated lens. He got it going and began snapping pictures of the different sections of the bristol boards, which he would convert into images he could splice into the video later, during post-production.

Walter came by and led me by the arm. "Okay, let's get you set up over here." He turned me around, raised the tweed at my rump, and clipped a microphone battery to the back of my slacks. He then walked me with the microphone cord, like a marionette, over to the director's chair. I sat in it, its canvas seat sinking like a hammock under the weight of my ass. Walter clipped the microphone to my lapel, just below Grace's poppy, and then tucked the cord out of sight.

Jerome looked at me through the viewfinder of the camera in front of me. "How you doin', Dr. Phil?"

"Don't call me that," I said.

"Okey-dokey, then." He made a few adjustments to his lens and then moved to the other camera, angled at my right. Raj took his place, looking through the first camera with a Spielbergian air. "Okay, light's good, colour's good," he said clinically. "Philip, we're just gonna get a level on your mic, okay?"

"Okay." I stared into the camera, that cold, glass eye in its black, telescopic bonnet. It felt kind of criminal, being this exposed to the world. Walter came by with the printout of the script, and I took it from him and rested it on my lap.

"I'm just gonna ask you some random questions," Raj said. "Let's, um, start with — what's your full name?"

"Philip Christopher Sharpe."

"Cool. Where were you born?"

"Charlottetown, PEI."

"Great. Where do you work?"

"At the University of Toronto."

"Nice. Let's see … um … What … what pop song best encapsulates you?"

I thought it over. "Oh hell," I said with a lopped grin. "Maybe 'Drunken Angel,' by Lucinda Williams."

With that, Raj's face jumped up from the viewfinder. "Oh shit — the drinks!" he said, moving to go. "I totally forgot the drinks!"

But I raised a hand to stop him. "Raj, let's wait," I said.

"What?"

"Let's wait until we're done."

"You wanna wait?"

I turned back to the lens, to the whole world ready to watch me on the other side of it.

"Yeah," I said. "Let's … let's wait till we're done."

Epilogue:
A Recipe for the Bloody Joseph

2	shots of Jameson Irish whiskey
4	shots of tomato juice
½	shot of freshly squeezed lemon juice
7	dashes of Tabasco sauce
1	(yes, you're reading correctly; do NOT skip this step) generous squeeze of Heinz ketchup
4	dashes of Lea & Perrins Worcestershire sauce
1	(don't lose your nerve now; you're almost done!) heaping spoonful of horseradish sauce
2	pinches of celery salt
2	pinches of black pepper

Combine all ingredients in a cocktail shaker with ice and shake vigorously for 20 seconds. Strain contents into large ice-filled Collins glass. Garnish with a stick of fresh celery.

Serves ONE (of the courageous)

Acknowledgements

I would like to thank the Canada Council for the Arts for its generous financial support during the writing of this book.

I would also like to thank my wife, Rebecca Rosenblum (to whom this novel is dedicated), and my good friend Patrick Hadley, both of whom read this manuscript at every stage and offered immeasurably valuable insights and suggestions.

I also need to give a big thanks to the members of the writing group I've recently joined: Sara Heinonen, Liz Ross, and Brahm Nathans, thank you all for your great suggestions.

For the chapter "Higher Learning," I'm indebted to Philippa Sheppard and A.J. Levin for sharing with me their experiences living in and studying at Oxford in the 1990s. In Oxford itself, I owe a huge thanks to Helen Taylor for her generous tour of Balliol College and Holywell Manor, and to Niels Sampath for his illuminating tour of the Oxford Union building.

For the chapter "The Midwife," I'm indebted to the Facebook hive mind for recommending the following tomes on home births: *Birthing from Within*, by Pam England; *Spiritual Midwifery*, by Ina May Gaskin; and *The Birth Partner*, by Penny Simkin. A big thanks, as well, to Corey Matthews, who allowed me to interview her about her experiences as a doula. This chapter was also heavily inspired by the incomparable birthing scene in J.G. Ballard's *The Kindness of Women*.

Numerous works of philosophy and philosophical history went into the formation of Philip and his inner world, but I want to single out one impressively exhaustive book in particular: *From Plato to NATO: The Idea of the West and Its Opponents*, by David Gress. I should also acknowledge *Civilization and Its Discontents*, by Sigmund Freud; *Foundations of the Metaphysics of Morals*, by Immanuel Kant; *Unruly Voices*, by Mark Kingwell; *On Liberty*, by John Stuart Mill; and *The Social Contract*, by Jean-Jacques Rousseau for providing much-needed inspiration and nourishment during the planning for this book.

Finally, a huge thank you to Shannon Whibbs and the whole Dundurn team for their continued support and excellence. These folks really swing for the fence when it comes to Canadian books.